To Tony

MW00929880

LOVE AND KISSES

(*Lady Arcana*)

ENJOY

Naomi

LOVE AND KISSES

(*Lady Arcana*)

Justine Rothman

Copyright © 2020 by Justine Rothman.
Cover Artwork by Naomi Rhoads

ISBN: Softcover   978-1-7960-8607-2
           eBook   978-1-7960-8616-4

All rights reserved. No part of this book may be reproduced or transmitted in
any form or by any means, electronic or mechanical, including photocopying,
recording, or by any information storage and retrieval system, without permission
in writing from the copyright owner.

This is a work of fiction. Names, characters, places and incidents either are the
product of the author's imagination or are used fictitiously, and any resemblance
to any actual persons, living or dead, events, or locales is entirely coincidental.

Any people depicted in stock imagery provided by Getty Images are models, and
such images are being used for illustrative purposes only.
Certain stock imagery © Getty Images.

Print information available on the last page.

Rev. date: 01/31/2020

To order additional copies of this book, contact:
Xlibris
1-888-795-4274
www.Xlibris.com
Orders@Xlibris.com
807678

Contents

Dedication vii

Chapter 1 1
Chapter 2 20
Chapter 3 32
Chapter 4 47
Chapter 5 59
Chapter 6 65
Chapter 7 77
Chapter 8 91
Chapter 9 104
Chapter 10 122
Chapter 11 151
Chapter 12 157
Chapter 13 177
Chapter 14 191
Chapter 15 203
Chapter 16 208
Chapter 17 224
Chapter 18 246
Chapter 19 268

Dedication

For my friend/s who tricked me into writing this book.

For Lady Arcana, the MUSE.

For Leo, whose love and devotion to music have been a lesson in feeling without words.

For my father and mother whose books never got written.

For my children and grandchildren.

For my teachers and my students......

Chapter 1

WELCOME TO ACADEMIA BOOKS!

The platonic tradition of dialogues on love are continued here by the professional censors of our generation. We maverick souls, a random selection deposited in these jobs, are exclusively concerned with the market. Scholarly conclusions and truths are trimmed until they conform with what the universities of our country will support financially.

ALL UNSALEABLE TRUTHS REGRETFULLY MUST BE REJECTED.

You may be surprised, as you enter the halls of Academia, to see a motionless figure sitting the office swivel chair hieratically as an Egyptian queen her throne. Irradiated by LSD, breathing slowly and almost imperceptibly, I depart somewhat from the normal deportment and appearance you may have been led to expect from office personnel. Your very happy receptionist, myself, is titled Ms. Alison Greaves.

Festively robed in an antique Janissaries vest of aged white satin with tarnished silver embroidery, (worn in celebration of our new volume of studies on *Military Strategy of the Ottoman Empire*), worn over a clinging black leotard, a Byzantine necklace of stamped pewter links casually peeks out from under my collar as though it were a mere kerchief. A pair of battered and faded dungarees, patched, embroidered and studded, clothes the lower half of my anatomy, and suede boots of a hot burnt sienna color with 1940 Cuban heels attend to my feet with luxurious comfort. A contrast between poverty and expensive slovenliness, I am enigmatically hard to assign a definition.

1

Especially if you look into the face of my beatitude, vacant of make-up but, nonetheless, thrilling with genuine delights, (mind elsewhere), and my hair which is curly red-brown, lots of it, and hasn't seen a barber in years, (the style is called hazards of naturalism)..... you may find my presence at Academia puzzling.

My Bachelor's degree in Painting has been negotiated for Secretary-ship to the Director. More important, I know nothing about publishing. What creativity I have is directed elsewhere, and I have no desire to climb the ladder of responsibility here. My opinions, which, admittedly, come from outer space, are not dictated by a concern for purchasability. I am an artist, laughing at the power of money. That's why I was hired.

A million hopeful literature majors, all trying to write or edit professionally, would give their eye-teeth and right hands for this job and its connections. Another unemployed million of careerists would kill for it. And they'd be a threat to this well-run organization with their desires to prove themselves worthy of power. They'd find faults, come up with improvements, and get in everybody's way.

I am ideal for this job. I only want the money. And to be allowed to be myself or to find myself, whichever. Intelligent enough to get the work over quickly and presentably, I also provide entertainment for our Director, Jack Livingston.

Perhaps you are already acquainted with Jack or rumors about him have reached you. But as the publishing industry well knows, one of his hobbies is helping people find themselves more quickly with his help. He is a collector of eccentric employees, and his kind intervention catalyzes their progression to further individuality within the bounds of functional madness.

Jack is a handsome 1940s model. His black and gray hair waves in choice striated curves about the form of his head.....very Art Deco. His custom-tailored suits in neutrally elegant colors all have the boxy shoulders of Leindecker fashion plates. This gentlemanly apparel covers the six-foot-four body of an ex-football player, still in working condition.

When this well-seasoned specimen of masculine virility confronted me at my interview, I almost forgot about needing the job, so dazzled was I by the possibilities. I had never conceived of bosses as being so attractive, not to mention sympathetic and charming. That was a popular myth to inspire young girls to go to secretarial school, or so I thought. But here it was in the radiant flesh. I swallowed hard and demonstrated all the qualifications I remembered, including that I needed money immediately and would be very *very* good if only he hired me.

Jack, living up to his reputation, knew immediately that I was the perfect secretary for him. (His standards you will discover, as I did, in time.) He hired me on the spot. Thus, my insecurities about where the money was going to come from disappeared instantly. Also, Jack didn't risk my slipping away from Academia Books by finding another job while he was making up his mind.

For the first few weeks, getting down the routine of the job took all my attention. I plugged myself into the typewriter and accustomed myself to the form of the business letter. Business letters limit creativity in the interests of economy and exchange, (time and money). One rejection letter is likely to be just like the next, only the name of the rejected author and the title of the book are different. Nevertheless, if a manuscript is good enough, I am instructed to tack on the one sentence of encouragement which is also standard: *We wish you all success with your work.*

Abbreviation of the letter, carried to the furthest extreme, can be reduced to the one word: *NO.* And that is the way Jack communicates it to me. He hands me a stack of correspondence with the letters **N O** written in red pencil at the top of each page. Having memorized the rejection formula, I operate the IBM electric typewriter, which then spits out a letter of regret every five minutes........ten, if I pause to read the correspondence and educate myself as to what might constitute a rejectable manuscript.

When Jack's business is completed, Elaine, his A/A, (Administrative Assistant), has second priority on me .....and when I have processed all their work, they lend me to the editors who pass me around until Jack or Elaine claim me again.

The office, which has not been redecorated for a long time, is deliberately designed to look like an office: it's a drag. The desks are all either steel gray or brown Formica imitation wood top. All the telephones are black push-button affairs. The walls are off-white monotony.....and the carpeting is institutional green short hair. The interior, to put it mildly, is purposeful bland dullness.

Even the letterhead, typographed to an impersonal businesslike conformity, excludes joy. I condition my body to robot automatism so that it will do the job on automatic pilot, freeing my mind to meditate. Gradually I notice that my fellow employees, the editorial and public relations departments, the accounting and production people, compensate with their idiosyncratic personalities and behavior for all the uninspiring surroundings.

Habitually, I arrive fifteen minutes early at the office. Solitary quiet is required before the idea of working penetrates thoroughly. It is hard for me to submit to the identity of secretary-hood. Breakfast has been eliminated because I don't want to get feverish or heartburned. The first hour or so is a struggle. A cup of coffee supplies all the energy. Like a votary, I make pilgrimage to the office percolator. It is situated in the back of the office in the innermost sanctum of the Accounting Department.

Benny is already nursing a cup of coffee, swaying in his green swivel chair with sybaritic lethargy. Since he was the first one in, he has already made the coffee.

Benny Frisch, Chief Accountant, is the veteran of Academia Books. His relationship is taken comfortably for granted as the benefit of the spiritual marriage of long years standing with this institution. He has seen everything. Nothing new to be found at Academia; therefore, he can handle everything.

4

The back office is his fief, for which he does occasional homage to our liege lord Jack Livingston. Benny benevolently oversees the accounting menage, even accommodating a dart board not for himself. Should Jack pay a visit to Benny's reserves, it is a safe diplomacy to engage him in sport. Jack's rampant and unlimited fantasy are better directed toward pleasure rather than left to roam, crying havoc in a system that is well under control.

Benny's thin graying hair flatly covers his squarish head. His white shirt protrudes over his belt in a discreet curve that suggests a paunch. His body is short but broad and very solid. He limps slowly with dignity, (a World War II injury), and has the refined resignation of a mathematically inclined aging Jew from Brooklyn.....aquiline nose and thin wide lips.

Benny is an absolute lecher, the pinching kind. He always gets in a good feel or a handful of your thigh if you are absent-minded enough to get close to him. And does he not know when to stop? Goddammit!

"But I *like* you, Greaves," explains Benny, "even if you don't give me a good Bang now and then. I'm not *in love* with you. I don't want anything from you..... just a good Bang now and then. You don't know how difficult life gets sometimes." He makes a grab for my skirt as I evasively slip by to the coffee-maker and set myself up with coffee and cream, no sugar. It is hard being angry with Benny. Jack Livingston has driven all the men in the office stark raving bananas with his overt sex mania. They all show different signs of coming apart at the seams.

As nicely as possible, I inform Benny there is just no way I can accommodate him in my schedule. Justifying *CELIBACY* in the office would be impossible. At Academia, they'd chalk it up as one more evidence of mental disturbance.

Benny has definitely assessed me as crazy, but he likes me. "Greaves, you're kooky..... just a nutty broad."

Today, after I tell him how *really* I was sick last week, he makes his daily pass for the record.

"How about all your sick days that I never mark down? You'd be really hard up if I did. Like I am! Hard up. You've seen my wife." (She is as short and boxy as Benny, hasn't aged gracefully at all.) "Come on," gets in a pat at my nylons, "let's go somewhere and *BANG*!"

Unclear to me where somewhere *is*. The boss says that if I ever took Benny up on his propositions, he'd be running in the other direction fast as the eye could see. I haven't the nerve to test this theory.

"Hey, be serious, Benny. Tell me. How was your weekend?"

For once, Benny looks troubled. "Well, we had a problem. Marion (his eldest daughter) is ditching her husband."

"Wow," I reply. "That's really rough. I mean, with a baby. Where is she? Has she moved in with you?"

"No," says he, "she's in her apartment. But the bastard, *(Marion's Ex),* switched locks on her when she was in the country with us. So we had to go and get them changed. And when we got in, we found he had completely cleaned out the apartment. No furniture! So we're taking him to court." He leans back in the swivel chair, carefully so as not to tip over, and lets out a reminiscent sigh.

"Then over the weekend, he comes knocking on the door, hanging his head. Sits on the floor and cries. I bet that's what he's done all his life, ever since he was a kid.....to get what he wants. That clever bastard has it all planned out in his head. Tick. Tick. Tick...... So then he sees the keys to the new locks lying on the kitchen counter, and he grabs them. Marion goes to stop him, so he tosses them out from the terrace onto the street. Then Laurie *(Daughter #2)*, who is in the next room because I told her "Stay with Marion in case there will be more trouble," she rushes out.

6

"There is a lamp which she picks up, but he gets it away from her. She gets hit, but then she gets it away from him. So then he runs out because he got hit, and immediately, he goes to the hospital. Then he goes to the police station to file an assault charge. Then Laurie files a counter charge, and now he is scared shitless."

Benny gives a thin smile of satisfaction, savoring his coffee and his vengeance. "Because an arrest on an accountant's record, man, that can really screw you out of quite a few jobs!"

"Wow....." I picture the entire scene as it has been recounted to me, complete with sound effects, thinking how friendly my own divorce has been in comparison.

"I tell Laurie not to drop it," Benny says smugly, "because I want that bastard to PAY. Alimony, of course. And tomorrow Marion goes to court for a writ of protection."

"She shouldn't let him in if he comes again," I advise. Divorces and separations have begun to fall into a familiar routine to me.

"*That's* what I told her already. Next time, she'll know." Benny puts milk in his second cup of coffee and stirs.

"She's really OK. She's a bright kid, Marion. She's got a job in Waldbaum's, part time. And when she's ready for full-time work again, she can go back to subbing. She's a biology teacher, you know. She makes forty to fifty dollars a day when she's working. She can support herself."

I calculate. All that money. What I could *do* with it! But the clock tells me it is time to be at my post in the front office. The happy receptionist who combs the morning mail. I stand to go, and Benny looks up and down at me.

"Listen. How about lunchtime we go somewhere? All I want is a good *BANG*....."

* * * * *

The front office is already populated. Elaine, my superior officer, is back from her business trip. She outranks me, as Assistant to the Director. I am only his Secretary, and often it feels as if I am more hers than his.

"Hi," I greet her. "I have bad news for you. I was sick Thursday and Friday last week and couldn't come in."

"How are you now?" she inquires, all concern.

"I think I'm all right. I'll know better at the end of today."

Elaine is the only one in the office who is in love with her job. It's only a crappy job, if you ask me, and hardly pays more than mine. But her romantic determination to make it an adventure carries even me away sometimes. Elaine is the Administrative Assistant because she has initiative. She has 'Attention to Detail', is a 'Self-Starter' and is business-minded, all the qualities I don't have.

"Now they're really letting women *DO* something," she tells me with a serious look on her beautiful face. "So be smart, Alison, and think about having a *career.*"

If numbers and business add up to career, I can't understand where the excitement is supposed to come from. I type her letters searching for the source of all this enthusiasm. One day I'll understand exactly how a publishing house is run. Someday, if I feel like it, I too may have a career. But I don't think so.

Elaine's letters are a paper portrait of her personality. They have good form and correct business style. They also seem to be irrelevant. Elaine's energy, though, as she hands me drafts of long letters to prospective authors, is enjoyable. She asks questions and gives advice. She doesn't know half the subjects she is discussing, if that much. She tells professors of esoteric disciplines, such as Utopian Urban Development or Invertebrate Psychology, how to rearrange their manuscripts. She may know nothing about the branch of knowledge, but she will know the market for it......university texts and college libraries. As for me? What do I care what it all means? I type every letter carefully, watching my spelling and adding at the bottom:

> *Sincerely yours,* (remarkable, but she is, she is)
> *(Miss) Elaine G. Greenlake, Assistant to the Director*
> *EGG/aeg*

With a hopeful smile, Elaine outlines a new plan to me. Her page boy of glossy black hair quivers with excitement, and her dark eyes glisten. Perhaps this will save Academia Books some money. A dollar here, a dollar there, and so her salary will be merited. Fine with me. Elaine is *M O T I V A T E D.* As you have already understood, the business of the job is neither my concern nor my avocation. I am just an appendage to the typewriter and the phones. The extra maneuvers Elaine wishes of me, I carry out without complaint simply because she is kind. This kindness, I find extraordinary. It would be nice to see her reap some points for herself. She tries so hard. Why not?

I know I don't sufficiently appreciate the position I'm in...... probably because I got it through an employment agency. Chance alone landed me in publishing. And the fact that I don't give a damn about it, which the boss thought should be a refreshing change. And it is an accident that Jack, with his bizarre sense of humor, was the person with the authority to hire me.

Jack has pointed out to me, though, in the interests of expanding my intellectual comprehension of the world, that Academia Books is a perfect vantage point from which to examine society. Also, he stresses that I should be aware, (as a related fact) that no one in our offices, (except Elaine) has any respect for authors, editors, professors, Ph.D.s, or anyone else.

"From which you may conclude," added he, "that the business

of publishing or not publishing ideas teaches us cynicism in the process." Easy to see what he means.

Today, for example, was another R.D., (Rejection Day). I had to do the letters and return the manuscripts of twenty-five poets. There was little time to do more than scan a few pages here and there to get the flavor of each personality. My.....my.... All these noble words..... I'd recite them aloud lingeringly if only time was available to spend on them. I *love* poetry. But it wouldn't do any good. The poetry doesn't sell. What a culture is ours where only dead and half-dead poets are respected.

Where are all these poets going to go? Why do they bother to send us their work in the first place? Why do they desire to be not only poets but published poets? And by Academia Books of all the available publishers? I mean, does it make such a vast difference in the work? Would the poems be any more expressive if they were published? And would any difference be for the better?

Almost all the poets appear to support themselves by teaching literature or language at some college or other. Here is a new picture for me of the professor as a hopeless romantic or cynic or dweller in trivia. You should see the ragged envelopes these accredited literati include to have their manuscripts mailed back to them. In the U.S. mail? If their papers get back intact to their ivy covered shelters, it will be a miracle.

As it is with the poets, so it is with the authors of prose. We are inundated with manuscripts from professori. Since Academia is mostly a scholarly press, the ones we publish end up being on arcane topics, such as: *The Cock and Bull Story: Hemingway's Theory of Christianity* or studies of emotional disturbances in societies of exclusively male monkeys......goodies like these. Just to develop a topic that is sufficiently cryptic requires many years of formal education, not to mention the necessity for being validated by respectable credentials.

As my stack of rejects grows smaller, I feel rather than see the boss drift by into his office. The boss, Jack, has my complete loyalty. No other employer, surely, would keep me on after the disasters that have flowed in my wake. (Fleeing through the halls of Academia in hysterical tears, publicly pursued by lovers with murderous intentions, wobbling in looking like the morning after, or simply non-explained non-appearances to list only a few.) And I have his approval, indeed, encouragement, to dress as I please. Ten strands of different varieties of colored and glittering beads, hand-embroidered peasant blouses redolent with authentic ethnicity, dungarees, new or aged, with and without holes, patches, add-ons, cut offs, studs,......and hair without benefit of beautician. He never complains.

I want the record set straight on Jack. Jack Livingston is a true humanitarian, even if it has turned out that he has a reputation as a sex maniac and an alcoholic. He keeps me on in the job. Doesn't force me to pretend to be somebody I'm not just to pay the bills. As for his drinking, it's a well-known fact that everyone in publishing drinks except for those who have seen a doctor and joined AA......though to be sure, few drink with Jack's tenacity and connoisseurship. You can't even claim he's wasting money doing it, because it all goes on the expense account.

I'm a special case at Academia Books. Generally, the staff goes crazy a month or two *after* they have been hired, just from being around Jack, who is contagious. I was well on my way before he interviewed me.

With his clairvoyant ability to sniff out tendencies toward insanity, Jack not only realized that I might really need his asylum, but that I would be a prize specimen for his collection. (Later he said something about my legs also having something to do with my getting the job. But that was minor.) Out of the goodness of his heart, he granted me sanctuary, a safe haven, and more liberty than usually goes along with a salary. His instinct for these things sensed that as a new divorcee with a daughter to support and a love life to mend, I needed the benefit of his tutelage.

My college background allows me to explain the psychedelic experience to Jack in language he can relate to, so he has cast me as spokeswoman for the Flower Children in our debates. As long as I answer the phones, get the letters out, and deal with the office chores, I can also type letters to my friends, make phone calls, and get taken to swanky restaurants once or twice a week on the expense account. Jack feels that sort of bonus is supposed to go along with the job.

My education has become Jack's personal responsibility. To be truly cultured, a knowledge of Paella, Moussaka, Tempura, Hoisin Sauce, and fancy French cuisine is of importance. Distinguishing a good wine from an ordinary wine is of importance. But *SEX*, how to do it, (*alternative ways*), when and with whom, and how to handle it, is Number One priority. Jack has decided my pitiful lack of experience is the main reason I get myself into so many messy situations.

My sex education is verbally conducted over sumptuous lunches and with no ulterior motives because, regretfully, the one rule Jack adheres to is: *"NO INTER-OFFICE FUCKING!"*

"Office relationships," Jack pontificates over a broiled sea bass, "are always a problem. They gum up the works. If they go wrong, there are all these tensions floating about......emotional attachments...... Pfeh. I always have a rule: *NO* inter-office fucking, at any time. Everywhere else, yes. In the office, no. Talk about it, why, yes. Talk is educational and harmless, even beneficial. Do it with your coworkers, no. Just too messy. THINK. Put yourself in my place. What if you had to end up firing someone who needed a job?"

I am forced to speculate on the survival of our colleagues elsewhere than Academia, and again Jack wins respect from me for his long-range thinking and self-control under provocation. You can see the qualities of leadership which make him an ideal Chief Executive.

Thusly, the boss and I are ruled out of having an affair with each other, which is fine with both of us. No problems with vacancies in the love lives. Across the gourmet food and fine linen, we make a date for an affair far in the future, should either of us be employed somewhere else. Years away, it is such a friendly and non-threatening proposition.

Meanwhile, the boss in anxious to make sure I get to try everything, gastronomically and sexually. He wants nothing for himself in my case, except the satisfaction of being my adviser. He becomes very religious as he discusses the subject. Slowly, he enlightens me into the mysteries of Tantra.....the cult of ancient sex worship that insists sex is the way to heaven almost regardless of whom you pick to do it with, except that it is preferable to select an adept as a partner. He never uses the word 'Tantra'.....but the manner in which he speaks is devoutly full of joy. So what else could he be talking about?

Tantra is a heterosexual art that insists the opposite sex represents your compliment, your 'Other', the whatever it is you need for completion. You should go out and to perfect sexual union surround it with all the sensual adornments, good food, fine wine, soft music, pleasant company..... Voila! God will come and visit you. To be truly spiritual about it, you knock yourself out making the invitation appropriately ceremonious and show the deity you are prepared to entertain as long as he/she stays.

Why, Jack Livingston is positive that if you are fully committed to sex, *(as a religion?)*, it can't fail to be a divine experience, ever. Your body should be allowed to gravitate to the appealing member of the opposite sex, (especially if they present a case of out and out need to you). Merely it is a question of hanging in there until everyone has had enough.....doing it in such an interesting way that no one is bored.....until you need to eat or sleep, or go to the bathroom. To Jack, sex provides everything, except a congenial way to make money. He thinks too much of sex to ever contaminate it with anything but pure altruism.

Sex should happen many times every day with as many different people as possible. Ten times a day for Jack is *nothing*.

"Most men don't realize they can do that, or are so stupid they can't find enough things to do to remain interested."

"Wow! Jack, I've never met a man who can handle all *that* much. Generally, men run out of steam way before I do."

"The wrong men!" Jack retorts as he ingests his Lo Mein, noodle by noodle. "You are an intelligent sensitive girl, Alison, who can feel things in a variety of ways.....so naturally you have a lot of possibilities. Your average person feels less, and has less. It is amazing, but so much of sex is in the head......"

My visions of male capacity are more optimistic now that Jack has started explaining how it works. He finds talking about sex is the next best thing to doing it. Would I have imagined a publishing executive, a boss, could be like him? Never. His ambitions are (1) to own a yacht and sail it around the world and (2) to someday set up a school where enjoyment of sex will be properly taught. "*MAKE LOVE, NOT WAR!* That is the one thing you Flower Children stand for that I can agree with," says Jack. "If people were only less inhibited..... If they didn't have so many hang-ups..... Yes! A proper freedom and enjoyment of sex would go much further to save the world than psychedelic drugs! It's all these uptight people who aren't getting any who are hostile." Regarding me as his most promising disciple, *(the only really committed one),* he supervises my curriculum with all the watchful zeal of a conscientious guardian.

Jack educates me. He tells me about his wife, what she does to him, how it feels, what she says she feels about it.....group orgies they have, etc. Techniques and anatomy are discussed with various free associations thrown in for good measure, (no pun intended).

"The *one* thing I tell anyone before I go to bed with them," Jack tells me so his record is clear, "is that my wife is *THE BEST.* I *owe* it to her to protect her. Can't have her disturbed by things people might say. Can't have the woman thinking she can change my relationship with my wife. My wife, Stretch, does give the best blow job I've ever had….. Isn't the greatest fuck though. One of the best, certainly….. but not the best."

Listening with wide open eyes and ears, the noodles swim like a school of eels in my soup. I stir them slowly and inhale the aroma. Mouthfuls of Essence of China melt and are sucked in along with Jack's philosophy. Slowly, the thoughts are spiced with a timeless mellow silence in which we both pay our respects to the food.

"Jack, you know, you ought to write a book. I did just what you told me, and the dude didn't know what hit him. You give the best instructions on blow job finessing I've ever come across."

"That's from my wife…..and because I talk with women freely," replies Jack, "although I could write many books if I had a mind to."

I assert Jack Livingston is a good guy, a pure man in spite of his alcoholism and vestiges of macho aesthetics. Why, he sees nothing wrong with expressing your personality as long as his letters go out. Even if I somnambulate through the office with a blurry countenance or if I come in resembling a walking orgy, so long as the letters have minimal typos, he considers I am carrying out the basic responsibilities of the job.

Alien to the very purpose of business and efficient only to get it over with sooner, I attend Jack's correspondence, the savage princess carrying out this and other menial tasks in the audience chamber of the king. The more barbarous and primitive my clothing and embellishments become, (as I gain confidence), the more Jack enjoys the astonishment of visiting executives. I urbanely conform with business etiquette, coming to an attentive stance and mouthing with dulcet sweetness the standard receptionist formalities:

> "Good morning. Can I help you?"
> "Yes, Mr. Livingston is expecting you."
> "Will you have coffee or tea?"
> "He'll be with you in just a moment."

The smoother my delivery gets, while the more outlandish my appearance, the greater Jack's entertainment. He is a monarch with a tiger on a leash of gold, delighting in predatory pets who define his own wild prowess by bringing the elemental instincts of the jungle into the headquarters of civilization: Academia Books.

There is more fun to be had in playing out these evolving roles than in all the business, which, alas, must be transacted. Seething emotions and secretarial efficiency personified, I happily perform my part. I'm only glad Jack prefers a live secretary to a dead one and has enough discernment to cultivate my style according to its own proclivities rather than forcing me into the suffocation of office impersonality.

Jack even takes care of my ego, making it clear that his passing up the golden opportunity I constitute is strictly connected with his business ethics, his experience, and the farsighted understanding that my income must be guaranteed. As with any philandering Casanova, women are regularly falling in love with him only because his sexual generosity terminates a starvation they were not even aware of. This is a lousy reason for love, Jack says, considering he is not the only man in the world.

As for Mr. Livingston, he considers he has a bargain: a live plant growing in the dry office soil, decorating the front desk. Unlike the plastic substitutes that look good from a distance but remain unresponsively the same, I require watering and consistent care. He spends the necessary time feeding me, watering me, and talking to me until I blossom exotically, perfuming the acrid business interior with the fragrance of feminine awareness.

Proud of his handiwork, Jack then introduces me to the parade of aging scholars and business luminaries that visit him with the satanic mischief of a Marquis de Sade. Even tired flesh will respond if the temptation is sufficiently appealing. Then, a gratified spectator, he watches the interplay. The atmosphere of the front office, with its suggestion of free love, illicit pleasures, and bohemian practices, benefits Academia as it gets people off balance, which gives Jack

16

a distinct advantage in business negotiations. The intensity and absorption with which I am dancing on the tightrope of sexual tension he has strung for me, (and with no safety net as insurance to catch me should I lose my footing), is what Jack likes about me most.

But it's very hard on the men in the office. You see, I'm not the only one who gets the benefit of Jack's counsel and advice. The boys in the back rooms, the men, don't appreciate this as much as I do; mostly they are a bunch of married commuters. Our public relations man, Bill, a very starched individual, has contracted a violent case of ulcers from Jack plus an addiction to blue movies.

"What are blue movies, Jack?"

"Porno flicks," he snaps with contempt. "A big waste of time. Why see it if you could be doing it? It's not like an orgy where you can join in if you want to. And the pity of it all is they do it so crudely, so clumsily. No taste. No appreciation..... Don't even bother going to see one, Alison. You're already beyond that bullshit. As for Bill," he adds, "he's a real sicko. He doesn't enjoy making love. That's why he has to watch it. Turning sex into a spectator sport, getting it secondhand. That's sick. Why, the man doesn't even enjoy *EATING!!!*"

* * * * *

"Do you believe the boss really can do all those things he says he can?" asks Tom, the Managing Editor, as he caresses the rear-end of his copy girl with longing eyes.

"Why not?" I answer. "He's dedicated enough, puts time and thought into it. Why, there are even special exercises....." Tom cuts me off with: "You're as crazy as he is and naive to boot."

Some pretty lady or other comes in to see the boss. Incredulously, the editors watch as the office door closes and locks. They listen for noises like little children outside of their parents' bedroom. An hour. It's the middle of the working day. An hour and still no one has come out of there. Imaginations take off. The men shift about,

17

ill at ease with themselves as if they were allowing some major part of their lives to atrophy. Before Jack went to work on them, though, they were perfectly happy with their wives and kids and houses in suburbia. Now they start inviting the copy girls out for drinks after work and buy them lunch with increasing frequency. The hungry looks I get as I pass the halls distributing memos...... Life is definitely hard or at least more complicated if you have the Jack Livingston aura pervading your workplace. Jack, with his sexual parading, strange transferences and verbal exhibitions, could make restraint very difficult even if you had a perfect marriage to your high school sweetheart. (Still, boss though he is, he's the only person at Academia I have any real affection for.)

* * * * *

"Writing a *BOOK*?" Surprised, Jack freezes in the process of raising his martini to his lips. "Whatever for?" That anyone who works at Academia can be so oblivious of the realities of the publishing world after a residence of more than a month at our establishment seems impossible to him. (Of course, it would be me.) "Writing a *BOOK*? What difference will it make to the world?"

"Oy, Jack," I hurry to explain. "That's not why I'm writing. I must write in order to grow into the *ME* I will be at the end of all the words. The words have a meaning beyond all the semantics..... The *feeling* behind all the words..... The way I feel....."

"I have a book inside me too." Jack contemplates his glass as if it were a crystal that revealed the future and not taking my book particularly seriously since it's been established in his mind as just a personal matter. "I have many books inside me.....good books....."

He does, he really does. I know he does. And I wonder why he hasn't bothered to write them all down. If I had only half his facility with words..... But with my pitifully small journal where I inscribe my daily weight, the list of what I ate, the list of what I refrained from eating, my physical health, who I slept with that day, and the current cause of depression, how can I presume to advise Jack who knows all about writing? About *WRITING*? But I do wonder about those unwritten books of his because they are important, and why he has not even started them......

Chapter 2

It is raining. Nature surrounds me with a falling sky. I feel like Chicken Little. Congruent to the environment, invisible tears flood my concentration. This sorrowful inundation of the emotions has been going on for days. On sunny days, though, I can manage to suppress my feelings and take care of the necessities. It is only when rain presents me with an external portrait of my depression magnified across the sky that my spiritual dams overflow.

I stand in the doorway, a medium-sized woman approaching thirty, stretching out my arms, testing the reality of the rain. As the drops drizzle slowly along my skin, ultimately falling from my fingertips, I weep along with them silently.

"…..*fruitless tears*…..," the phrase occurs to me. Rubbing my eyes, wiping my hands on the back of my pants, I retreat indoors. My table, littered with an assortment of papers, is a discouragement. When will there be time to clean it? The typewriter presents me with a single sheet of white paper on which I have been able to type a single sentence:

Paradise Valley is a desert. Constantly thirsty.

Of course I would pick a rainy day to write about dry places. I compose a mental picture of a desert landscape of the southwest. If I can make myself visualize it, I will be able to pick out a description:

> *Flat plains of rock are compacted into red earth sprinkled sparsely with vegetation. The ground is left balding and nearly naked.*

"Like some giant desiccated mummy," I muse to myself. "The

skeleton and some of the skin covering it have been preserved. But it's lost all of its flesh….."

"Dammit!" Swearing aloud I cross my legs. "No time for morbid thoughts." A contemporary Buddha, I roost on a kitchen chair in the lotus position, (not so easy in tight dungarees), and resume typing:

> *The blank sky is an infinity uninterrupted by flat cities. It is a horizontal land; all the architecture hugs the ground. Outside the city limits, the fierce heat of the sun rouses primeval totems: the cactuses…..upright exclamation marks on an empty plain….vertical and self-contained…..*

The perverse eye of my mind immediately transforms a cactus into an erect green prick covered with spikes. I don't want to be reminded of anything connected with sex! "No way!" My hands cover my eyes, attempting to obscure this image. Methodically, I conjure a Saguaro as a replacement, its many arms invoking the sky. Better. Saguaros always assume a reverent pose, always seem to be praying.

I continue

> *The tough skin of the cactus, thorned and barbed, is the desert's comment on the scantiness of water. Survival in this furnace means fluid must be guaranteed, cherished and protected…..*

Propping my feet on a garbage can filled with shredded paper, tucked under the table, I listen to the falling rain. Poems and novels invariably link the rain with cleansing, but they are, after all, fiction. Can the rain be depended upon to cleanse anything?

Yesterday the kid barged into my bedroom, where I was skulking, hoping for privacy, and announced:

"It's going to rain, Mommy."

Animated by the prospect of change, she runs outside for evidence, to check the sky. Every noise she makes running through the house sends electric shocks up my spine. In the amusement park there is a pedal you hit with a sledge hammer which sends a ball up a wire. If you hit hard enough, it reaches and rings a bell. I feel just like that. My spine is the wire, and loud noises of the kid jolt my spinal cord, crashing into the base of my brain, there setting off some unpleasant explosions. The immanence of rain upsets me also.

"By morning, everything will be dry, probably. So what's the use?" My thoughts diffuse into an interference pattern as bumping, knocking, and muffled exclamations filter through the thin sheetrock wall. Is Babette fighting with her friend again? Living with her continual battles erodes my self-control. Sooner or later I will come out of my corner, screaming. Then I will have a sore throat and nothing will change. How not to be driven crazy?

How long can I survive Babette's childhood? Will life ever give me the Grand Prize: 'PERMANENT PEACE OF MIND'?

I recline on my mattress, waiting for the rain to materialize. I made my own quilt, (because I didn't have the money to buy a real one), stripes of different black materials quilted in parallel lines, hoping to dignify this mattress on the floor into a bed. Wind and rain begin to hiss and splash against the window. The dark glass reflects my face to me, blurry with distortion, sprinkled with raindrops, isolated and disfigured by the rain..... In New York City.....dark murky gray haze.....oppressive air sandwiched by tall buildings stained gray with soot.....rain freezing into slippery traps on gray concrete pavements; people falling.....streams of dirty gray rain swirling debris of too many people into the gutters.......

When I feel so rotten, I retreat to sleep for lack of anything else. Emotional exhaustion makes consciousness itself abrasive. Mechanically I assume the formal posture of a mummy on a sarcophagus, arms folded neatly over my breasts. I count my breaths: one, two, three, four, five, (inhale and hold.....exhale), one, two, three, four, five. What better way to bridge the interval between retirement and being taken away?

Gradually, a presence makes itself felt. A woman, swathed in white drapery, leaning next to an institutional table, confronts me. As focus sharpens into detail, a pale mask stares at me with deep-set eyes of extraordinary blue radiance. The effect is lapis lazuli inlay in Greek polychrome marble. The planes of the features are expressionlessly symmetrical.....high forehead, high cheekbones, and straight even nose. The sculptured full lips curve even in repose. Long tangled hair surrounds the face in a profusion of wild brown waves. This unmanicured mane is splendid, and red and blonde highlights gleam from the snarled filaments. Reminiscent of classical art, the face presents a haunting spectacle. By Hollywood standards, you could not call this face pretty, perhaps not even feminine. The intelligence and willfulness projected do not conform to the fashionable stereotype of a pretty girl.

As the shock of the intrusion ebbs, I find myself pleasantly warmed by this woman's style. I search for a name. She seems familiar to me.

The white cloth draping her is revealed by examination to be a Mexican robe of unbleached and handwoven material; a kind of loose sack. Tiny men and women are elaborately embroidered in green and red cross-stitching around the yoke; and then it falls in simple folds to the floor. Fred Leighton Imports! Recognition arrives in a dizzying collision of trivia: this is my favorite dress. The woman must therefore be *ME*, Alison. I must be in a dream.

The executives at work who feel any kind of a loose dress cheats them of their prerogative, body-watching, tease me about wearing a postulant's garb.....or a potato sack.

"But of course," I retort. "A potato sack, naturally, but one of the highest quality. Would you have me settle for a common potato sack? *NO.*"

I patiently assemble clues from the dream to resolve where I am. Usually when I look in the mirror, I have trouble recognizing myself, and I don't like it. It is a pleasure to remember how favorably impressed I was with the lady until I identified her as myself. This augers well for the dream.

Surroundings are modern institutional.....blankness. Could be a school, business office, staff lounge, community center. An electric percolator which has already reached the stage of quiescence dominates the table which is stacked with rows of cheap paper cups.

Aha! This is Babette's day care center. Construction paper ornaments, the hieroglyphics of children's drawings, and low cubbies with hooks for coats and separate compartments for rubbers all spell: *DAY CARE CENTER CLASSROOM.* The coffee defines the occasion as a Parent Teachers Meeting.

All right. I can accept this. But why are Joan Baez and Bob Dylan here? And what is my boss Jack doing here? His kids have grown up long ago. I look about and find some more inconsistent participants; my best friends Petra and Ruthy, (who don't even have any kids), and Pierre from the leather store. (He doesn't have kids either, although he would like some).

"It's going to turn out all right. Dreams have a logic of their own, a la Shakespeare, Jung, and Carlos Castaneda....." I reassure myself and list every observation hoping I'll remember it when I wake up. It could be of importance.

Chocolate covered Mallomars. A paper plate of chocolate cookies, such as I bought for Babette on a whim just the other day. This plate is ceremoniously being passed from hand to hand. Everyone is helping themselves and eating with gusto. The plate reaches me. I pass the plate along without taking anything. A hush and stopped motion. Everybody is staring at me as if I have violated some collective etiquette, waiting for me to account for my anti-social abstinence.

"PEOPLE WHO CAN'T CONTROL THEIR APPETITES SHOULDN'T HAVE COOKIES!" I hear myself declaim in a too loud voice as if reiterating a familiar aphorism.

"If you eat too many cookies, you get a stomach ache," I elaborate hopefully. "And you shouldn't start eating cookies in the first place, unless you know you have the will power to stop."

Everyone turns away from me. Was there anything insulting in what I said? Maybe I'm talking too much? Or hanging around children too much so that I'm talking like an idiot? What would Carl Jung think of this dream? Perhaps no-cookie-taking is self-evident, and I am only repeating what everybody knows, thus revealing myself to be a bore and a ridiculous fool? A roomful of happy cookie-eaters surrounds me, munching, none of whom seem to be suffering any ill consequences. They are stuffing a never-ending supply of Mallomars into their mouths at a rapid pace, ignoring me and my unfortunate speech. I cannot imagine how they avoid being sick. I could never cram into myself the quantities I see being put away.....

Frustrated and hungry, in a cloud of chocolate vapor, I move off by myself, away from Bob Dylan and Joan Baez, away from Jack and Petra and Ruth.......putting a distance between the plate of temptation and myself. And something I read by Richard Alpert comes back to me: when you start getting straight with yourself and find the here-and-now, your hang-ups and desires will easily fall away. I've been waiting for the hang-ups to fall away ever since I read this, but they haven't. Now, suddenly, in my dream, I get illuminated. *Satori. Nirvana.* I no longer want cookies. Have lost the need for cookies. Can't imagine ever wanting to eat cookies again. Exhilaration. Freedom. Just like that! It is so simple. Just as Alpert said it could be. The enemy, cookies, has surrendered. Cookies, as a social pressure, have been overcome. Even subliminal messages beamed from the TV or by satellite into my subconscious can never force me to eat cookies again.

THOSE WHO CAN'T CONTROL THEIR APPETITES SHOULDN'T START EATING COOKIES echoes the voice of the

Guru again and again within the center of my soul. I have heard the voice of the Guru within. I've been hunting for the Guru for years, never found him before. But now my course is plain. I murmur this dream mantra with dutiful gratitude. I have received personally the first commandment: **THOU SHALT NOT EAT MALLOMARS OR ANY OTHER COOKIES**. So let it be written. No cookies! So let it be done. Amen. Selah!

* * * * *

My shoulder is shaking. Someone is shaking my shoulder. The heavenly voice ceases its whisper. Tapping me with her little hand is a midget willow-of-the-wisp in a flowered flannel nightgown. Tiny pink roses on linty white flannel. Babette, my four-year-old daughter. The clock reads three-in-the-morning.

"Whaaat?" I groan, trying to separate from the dream.

"I want to sleep in *YOUR* bed, Mommy!" Babette declares with a good deal of assumed cheerfulness. She scuttles in beside me, wriggling until a satisfactory nest has been arranged in my side.

Still in the half-coma of interrupted sleep, I mumble as firmly as I can contrive, "Good night, now. Really, no more talking." The child isn't permitted to sleep with me. But her softness is soothing and pleasant. Just once can do no harm. A soft bell-like tone floats up from under the blanket.

"OK, Mommy. I like you a whole lot, Mommy. I like you all the time."

The kid's presence ameliorates the memory of the cookie-dream with the comforting cushion of affection. But why is my unconscious producing such classics? Every time after I read Jung, I can expect a dream to order, symbols hovering within reach with a million archetypal positive and negative significances. "What do the cookies stand for?" What a dumb question. Everybody knows that everything in a dream is a part of yourself. "So what do the cookies stand for?" I cling to my sleeping daughter, wishing for her unchallenged self-belief.....the self-belief of a four-year-old without benefit of an Introduction to Psychology course.....and wishing the Mallomars would go away forever.

Babette is an aesthetic experience. She is Little Lady Fauntleroy. As she runs in the park, the glittering spirals of her red gold curls mesh with the light, crowning her with a copper nimbus.

"What magnificent hair! Do you know how lucky you are?" exclaims the proverbial old lady passing by. Kids are magnets to old ladies. Babette speeds over, nearly stamping her vanilla ice cream cone onto the lady's old black coat.

"Don't you speak to my Mommy." She bristles with greed, totally unwilling to share. Hastily, I make a grab for her.

"Why not?" coos the old woman with the tolerance of age.

"Ummmmmmmm.....my Mommy doesn't want you to!" Rubber knees bounce down the street: *zoyng, zoyng, zoyng*, like a pink rubber ball.

"You are so lucky," repeats the old woman, reluctant to let me go. I follow Babette, sedately having a hard time with the old-lady view of my life. Just because I am young? (*relatively*), and have a pretty child, automatically I am fortunate? Alison, the fortunate?

Instead of dropping off to sleep, Babette stirs and pokes me. "I have to go wee-wee." Motherhood equals responsibility for everything.

"Go then," and I add, (toilet training must be reaffirmed per Dr. Spock), "I'm very proud of you, very proud....." A few minutes later, a plaintive squeak from the bathroom intrudes on my dozing.

"Wipe me."

I hoist my body from the bed, reminding myself how lucky we are she has made it to the bathroom. I dab at the diminutive little ass. It is as plump and pink as a chicken breast in a supermarket and has a fine little shape. This task accomplished, Babette demands in a regal tone: "Juisssssssss."

"We drank up all the juice," I remind her. She agreeably consents to milk. I grope my way to the kitchen, turning on the light as I step in. A convocation of roaches refuses to move out of the way. Damn my lack of housekeeping. I have not been able to get rid of them.

Why do they have to choose *MY* house? My grandmother never had roaches. Roaches don't bother me as much as they do some people. Still who enjoys seeing them? Armed with a paper towel, I attack the kitchen counter. The roaches start to run. I am successful in squashing a few of them.

"I didn't invite you. I don't care if you were my grandmother in a previous life. You have no business here!"

No. I am not going through the scene with the roaches tonight. I've had a little token respect. I got them on the run. All I want is a good night's sleep. I return to Babette with a cup.

"*Don't* spill. And when you've finished, come back to bed. *This* time we really are going nighty-night."

"Stay with me, Mommy," pipes Babette in her I-am-a-little-little-girl-protect-me voice which she knows sometimes works.

"But I can see you from the bed."

"Noooooo. Stay with me....."

"Oh, Babette....."

"Oh, Mommy......"

No, I do not get annoyed. Though ardently longing for a reunion with sleep, though deeply yearning for every second of delicious pure sleep as a miser treasures his coin collection, I do not, (*REPEAT: do not*), get annoyed.

"Motherhood," my father repeatedly tells me, "is an essential responsibility. You must live for your child or for your children. And make a life for <u>them</u>." Perhaps. I hold onto Babette in the darkness.....the child who looks to me for answers.....irony. I pray for the temporary death that is dreamless sleep and the resurrection of a clean new morning.

* * * * *

Knowing your sanity is in the balance is enough to make you crazy. I am not paranoid. How do I know I am going crazy? Ida, my father's wife, (who will not let me call her stepmother because it makes her feel wicked), told me I was.

"Thank you very much," I said as politely as I could under the circumstances. (Ground rule #1: One must always be nice to stepmothers so as not to create problems in Dad's marriage.) "But couldn't you tell me instead that I am going *SANE* or at least getting saner? That would help a lot more."

"I really couldn't do that," she says with virtue and psychiatric expertise reeking from every pore. "I know what you want to hear. But I can't tell you that because I don't really believe it."

My father sits dumbly trapped between us, knowing anything he says is going to be wrong for one of us. So he says nothing. Probably he thinks we are both crazy. Why isn't he intervening on my behalf though? Or does he really think I'm crazy too? After all, *HE* never had to have a divorce. The floor of my childhood faith has vanished, and I'm floating in space. And since this time, when she brought the matter to my attention across a chocolate malted in the ice-cream parlor, I watch my craziness swell or shrink. Some days I'm not in danger of a nervous breakdown..... Other days.....

"It could happen to you any time now. Maybe it would be the best thing for you that it could happen. Then you would go and get it taken care of." Thanks, Ida. She is so self-complacent. She doesn't know what she's doing to me, or does she?

* * * * *

At night, sometimes the voices start. After Babette has been put to bed, when the responsibilities have all been taken care of. Suggestive voices quietly spread the red carpet of self-destruction for me, seductively as though it were "a consummation devoutly to be wished ....." (Inflections of Laurence Olivier).

"To be, or not to be. That is the question."

Oh, this is all very noble in the mind up on a stage or in the movies. But it hurts when it's happening to me. There is nothing 'noble' about this. Instructions in iambic pentameter that have a contagious rhythm and will not be shut off. "How to do the Deed in ten easy steps." Simple Simon says, "Now, take just one giant step."

Take nine little steps. Take eight. Take seven. I didn't say, "Simple Simon says." Uh oh..... Everything in the house suddenly is seen as a weapon; the oven, the kitchen utensils, my sewing shears, the can opener..... What a dangerous place to be, my own house!

A galaxy of disconnected tools knives, scissors, wires, pill bottles, window ledges, razor blades, spin through my mind like a roulette wheel. "Which one to use?" Multiplying and dancing in intricate patterns.....a bizarre corps de ballet, (or CORPSE de ballet = pun intentional), a Busby Berkeley production number.....*spectacle des instruments des* death.. "Take your pick."

"Phooey." Knowing I'm crazy doesn't make the visions go away. Identifying the classic schizoid symptoms doesn't make the voices recede. So what use a shrink?

Phosphorescent skeletal ghosts with grotesquely threatening

anatomic abstracted grimaces loom from the blackness...... This is hideous!

"I will never, never, never let a monster in the house." I was explaining this to Babette only last night when she woke up with a monster dream. "Trust me!" How can I believe myself now? Babette is of the Sesame Street generation. Her cookie monster is fuzzy and easily tractable, and when Mommy says "Go away!" it goes.

"Go away!" Doesn't work if the monster is real. Better not let the kid find this out; she'll never sleep again. And then I won't sleep. Well, this would make some surrealist painting, wouldn't it? Utterly garish, though. Still, if nasty apparitions are going to make themselves a part of your daily life, why not find them a job? Artist's models: employment for ugly ghosts. At least one doesn't have to pay them.

Episodes from the past, recurrent bad dreams, insist on replaying themselves again and again through my memory, every night. Again and again and again and again: *The Scenes I Would Most Like To Forget.*

Chapter 3

Here I am. Waiting for my divorce in the year of separation New York State is requiring before they give it to you for incompatibility. He, the ex-husband, is taking care of the legal details. Dave knows about lawyers; I do not. It will happen sooner or later that papers will come in the mail. Then I will be checking X in the box next to DIV instead of checking next to SEP on application forms that inquire about marital status. The divorce, though, is not the cause of my precarious mental state. I'm sure of that. This divorce has been a total rebirth, restoring to me a self that had been submerged or repressed piece by piece into the unconscious.....

I didn't notice losing myself at all. I was too busy believing in Dave's pronouncements as if he were an oracle, looking up to him as if he were on a pedestal (like the Statue of Liberty), and in trying to keep up with his demands.

"Yet I really don't love him anymore," I consider with some surprise. "I don't know if I ever loved him after all. How painful that I am capable of lying to myself that way. Why was I so stubborn?" and then, "How can I trust myself to know how I feel ever again?" I bitterly reflect that Dave started out lying to himself from the beginning.

"He never loved me at all. What a big lie all around."

Dave had looked more like a twin brother than a husband. Everyone said we were narcissists, being married to each other, because our coloring was identical, auburn hair and blue eyes. Our features were as similar as if we belonged to the same family. It seemed familiar and natural to be together. (We never for a moment considered that people could be right on target about the narcissism because we could not possibly fall in love....with.....ourselves.)

Dave and I met over a chessboard, where he distinguished himself by winning three times in succession. I had spent that summer living in the Fat Black Pussycat, a Greenwich Village cafe and chess house, trimming preppie egos by challenging them to play and winning fairly easily. Of course I didn't mention I had been playing chess since I was eight years old with my father, (who, lacking a son, was reduced to playing with me.) I also didn't mention that once he taught me the elementary principles of strategy, I beat him regularly and therefore had been playing with my uncles who were serious woodpushers. No, and I didn't mention that I belonged to a chess club. I just hung out in the cafes, looking as cute and dumb as possible, and waited for a pin-striped-crew-cut-college-preppie-type to come along, complete with that automatic assumption of superiority. This was the Sixties and women didn't play chess then, or, if they did, they were considered to be incapable of logic. Ergo, an easy win, and then the satisfaction of some masculine preening at the girl's expense. If he was a nice guy, he might even take the trouble to replay a few moves and show the girl where she went wrong, not that it would do any good. Thinking was not what a woman was valued for by young college men of the Sixties.

My mother's death (two years before) was still haunting me, and I was killing as many opponents in the Game of Kings as possible to try to make up for it, not that it ever did. Since in the entire summer I had never encountered any other young men capable of beating me three times in a row, Dave was instantaneously credited with the charisma of superior intelligence. As the veneer of Andover and Yale lent him a seeming maturity he didn't hesitate to exploit, Dave swept me off my feet. We courted after the manner of F. Scott Fitzgerald and Zelda. I sent him a painting for his wall at Yale. He sent me a series of pithy postcards which, with a scathing wit, satirized the conventions of the university. Packing an attache case with hollow-stemmed champagne glasses, silver candlesticks, candles, a vase, several long stemmed red roses and (most important) a bottle of Piper Heidsieck, we chose to have our evening picnic during the heat of final exam week.....right after dinner hour at Yale on the veranda outside the mess hall. Of course we were dispersed. After a few more little dramas filled with charm and some wilder escapades, we reached the inevitable conclusion: we married. Later, having discovered F. Scott was Dave's favorite American author (and role model), I read his novels and short stories and discovered that our courtship had been acting out a script I hadn't even known about..... and Dave's ideas of what was romantic weren't even his own. I'm not so sure it made a difference who the girl was either, as long as she was some wild-dancing-artist-non-conforming-bohemian-type, and I was all those things. Zelda went crazy too.....a prognosis I didn't find too comforting in retrospect.

As the Anti-Vietnam War Movement spread across the nation's campuses, ("a specter is haunting the nations of Europe,"..... well, in this case, America), Dave immediately rose from the ranks to become a nationally recognized student leader and spokesman for the young left wing. Immediately, he gave up his creative writing for polemics and assembled a Marxist library. Overnight, Dave became a left-wing oracle. He gave *Das Kapital* to himself with such intensity that he read through all three volumes, himself, in one long consecutive sitting, understood them, and had a point of view about them.

I struggle through the chapter in Volume 1 on the *'Fetishism of Commodities'* in the original unexpurgated form Marx wrote it in. Marx is a typical German writer, so the philosophy unfolds in a rich Wagnerian orchestration of quotations in different languages which span all the semantic systems of Europe. From the dawn of philosophy, dropping names and allusions, he traces the steps of philosophy from primitivism to truth. All the antecedents of Marxian Dialectical Materialism are actively dancing in front of me. Dave has clarity about this, but I am dizzy. Every sentence is impacted with multiple associations and philosophic correlations, all of which define how society has arranged the thought structure of human beings as they relate to objects. Material realities = commodities. And then Marx explains how the material division of these objects exacts a vengeance by dividing humanity from each other. And I could tell the line that divided me from Dave because he found all this very easy to understand; I found it hard.

Dave was uniquely equipped to dive into this cataract of reasoning because he had been a swimming champion. Before I knew it, he was in and out of the books, having covered the distance and was standing on the opposite shore trying to tell me what time it was with a stop-watch in his hand.

Since Dave was so interested in saving time, politically, and since he lived right there in the same house with me, I didn't quite see the need, (*nor did he*), why our labors must be duplicated. He assumed the post of Resident Ideologist and I agreed with his conclusions without argument and immediately translated them into action.

That the world made no sense had been apparent to me from early childhood. And to build a society where all could live happily, I could see that love of humanity was the way. Not only must the distinctions of class be defied, but also those of sex, occupation, or any other barrier which prevents people from identifying with each other. At once, I was denoted a *LIBERAL*, having 'liberal *tendencies.*' I was someone who could easily fall into the error of liking people for themselves, which could be dangerous.

The process of working toward a settlement of the world's problems within a group creates its own micro-society which produces human beings in the image of that process. Thus Marxism produces the dictatorship of the proletariat, (in our house, that meant Dave), and the Women's Lib movement produces 'sisters'. A loving family produces romantics and art-classes produce people who think beauty is important to have in the world.

I was badgered to give up my post-expressionist painting, (which wasn't going very well anyway), in order to "do something for the working class." ("It's not as if you could draw well enough to do political posters or cartoons for our newspaper.....") The fear that I might be untalented was too painful to contemplate. Terrified that if I worked at art I'd have real proof of not being any good and badly needing Dave's approval, I decided to go along and give it up. It is better to serve. And easier to remain a might-have-been.

My philosophic encounters with Dave were definitely complicated by marriage to him. Not only was he Resident Ideologist, but also **HUSBAND**. He decided where to live, what music to listen to, how and when to eat, and who our friends were to be..... I could have friends on the side, but he shared very few of these friendships because my estimates of who was likely to become a friend of the working-class were so clouded by my liberalism. I became very depressed by how little sharing there, in fact, was, but there is no way for me to explain my view to him in ideologically valid statements since I had seceded from thinking as of when he started doing it for us both.

A child is born. I am transformed into a housewife, organizing other housewives and watching soap operas so that I can blend in with the neighborhood. The plots are very difficult for me to follow. It all seems so torturous, and these families, their behavior, their clothes, are like nothing I've ever seen. I'm fascinated. Is that what most of America is like? All the ladies buy 'Ladies' Magazines' at the supermarkets, *Woman's Day* and *Good Housekeeping*, and do little projects that cheer you up and make you feel very creative. We turn cornstarch into play dough for our kids, wind string around cans and bottles to decorate them, and knit sweaters.

Dave is busy organizing students, who he brings home at meal-times. They treat me better than he does. (Their parents have thrown them out because new converts to the left tend to be arrogant, opinionated and obnoxious......to their parents and relatives who have done everything wrong, though not to each other, of course.) They are glad of a home-cooked meal and a family atmosphere where they are greeted with some appreciation. Yes, Dave's students are very nice to me. Dave and I need people to be there so that we are not alone with each other.

Dave and I sit on opposite sides of the bed. He is dressing to leave the house. It is cheerless and a bit of a mess. I have no spirit to keep up with it. Trying to confront him inarticulately with the problems in our relationship, I am rousing his anger. He would prefer to ignore them.

DAVE: Not *now.*

ALISON: *That's what you always say.*

DAVE: *All you ever want to talk about is our 'relationship.'*

ALISON: *That's not true. I talk about the kid.*

DAVE: *(Interrupting me:) She's part of our relationship…. You don't talk about politics. You don't talk about culture. You don't talk about anything, except our relationship….*

ALISON: *(Very hurt:) YOU don't talk to me about ANYTHING….. politics, culture, our relationship, or anything else…..*

DAVE: *Look. I have to go to a meeting…..*

The struggle for a 'better world' keeps us together at first. Don't we share the same ideals, the same risks? We share the relatives' disapproval and scolding, the excitement of having the FBI ringing our doorbell at six o'clock on Sunday morning, the subpoenas by HUAC and the Grand Juries…..having to raise money to pay for our friends' lawyers and bail. Politics keeps us busy with meetings and projects. Who has time to see the erosion of our relationship, the relationship that never really was between real people at all. Camaraderie prevents acknowledging it. Comrades, as commonly agreed by the left, have real and meaningful relationships with each other, unlike those that stem from the patriarchal family, private property, and The State. The state of our marriage, though, leaves something to be desired.

Mountainously pregnant with our child-to-be, lying next to Dave in our king-size bed, I hear him say, "It's all your fault." He looks at me with hostility. "You aren't interesting to me. You're not sexy. I don't even like to touch you. You are so *UN*-sexy that a man can lie next to you naked and not only not get turned on….. he'll get repelled. Look at you, nervous, shaking, cold, dry….."

Dave has always been right about everything, *(like my father)*. His political leadership confers an authority to all his other pronouncements......and it is very hard to defend yourself when you know the other person is always right. So I can't find the answers to speak, don't understand why this has happened to me, and it is pretty obvious I am all the things he says I am. ("Mother," I call silently, "if you were here, this wouldn't be happening. If you were alive, I'd have someone to run to......someone to love me and take the pain away.") Dave doesn't love me.

But somehow we get over the crisis of pregnancy; we have a baby. And for all our high and mighty ideals and commitments we're pretty middle-class, Dave and I. Inexperienced too since we have experimented with sex exclusively with each other. When she discovered this, Ida, my father's wife, helpfully gave me some *'How-To-Do-It'* books so that life with Dave could be nicer, explaining all the anatomy and technical ways. Ida enjoys being an authority on everything, from home decoration to politics and psychology. Sexual problems can be easily solved by reading the right books! But Dave refuses to read the books because he already knows how. Besides, the problem is mine, with my inhibitions and my frigidity.

I become a cardboard wife. I cook five-course meals for Dave and his friends while sticking to the Stillman Diet and having nothing but a few eggs and six eight ounce glasses of water a day. I feel more empty emotionally than my stomach does because it is sloshing around, making me seasick. I always thought of myself as a passionate person, so it is a real paradox for me that Dave thinks I am such a dud. I sew nightgowns for the child to save a few pennies using the patterns they give in *Family Circle* and wait for a small sign that Dave cares about me. Dave virtuously helps with the housework, pointing out to me that this is positive proof he is <u>not</u> a male chauvinist pig. (Other husbands help their wives because they love them; mine does it to be politically correct.) He babysits with the kid so I have time to go out to political meetings, so I will be a credit to him. All I want is some affection, a sign that says I'm something more than just a 'wife'. It's obvious Dave wishes I would get off his back with my waiting. What I want from him is not something he has available. Relationship discussions are a drag. If I start them, he throws everything he can in my face: dowdiness, fatness, helplessness, clumsiness, ineptitude, and bourgeois tendencies. With each word I retreat deeper inside myself. I am unable to confide these humiliations to anyone. I stop talking…..except to my oven, my washing machine and my baby. I hardly hear music anymore and I stop seeing in color. Dave sees everything as either black or white; I see everything as gray.

And on the streets, wheeling Babette around the neighborhood in her stroller, I have become the invisible gray woman. Men never notice me. I notice them not noticing…..which is more comfortable than not, except that it is proof that Dave is right. Really, there must be something wrong with me.

In the crumbling apartment Dave has moved us into, (so that we can live in a suitable working-class neighborhood), Dave gives me the news. "Tonight my club discussed your paintings, and they all agreed."

It's been years since I painted, and just as many since anyone acknowledged the souvenirs of my college days hanging on the walls, reminders of when I thought what I felt was important enough to try and look at it. I'm still fond of these mementos, remembering the excitement, the aliveness behind each stroke of the brush, the jolt of electricity down my arm, and the tingle of happiness in my stomach. In those days, I didn't need food to feel full.

"What do they think?" I ask, hopeful of some positive recognition.

"Your paintings are **BOURGEOISE.** They are all about alienation. They are sensual and vulgar and emphasize lack of communication. They are one hundred percent (100%) Bourgeoise. I know I didn't always think so, but now I don't even like to look at them anymore."

Noticing he has disturbed me, he throws me a sop. "That's all right though. I can't help it. You can leave them on the walls. I'm sure I'll be able to ignore them. I just won't look at them."

I can't believe this is happening. The paintings are me; they're a part of me. Even if I'm not an artist, just an organizer of housewives; even if they aren't any good artistically. "My own husband and his club of students, now they are art critics!" The paintings are like a diary; they are a journal. I am being judged.....by my husband..... and look, I am 100% denied. By my only husband. Rather a blank wall than a souvenir of who I was.....when he supposedly fell in love with me.

As I assimilate the full extent of the rejection, I start crying. "Are you positive?" I beg him.

"Dave, I mean.....isn't there even a one percent possibility of something decent in them? How about fifty-fifty? Half the painting could be *OK*? Think about it. Think carefully. It's important to me. How about.....", breathing carefully, "99% Bourgeoise. Can't there be at least a one percent doubt?"

Dave cogitates. His judgements have to be ideologically correct. There must be appropriate intellectual substantiation. Calmly he looks me in the eye, unmoved by the tears streaking my face, and states with grandeur: "It is like pregnancy. You either are or you aren't. And your paintings are one hundred percent (100%) Bourgeoise. I'm sorry. I didn't know you cared about them that much anymore. If I had known, I wouldn't have upset you by telling you about this. Try to calm down."

All through the night, I cry into the blue sheets on the king-sized bed. Hysterical, I feel as if I'm going to die of misery any minute. By morning, my eyes are so puffed I can barely see out of them, but I do have at least one clear insight. I am positive, and know for the first time, absolutely, that Superman has made a mistake. And if he mesmerized his club so that they agree with him, they have also made a mistake.

I can't blame the left because my husband doesn't love me. The revolution must go on. For the sake of the starving, the poverty-stricken, the illiterate, the diseased, to eliminate racism..... and all forms of chauvinism….. the revolution must go on. But without me. In this new society and in the group that Dave is leading, there is no place for me. And though it is hard, I finally admit the thought that Dave does not love me.

As for my paintings, done when I was coming to a radical view of the world…..Dave is wrong, without question. They are certainly not 100% Bourgeoise.

I begin to have headaches at bedtime or late movies I can't possibly miss. Dave manages to have to read Ian Fleming on those nights I fall asleep before him. James Bond, even though he is the wrong political complexion, turns Dave on. Many nights I sleep in the guest room with a historical novel. Romance and love in the far, far distant past, complete with costumes and poetic declarations.

"I don't want my reading to keep you awake, Dave." It is not mentioned between us that we never make love anymore.

* * * * *

When I retired from active politics to tie-dying and embroidering wearable collages, it wasn't because I thought there was anything wrong with Marxism-Leninism. In spite of the fact that my father always said, "If you're miserable, you should concentrate on other people and do something for them," this therapy just didn't seem to work for me. So I stopped selling the newspaper and going to meetings. (Besides, Dave was taking care of the working class.) I still cooked communal meals for Dave's students and went on watching soap operas so that I could communicate with the members of my babysitting co-op.

Two students (who Dave brought home) attach themselves to me…..young women. "What wonderful blue eyes you have," Ruthy says to me, "I wanted to get to know you right away."

I listen timidly, wonderingly…..someone likes me. How strong and lively and young they are. How old I feel and I'm not even thirty.

I clutch at their gusto for life even while I'm dubious about the grass and drugs I discover.

"We don't really do a lot of drugs. That's just a rumor," Petra says as she tastes the turkey stuffing I am making. Stuffing isn't on the Stillman Diet, so I need to have a 'taster.' My life as an activist has ruled out all illegal activities, drugs as well as excessive drinking and promiscuity. *(No sleeping with your neighbor's wife. Live the kind of life the workers can respect!)*

Ruthy and Petra are discussing the merits of spreading cream cheese as opposed to honey on your lover's body and licking it off. Both of them decide in favor of cream cheese. I have no idea of what they are talking about, except it sounds sticky, and it's not on the Stillman Diet. I can't imagine ever wanting to do something like that to Dave. Of course, if I told him about it, he might want to try it; and if he liked it and I didn't..... Still, it is interesting to listen to them.

Ruthy and Petra know the words to all the songs on the radio. They know how to dance. They dance around my house. I try it and am clumsy; they don't do it the way it was done when I was in college.

"The point is just enjoy yourself." Ruthy undulates around my living room, rippling like a belly dancer. Trying to imitate her I feel gawky and foolish. I'm such a jerk.

"You're just new at it," says Petra, strutting a complicated pattern across the rug. "You'll be surprised how fast you'll learn if you just keep trying. There aren't any steps, really. Listen to the music. Then make up the steps as you go along."

"Oh, Alison," I say to myself as I try out my feet which have forgotten how to make things up. "A dance without any steps. I always thought there were steps. No wonder I was doing it wrong."

"Swinburne's poetry is a gas!" Ruth is an English Lit major. Taking the pins she hands me and fixing Babette's diaper, I confess

42

that I vaguely remember liking Swinburne when I read him long ago. "Wasn't he a poet-laureate or something? I don't seem able to remember anything I read….." Not only am I not up-to-date, I'm not even in touch with being behind-the-times.

"Grass isn't bad for you; it's just illegal." Petra stuffs the left-over turkey into a container and stashes it in my refrigerator. She is a German language major who is working her way through school as a technician in a laboratory. She relays a list of scientific statistics to confirm the innocence of Cannabis. What can I say? I used to agree with Dave, but he's wrong about painting. He's wrong about Petra…. He's been calling her a junkie, and I can see she's just a college student.

* * * * *

The marriage is finished. Dave can't go on with it, and neither can I. I am not only emotionally starved….. I haven't eaten for days. The energy is all gone…..not to mention the thrill. I'm tired of waiting for love to come from Dave. Like Ishmael, the tribe casts me out, not so formally in words, but that's what happens. I am dropped by the entire lot of them. None of the comrades, who had 'truly meaningful relationships' with me, seem to find them meaningful anymore. Dave is active and I am not. I guess they have to make a choice, and it isn't going to be me. The housewives don't seem to want a divorced lady around their susceptible husbands. Only Ruthy and Petra remain to help me move my furniture out of the apartment.

My father says, "Dave is a bastard. Don't worry. I'll back you up all the way." The separation becomes a grand new project for him and Ida. They find me an apartment in a luxury Fifth Avenue high-rise building in the Village. The previous occupant has just died. That's how we are able to get it at such a good rent. They tell me I am lucky to get it. I feel lucky to have moved out of the hell-hole that was my life with Dave. It is only a one bedroom apartment, and Babette is assigned the bedroom.

"You must live in a doorman building," my father insists. A

doorman building, he says, is essential for a young woman living alone with a young child. A few pieces of second-hand furniture come with the apartment. "But they are new for you," points out Ida cheerfully, as she proceeds to demonstrate how the furniture can be arranged to give the feeling of more space. I am too numb to question, and have been living in a gray fog for years, so I don't have any ideas at all about what my environment should look like. I accept everything. I accept a box of secondhand clothing, (*Ida's castaways*), to start my life as a woman anew.

* * * * *

Ruthy and Petra arrive to visit armed with record albums. "The Rolling Stones? The Jefferson Airplane? and who is The Who?" Woodstock passed me by without any of the comrades pointing it out to me. I was too busy agitating with the neighborhood mothers to get the Parks Department to put safety matting under the jungle gym and sliding pond in the local playground to know that it was happening. Now I live in a different neighborhood, and there isn't any safety matting in the playground to prevent the kid from splitting her head open should she take a fall, and I know nothing about music at all. Petra and Ruthy assure me I can make up for lost time.....

The marriage is a dead experience like the split skin of a caterpillar, no longer able to encase me. I examine the empty shell, marveling...... Without its spirit, it is just a hollow transparent mold, dry, and not too interesting. I am a metamorphosed being with a new and tender skin.....

I find myself in a new house. I have almost no money and can't afford to tip the doormen each time I go in and out. Quickly the building staff decide I am not worth very much. Even the fact that I have a little girl is no help. The continual visits of the street people, hippies, assorted black and white musicians, dopers, and other non-straight types who visit me spoils the image of the apartment house. All these strange ones I have met in Washington Square Park.

I take Babette to the playground there every day, and I stop and listen to the street singers, the guitar players, and talk to the people. Before I realize that they are not the working class, I see life in them and find I like them.

The first time a man stays overnight, I see the doormen smirk at each other as I pass through the lobby the next morning. They go on smirking.

Men can't keep away from me. It's quite extraordinary how I seem to attract them now that Dave is no longer around.

So the doormen have plenty to talk about.

My father, stating how insupportable my life has become, (he thought without Dave maybe I could live like a nun), cuts his financial assistance. But Jack Livingston comes to the rescue, and when an employment agency sends me to interview with him, he sees that I need help. All kinds of help. And he gives it to me, a job with Academia Books.....and encouragement to go out and explore the brave new world of men and sex and dope, (although Jack doesn't really approve of dope. He prefers martinis.)

A complete Canadian rock band, with chunks of hash sufficient to stone a herd of elephants, spends the night Jimi Hendrix died, grieving for him in my apartment. A young black musician upsets the neighbors with his color and his loud electric guitar, and upsets me by trying to choke me to death in the laundry room down the hall. Laundry has now become a trauma, so I am slightly more cautious about who I associate with. Sundry husbands from the old neighborhood make surprise visits to see how I am doing now that I am single. (So their wives were right! Divorce, I thought, was going to make me repulsive, but I begin to see it is the other way around.) I haven't given them any particular encouragement either, aside from treating them like they were people.

Of course, in due time, (now that the left-wing dictum about no illegal substances doesn't apply anymore), I get turned on to grass, hash, mescaline, peyote and acid.....assorted psychedelia.....all of which I like very much. I trip out, meet God, am rendered utterly vulnerable to everything. The colors return. I see them as I have never seen them before, and I cry now with joy. Because after living gray for so many years, this is more than having your consciousness expanded.....it's like being alive after being dead. Oh yes, being married to Dave was like being condemned to being a living corpse. But the generation gap between me and my father is widening as I feel myself growing younger every day. So I am half-crazy, living without foundations to support my world, living without any certainty.....but at least I am free.

It is possible to be friendly with Dave when he visits the kid or takes her on alternate weekends. What a model ex-husband: he pays and he visits. I am so lucky. With the pressure off him, he is much nicer. He begins to seem almost like a cousin. His life goes on pretty much as it always had, the political work and all. He has found himself a lady. He doesn't put me down so often. I am no longer an obligation he cannot fulfill.

It's so clear to me now that what happened in bed was not my fault. I can't even continue to hate Dave for the pain he caused. I am a butterfly..... I am a spectrum of color..... I am an eternal blue flame stalking the speed of light.... The gray frigidity that Dave turned off was another person. That there was no real love for each other is perhaps proved by the fact that neither of us makes the smallest sexual gesture toward each other after the separation.

Chapter 4

I lie in the dark, reviewing my present state of affairs, (No pun intended. Really.) I have my kid. I have a decent job. This month, I have a new cause. **CELIBACY**. Yes, now I have sworn myself to *CELIBACY*. Why the blanket slogan? Is it a fit of religious extremism? Am I perchance undergoing enlightenment? Preparation for leaving the world altogether? I only hope the world will believe me when I say I am *'COMMITTED' to CELIBACY'* and leave me alone. Especially the male half. I need a break.

My gynecologist says I need a break. He knows. He's an expert on who needs breaks. I go for a check-up. What a nice man he is. He has a grey shorter-than-crew-cut on his chiseled head. Piercing gray eyes of humor and intelligence gaze out at you. The usual pictures of a healthy happy family reside on his desk. Prosperity equals having life in control. You can have confidence in Dr. Davis.

He is even smart enough to treat me as if I am not dumb, the first obstetrician who hasn't addressed me in the plural. *("And how are we feeling today?")* They get it from confusing the mother with the baby, I suppose, but it still grates on my nerves. The doctor who delivered Babette would subject me to a myopic stare and say, "Has the little mother eaten her leafy greens?" (a euphemism for spinach). I hate being talked down to by these white-coated diploma collectors who feel that just because they have a license to meddle with your guts and, in this case, your equipment, automatically, they can treat you as if you don't have any brains. Dr. Davis is the head of the Gynecology Department of a med-school hospital. So he has to be at the forefront of medical research and reading all the latest literature. One has to in order to keep up with the students who are generally pretty sharp. He cultivates smarts instead of bedside placebos.

"When you end this cycle of pills," says the doctor scanning my file, "I want you to take a month off."

"A month off?" *(from pills or sex?)*

My body needs a chance to re-establish itself, he explains and a whole lot of medicalese he gives me to back this up, which I immediately forget. Then he reviews all the alternatives, all the gadgets one can use so as not to get pregnant. This all adds up to only one way as far as I am concerned. Only one foolproof method, aside from the pill, and I hesitate not. I figure: "I love no one. Ergo..... no real need to screw." I am a *Celibacy Crusader.*

To my favorite hangout I go, the leather store, and announce to all the friends........**CELIBACY.....**is where it's at. This creates quite a stir.

"Alison Greaves, you have got to be crazy."

"Well, we knew that."

"Crazier than even we thought."

The leather store is operated by Pierre and Maryann. It is a friendly haven located in the warren that is the West Village, surrounded by tourist traps, head shops, souvlaki stands, import stores, and cafes. The leather store has its own coterie. Your*SELF* is welcome here. No subterranean gaming. All games are 'innocent'......no one hurts anyone else. The true Flower Children's paradise. Pierre, the owner, is a Henry Miller freak, which is to say a disciple. Henry is God. Pierre is his Prophet. The bunch of lively souls who lie on the waterbed in the backroom in nests of ten accept this. They undulate back and forth to the music of Neil Young, share grass, and breathe in contentment. They are street philosophers, artisans, poets, actors, and amateur musicians.

I thread through the narrow Village streets and peer through the glass. Can they ALL be out for dinner? Nope. There is life inside.

Good. I can be with my friends and wait for "Something to Happen" which we do quite a lot. Perhaps nothing at all will happen, but in good company, even this has turned out to be acceptable and nourishing.

Pierre is out somewhere. That's good. Henry M. is for continual sex, and Pierre preaches that you have to be 'in touch' with it. Part of my attraction for him, I know, is the wild life I've led this winter..... Why I could be a character straight out of *Sexus*, *Nexus*, or *Plexus*.

I'm now in the middle of *Tropic of Cancer* lent to me by Pierre. I have mingled feelings about it. I love the writing but resent everything he is saying. Pierre takes it as the gospel. All of his friends must read Henry Miller in order to understand him. Pierre insists.

Tonight I join the circle passing around the bottle of Boone's Farm apple wine, which is standard fare for weeknights. "Gang," I declare, "As of right now, I wish to say......to let you know ....that I'm not fucking no more."

"Ohhhh....." This is enough to set the theme for the evening.

They have already exhausted their repertoire of folk songs and are floating. John is strumming a guitar with righteous enthusiasm, (fairly smoothly for an amateur). "Whatta line," he grins.. "Whatta beautiful line."

Just for me, John breaks into raucous song. The companions are all so delighted at the novel approach his composition is taking, they join in the chorus as a new anthem. Throats, well lubricated, have voices that will travel; and so the word travels into the street. Passers-by, curious to trace the source, stare in the door incredulously. What is this weirdness? Are all these hippies insane?

Leather Store Chorus, with animation:

> *I'm not fuckin' no more, no more.*
> *I'm not fuckin' no more, no more.*
> *I'm not fuckin' no more, no more.*
> *AND I'm not fuckin' no more!*

From the cadence, you have guessed correctly that this is a New Age folk song. Another classic from Anonymous.

Me, Alison, with commitment:

> *Ain't gonna take the Pill no more.*
> *Ain't gonna take the Pill no more.*
> *Since I ain't covered no more, no more,*
> *Ain't gonna fuck no more.*

Chorus, the gang, the leather crew, have fallen in love with the song, ourselves, the commotion we are making. We savor the shock on tourist faces, the street reaction, with appreciation. Displaying to tourists is fine sport, especially when they come from out of town. They have no cause for their arrogance. Just because they have money to spend. To buy Pierre's frontier leather jackets with their Indian beads and feather trimmings, which none of us, his friends, can afford. Tourists aren't, after all, rock stars. (As Village shoppees, we get to see some of the musical kings and queens of the day pass by. They help make it a spacier world. We treat them with respect, even if they are ego tripping. At least they have their own very definite personalities, instead of being carbon copies of somebody else.)

John, with inspiration from *Where Have All The Flowers Gone*:

> *Lost his penis in the war.*
> *Lost his penis in the war.*
> *Lost his penis in the war,*
> *and HE's not fuckin' no more.*

(Shades of Tyrone Power and Ava Gardner.........*FFFor Whom The Bell Tolls*.....the last time I saw Paris.....*La Vie Boheme...*)

Linda, John's wife, titters and claps him on the back. She is a model hip beauty, gorgeous with long straight blond hair, and long straight legs encased in blue denim. Linda helps Maryann around the store as well as being a decoration.

The religious perspective invades......

> *Fucking is the original sin.*
> *Fucking is the original sin.*
> *Fucking is the original sin,*
> *So......I'm not fucking no more!*

"Who wants to be original?" "We do!" "Wait, you have it all mixed up ....."

John, the irreverent note you can depend on:

> *The Virgin Mary never fucked.*
> *The Virgin Mary never fucked.*
> *The Virgin Mary never fucked,*
> *(angelic harmony),*
> *So....... I'm not fuckin' no more.*

"Wait!" He gasps, "I'm not finished....I have another one." John, he is beautiful, he is gentle. He is normally shy but friendly. His happiness, his peace, his air of innocence feeds all of us. Strumming his guitar, always, John. Enamoured by the possibilities Catholicism offers the song, he makes an effort to maintain a serious face and sings.

John, reverently:

> *The Pope never fucks at all.*
> *The Pope never fucks at all.*
> *The Pope never fucks at all?* (Laughter)
> *Well.......I'm not fuckin' no more......*

"You don't know that, John." "Hey, don't stop there, man." A new art form has been discovered............ "The Fucking Song, man ...... the Fucking Song...."

Linda, with gusto:

> *Why don't you go and fuck yourself?*
> *Why don't you go and fuck yourself?*
> (I join her.)
> *Just go away and fuck yourself*
> And, in two-part harmony:
> *Cause I'm not fuckin' NO MORE!*

"Hey, Ladies, are you for real? "No, man, it's just an *ATTITUDE.*" "Yeah, but Alison means it." (Ha, ha, ha.)" "Like hell she does . . ."

The gang doesn't believe me, I can tell. All they do is laugh.

"Friends, *FRIENDS* are supposed to give you support. Morale support. Moral support," I scold them. "Hey, it's for a good cause...... **CELIBACY**......you scoffers!"

More friends wander in. What is all this hilarity? Whence the rosy flush that dyes the communal cheeks? Uh oh, got to do it all over again for them......no other way to really explain why everyone has flaked out.

Encores galore.....

Humble John of the streets to educated Mike of the computers, modestly:

> *No one ever taught me how to fuck.*
> *No one ever taught me how to fuck.*
> *No one ever taught me how to fuck.*
> (gaily).......*So how can I fuck at all?*

"That's right!" "They ought to set up a school for it." "Beginning,

Intermediate, and Advanced -- three credits..." "Can you dig it, man?" "What did you study this semester?"

"Well.............."

* * * * *

I shudder and grow silent. All very well do I remember how I finally learned and who taught me.

"It's a good thing Pierre isn't here," I think. "This isn't his ideology at all. Oh no. We've discussed it....."

Pierre and I have a policy of not seeing each other. He tells me he likes me so much he is afraid if he sees more of me, he will not like me at all.

"What petty bullshit dramatics is this?" I ask.

Pierre's dark eyes glow as he hovers over his piece of leather with his awl. Dark skin, black wavy hair flowing down on either side of his head from a center part. Behind him, silently flowing like a slow but never-ending river is his wife, Maryann. Her long hair flows down her back, her smile flows from her eyes, her good will and amiability flow all over the leather store, bathing everyone in it and making it a comfortable place. She is a *WIFE*. Her personality is recessive to Pierre's, but is there in support. She is so quiet, it is hard to decide whether or not she is intelligent. Yet she is not shy. She is not beautiful, either, but very pleasant in appearance: strong and solidly built. She looks like a fertility figure. She is much taller than Pierre. (Of course, almost everybody is.)

Maryann is the mother figure of the companions.......ironically, much more so than me who have a child. When I bring Babette to the store, Maryann sets her up in a 'good' place with a can of large colored beads and some leather thongs to string them on, and the kid settles down happily and doesn't make any problems. Maryann smiles at everyone, creating the impression she really sees everything and accepts. Maryann accepts, for example, all the crazy stuff Pierre hands out.

"I was a Plains Indian in a previous life," Pierre will say, looking very much like one in his deerskin shirt with leather fringes ornamented with beads, (made by himself). He turns out shirts, moccasins, leggings, ornaments that seem to have stepped out of the pages of James Fenimore Cooper. Most of the leather goods stores in the West Village are upbeat, hip, and proto-modern. Not Pierre's; his looks like a trading post. I've given up questioning Pierre's dreams. He backs them up too well.

"Deja Vu," he remarks in explanation. "You know about Deja Vu?"

Pierre gleams inscrutably behind his counter. "What I want to know, Alison, is: *ARE YOU FOR REAL?"*

I am irritated. The first day I walked into Pierre's store I wore this poncho which I had designed and covered with embroidery. It took weeks. I was disguised with sunglasses which Pierre invited me to remove once he had established that I made that 'thing' myself. The poncho qualified me as a fellow craftsperson and also a human. (A good sort of calling card for creatures of some similar persuasion.) It was based on motifs in Mexican needlework, (because it was an attempt to make for myself what I was too impoverished to buy), and had an attention to surface variation and textural effects that was certainly the product of a modern art school. It was unique, my pass to Pierre's domain.

Now he is sitting there on his stool, asking me: Am I for real? What is going on in his mind? Is he teasing, inviting a debate, or just goading at me? I find myself asking in my head, over and over: "Am I for real? Am I for real? Are you for real? What is *REAL*? Is this the koan for the day?" Self-conscious and somewhat resentful, I accept the role of defense attorney. Just to answer Pierre, I launch into a theoretical exposition on the nature of reality. He approves it as an improvisation but finds it only temporarily satisfying.

"Why do I have to answer questions like this? And why am I supposed to agree with every word Henry Miller ever wrote?" I exclaim, becoming more annoyed.

Pierre is afraid he will or won't like me. "We should try to avoid each other as much as possible," he somberly legislates in a velvet voice. I am not to be, of course, banned from the leather store. It is accepted that this would be *UN*-fair. I belong here. It is only that when Pierre is here that I must try to be someplace else.

Tonight it is Pierre who is someplace else, and John and Linda, the whole crowd, even Maryann, are blasting the 'Fuckin' Song' into the only immortality it will ever know. Tomorrow we are all likely to have forgotten it.

Gang: in unison, with benefit of a night's rehearsal and the atrophy of cumulative stoning:

> *Don't want to fuck and don't want to screw.*
> *Don't want anything to do with you.*
> *You'll find a better partner in the Zoo.*
> *And I ain't fuckin' no more.*
> > *(Hear me talkin' to yah.....)*
> *And one more time.....*

Without a doubt the funniest song we've ever made. It's our own rebellion against society, against **HENRY M.,** resident deity; against the authority of Pierre. (We all love him, but he has been known to be tedious on certain subjects: my personal revolution against the plague of men infesting my life, always wanting to fuck me. I hope I can work out of this vicious circle.)

The night ends. The group separates after locking up the store and go their respective ways home. I go alone. Carefully I navigate to my apartment. I am really good about finding my way back under any conditions. I have to. Dave, the *EX,* can go home now. He's been the babysitter. "See you next Sunday," he says as he puts on his coat and picks up his briefcase. He doesn't make any comments about my condition. Whew..... It is still difficult when he criticizes. I am glad to have him babysit though. Otherwise, I couldn't afford to go out much.

* * * * *

The aloneness comes back on me when the door closes, and the disorientation. I have another internal battle. I try not to notice, to go to sleep. The self I don't have all in one piece fragments still further into a confusion of arguing voices and makes sleep impossible, even though stoned. Still it's a small victory, a night of *CELIBACY*.......my first 'accomplishment'.

Every morning I wake Babette up in time for her cereal. She is hungry and wants to eat right away. Sometimes she leaves the table to kill roaches. She brings them to me to show me.

"Why are you so ready to get angry in the morning?" Babette wants to know.

"We have to hurry so I won't be late for work. My boss says I have to be on time." I explain if I am not on time, I will lose the job. Babette doesn't understand this and wants candy. "No candy in the morning. There's no candy in the house." Babette asks for me to buy some.

"Stand still so I can brush your hair."

Babette doesn't like to stand still, and she doesn't like to have her hair brushed.

Wow. I admire my perfect child, my handiwork. Her hair is so variegated, shades from hot orange-red to honey-gold...cinnamon hair glinting in the morning sun...texture of child-skin, glows like alabaster, feels like suede...soft and clear. Getting up in the morning is more fun than sleeping.... alone.

Dear Pierre:

WHAT IS REAL, really?

Life is just a nightmare to me..... a random parade of incomprehensibility.... Everything is spontaneous.....There is no reason for anything. Why do you make me spend so much time hunting for a cement when the pieces won't fit?

Marx has a passage about the fetishism of commodities, where a table assumes an overwhelmingly grotesque significance..... namely, IT is REAL. I mean it's out there independently (of you or me). Going through its own trip. Plato would tell you first the table was in your head. And so much for abbreviated philosophy. My head is so full of furniture and keepsakes and clutter by now.....and you expect consistency from me..... Yeek Gods.

I had a long rap with John. I have a bit more understanding of you now. But really you're being very silly. It bugs me that I can't 'see' you. It's as annoying as when I have to change a typewriter ribbon in the middle of writing something that is going well..... The interference of mechanics.

My kid is just fine, thank you. Babette, the little goddess, was eating this orange, see. Mashing it in her face, bathing in the juice. It was all over her cheeks and her chin and dribbling onto her clothes; one sticky mess. Meanwhile, there is this big happy grin all over her face as she is registering the attitudes of everyone watching her. The more dismay and shock the kid sees, the more she enjoys smearing herself with the orange. A natural, un enfant provocateur. And here are we adults, shocked because of all the ingrained "DOs" and "DON'Ts" that make us react 'Yech!' when we get spritzed by a spray of fruit juice we know is going to stain us. Babette is like Eve. If something makes her feel good, she likes it. She rejects the voice of civilization which is the voice of the slave (who has to clean up later.) I know it should be my voice. I should be saying: 'Be Neat.'

Don't forget. She has no hang-ups to start with. She doesn't need to create Miller-like symbols, such as "I love everything juicy and flowing = SEX," to love an orange. It's just an orange to her, and she enjoys it more than most people enjoy whatever. Life is too short. Let her enjoy it before it becomes too complicated. Don't ask her if it is a 'real' orange? Come to think of it, don't ask me........

Chapter 5

Typical evening, middle of the week.

I collect my kid from the day care center and take her home. I am a model mother, feeding her, reading to her, and putting her to bed. I wait out the bedtime conflicts. As soon as the sounds from her room die off, my mind starts dictating to me:

> *Once I was a tiny egg. Spherical, like the world. Then I got perforated. Some things haven't changed. (What a feminine image!) Then the dreams of my mother and the dreams of my father blended together into a nightmare of random selection.....and that's me. And if the chromosomes had fallen into a different pattern, (like someone throwing a set of pick-up sticks or, more apropos, yarrow sticks), I could have been a very different sort of person.*

I construct a series of composites of my mother's and father's traits and imagine myself as all these alternate personas.

The downstairs buzzer calls me to the intercom. It is Tommy with a friend and they want to know: Is it all right if they come up? "Sure," I tell the intercom and rush to fix my hair and polish the face before the elevator delivers the guests to me.

The bell rings. Bong. There is my palm tree, Tommy. Seven feet tall, platinum blonde (natural) long hair, radiating like a street lamp on a hazy night, encircled with rainbows. He's definitely charged up on something. Tommy is a street musician, (guitar), who also deals. Somehow he is a source of all manner of psychedelics to the rock-and-roll community, including the residents of *Electric Ladyland*.

Beside him, (underneath), is a genial looking person smiling shyly at me from behind a pair of steel-rimmed glasses (a la French intellectual). He's got mousy brown hair that reaches his neck in lyrical waves and is dressed in a beat-up navy blue coat cut stylishly (again, Paris, early 1900s.) Once it was probably elegant, but it looks as if it has been recycled through several wars. He has a mustache in a style I have never seen before (Fu Manchu, I am told later). He looks funny and friendly. Something inside me is happy just from seeing him. Yes, friendly. The archetypal **FRIEND.**

"This," Tommy gestures toward his companion, "is Leo." The Leo person simply stood there smiling away under the shadow of his mustache as if someone had just told him a good joke, but it was private.

"Hi, Leo," I continue, registering his appearance and hoping for a clue to his being.

"Hello," he answers me in a voice that sounds as if he's trying very hard not to laugh and also as if he has just given me a spiritual gift.

"What a nice young man," I think to myself as we go into the living room. *A great big smile has just walked into my house carrying a guitar case. I am a sucker for musicians. I only hope he is good.*

Tommy, mammoth as always, settles himself on my braided rug, beaming as if he has just succeeded in pulling off a rare coup.

"Leo is my jamming buddy," as he crosses his legs. "Is it *OK* if we jam here? I thought it might be fun for you. You haven't been going out much lately, and what with the kid and all....."

I start doing the hostess bit, filled with anticipation and pleasure. Live music is a passion with me. I wallow in it, allowing all pretenses of coolness to be washed away. I play...with the sound, tossing it like a volleyball from one set of nerves to another. I eat the vibrations, swallowing and digesting the music. It perfumes my brain. Luxury is nothing more than a good jam session, something that happens in the **NOW** and maybe never again. Musicians like me because I listen hard.

"I'm glad you came, Tommy. I've been missing you and worrying. Please make yourself comfortable, Leo. I wasn't expecting visitors. My house is a mess. You'll just have to take things the way you find them." I start lighting candles, incense, and bustling around, adjusting pictures, and collecting bits of paper. The two reassure me that everything is just fine. I should sit down, be comfortable, and not be running around on their account.

"First," announces Tommy, "we have here some super-special opiated grass. Let's tum on. I know you haven't been smoking lately, but I don't want you to miss this. You'll really get off on it. I want to share it with you..... Come on.....'

I haven't been smoking grass since I've discovered that I'm becoming over sensitive to it, but this situation feels *OK*. The invitation is not to be resisted. The joint circulates slowly between the three of us. I lay back on the sofa. I am magnificent. Tommy's the world's most generous soul. The new Leo '*friend*' pacifically blends into the environment, gently, easily, and all is right with the world.

They start to play, tuning up, agreeing on chords, easing into "*Wooden Ships*." Exchanging rhythm and lead, the melodies weave in and out sonorously. They really are very good together, and, (surprise), this Leo can really sing, though he's very quiet about it, (very 'laid back').

"When you smile at me, I can understand....." His voice has got something.....

Though I've heard the song before, there is something new about it. Leo sings without any visible strain, yet there is a yearning sincerity to his voice as if the words were rising to the surface for the very first time.....this delicate something different between his rendition and that of your usual street musician........

Tommy has really scored for me this time. He has brought *TALENT* into the house. I fantasize a drum and bass accompaniment, and am thoroughly satisfied. "*Wild Horses,*" "*A Day In The Life,*" and several Dylan songs follow. Tensing and relaxing as emotions respond to the sequence of notes, I am floating in the harmony..... but something is wrong.

I am beginning to sweat. My hair is soaked, and my forehead feels red hot. Something doesn't agree with me. I think I've got a fever. Shivering and heaving, I race for the bathroom. I slam the door shut and immediately start retching into the toilet. I soak a towel with water, wrap it around my burning head, and emerge, still shaking.

"What's the matter, Alison?" asks Tommy, seeing that something is not as usual. "Are you all right?"

I lay myself down gingerly, and my teeth start chattering as ripples of electricity charge through me. "I think I'm flipping out....."

Tommy lays down his guitar and comes to sit beside me, holding my hand and looking anxiously into my face. He's not used to delicate systems as he can take any amount of dope and hardly know it. I must look a sight under my dripping turban, and I'm embarrassed.

"Take it easy," soothes Tommy. "Just tell me if there is anything I can do to help. You have to tell me though. Earlier, before we came, Leo and I dropped some acid, so we're tripping..... I'm not exactly sure what is going on. So you have to tell me. What should I do?"

"I'm not sure. What did you say was in this grass?"

"Opium," he says. "It generally slows you down.....but the acid may have speed in it."

"Maybe it is a contact overdose," I gasp at him, trying to cover my disintegration with a joke. "I need blankets. I'm cold....." It is freezing, and I'm shaking with chills. Tommy locates blankets for me and tucks them in carefully around me. He's worried.

On the rug, in a white Indian shirt that hands gracefully on his slender torso, sits the Leo person bathed in a dim light, playing his guitar. Playing alone now, his music takes on a different quality than when he was jamming with Tommy. He trips into it as if he was bringing a love offering to a God, a loving God, in whom you could have perfect trust. His music is a passion and a portrait, incredible nuances of feeling expressed in eloquent musical vocabulary until the emotions he extracts from himself shimmer like a rainbow in flames. The music is so human, it almost has a physical presence. I have never before heard anyone improvise like this, with such humility and such honesty. A naked personality is baring itself beyond words and beyond thoughts, and it is unbearably beautiful.

With every phrase, a new round of shivers begins, and the music is carrying me over the borderline of control into convulsions. I am afraid I will die. I beg Leo to stop.

He comes to me. "Is something wrong? I was trying to help, with the music. Make you better somehow....."

"Please excuse me," I gasp at him, shaking violently. "The music was lovely, perfectly lovely.....too much lovely.....and I'm flipping out on it..... I'm sorry you should see me like this ..... the first time we meet. I'm not like this at all, am I, Tommy?"

"No. No." Tommy reassures me, gripping my hand and seeming to feel guilty for giving me the grass.

"I'll be all right if it's quiet for a while....." I clench his fingers. "Just stay with me. And tell me I'll come out of it in fifteen minutes."

"What?"

"Just tell me I'll be all right in fifteen minutes. If you tell me that, maybe it will happen. I'm in a suggestible frame of mind, so if you tell me I'll be all right, I'll be all right."

The two young men are having trouble focusing through their

trips, but they accept this as reasonable. They do their best, comforting me and assuring me they don't mind what I look like and everything will be fine soon.

Tommy goes into the kitchen and returns with hot tea in mugs. We drink together in silence. The shuddering subsides, and I become drowsy. They leave me wrapped in my blankets on the sofa, softly tip-toeing to the door, gathering their belongings.

"Please come back soon," I call after them. "I want so much to hear you when I can really listen. Sorry about making such a scene....."

"Don't worry about a thing," Tommy replies, "and I'll call you tomorrow."

Chapter 6

Lunch hour is a brief escape from the subservience of a job-job. As I exit the office building, I pass Angel who has stationed himself outside, leaning against the concrete wall. Massive and motionless, he is a monument to sensations I do not wish to acknowledge. Large sunglasses mask my eyes, and I still avoid looking at him.

A green covered sketch-book is under my arm, sandals and bare legs. I feel his gaze follow my legs up under the skirt. My thighs tingle with the intimations of nakedness and vulnerability that Angel is deliberately projecting my way. I wish I had worn slacks.

"You look very sweet today," he offers. I don't want to hear it.

All through the winter, Angel was my favorite man. I persisted in seeing others as a precaution. I did not want to ever depend on Angel and carefully took measures never to allow him to be sure of me. Unquestionably, Angel was my 'favorite.' He was a professional stud. Formerly a pimp, he gave up the life claiming it bored him to have to keep tabs on so many women. Satiation was a carefully developed technique to keep his women on the hook.

Petra once said to me, "I know I'm here because it hurts so much....." The awareness of Angel's bulging muscles, biceps solid and larger than my thighs, brings pain. Haunting memories of our affair invade my will to block out remembrance and lead me to question the decision I made.....never to see him again.

"By the way, what have you done with those sketches of me? Have you thrown them out? If you don't want them, let me have them!"

NEVER, I resolve. Those souvenirs were too expensive for me to just give away. When he was naked and asleep, (often), sometimes draped in a sheet, I drew him. When he was helpless and snoring, face slack, mouth drooling, I would ease out of bed and, with a pencil in my hand, change the balance of power. Preserved representations of Angel in terracotta conte crayon, deceptively gentle, sleeping on newsprint with a childish look, or drawn in pencil on canvas board, sleeping again, an African tribal figure......

"What's the matter? Can't I even talk to you? After all, we're still friends. Aren't we?"

"Are we?" I question myself, concentrating on a fast departure. "You were probably so drunk, you don't even remember what you said on the phone."

"Go think about it all day....." he calls after me as my make my dizzy retreat, nauseated, forming the untraceable steps away from him with bitter resolutions of *'NEVER AGAIN.'*

Tommy has been with me throughout the course of the affair, a strange chaperone. Now that I'm down and discouraged by the empty place in my love life, Tommy holds my hand and escorts me to and fro.....feeling needed and therefore pleased with himself.

"I should meet some straight people, I think." I turn to him. "I mean, there must be someone out there, some regular man, a grown-up, who can take care of himself......and is single. Don't you think?"

"Today I don't know about anything," Tommy responds. "I'm crashing. But anything is possible."

I decide to investigate the world of normal people, and following advice from various normals, such as Ida (my father's wife), I locate a meeting of *Parents Without Partners*. Will I find someone there to take my mind off Angel ? A settled person, understanding of children, willing to undertake responsibility, full of the prerequisite courtesies?

"Tommy, I'm nervous. I'm not going to know anyone there. How do I just walk in? What if I don't like it?"

"You want to go somewhere? I'll walk you over."

We stand together on the sidewalk in front of the luxury brick building, blankly looking at each other. What now? We are a bizarre couple. I, in an old fur-lined black wool coat over a cocktail dress; Tommy, in his rags, battered old Navy jacket and headband.

"You go on inside now," he directs me. I flash alarm and insecurity. "Don't worry. I'll stay here for five or ten minutes. If you don't like it in there, just walk out. "I'll see you back to your house. And," he smiles wistfully, empathizing with my hope, "if you don't show, I'll know you're having a good time, and I'll split."

Five minutes later, I emerge in haste, grabbing for Tommy's arm. "They are all *BUSINESS* types in there.....middle aged, middle class, and most of them fat. None of the other women look like anything at all. I could see this movement in my direction and I freaked." I'm very depressed. "I wouldn't have known what to say. They looked half-dead already. They looked *worse* than all the people at my job." A doleful coup de gras.

"That's OK, Alison," and Tommy begins to ease me down the street. "We'll just walk around the Village.....see some things, maybe bump into some friends.....then I'll take you home."

"What if we run into Angel? He's different at night! I don't want any trouble."

"Angel wouldn't fight me," reassures Tommy, drawing himself up to full height. He seems secure about this, so we perambulate the Village, looking in store windows, feeling the movement of pedestrian traffic whooshing by, apparently goal-oriented, going somewhere. Both Tommy and I are wishing we had a somewhere we really wanted to be, instead of places to run from.

Next morning, Jack advises me I am to have a treat. He has been in the back room playing darts with Bill and Jean-Claude..... Jean-Claude, our *tres* debonair Accounting Assistant from the islands, (Martinique), and Bill, our ulcerous P.R. man. They've been laying bets. Naturally, the boss has a system for darts, and he's been winning. He is full of ebullient good will.

"You," he authorizes, will be allowed to do a stipple drawing of the head of F. Scott Fitzgerald for a book cover."

(Stipple drawing? F. Scott? Book cover?)

"What did you say, Jack?" I'm very confused and not knowing at all where to begin.

"I said we might as well make use of your talent. We want you to try your hand at drawing. If it works out, we can save money." (Oh.)

He hands me a photograph of F. Scott and says, "Here you go. Take a whack at it."

Great attack of nerves. I can't do this in the front office. Not with the ever-ringing telephones and million odd jobs they throw at me. Granting that I can do it at all. Advising Elaine I will be found in the Production Room, I beat it. The girl who used to do this work has gone to another publishing house, stepping into a better-paying job. She has left an empty drawing board. Nobody contests my moving in.

"You need the drawing board? No problem,"

I go, go, go. I make a xerox copy of the photograph so I don't spill on the original and settle in behind the drawing board with a coffee cup for support.

The Production Room has two windows and is a corner office. One window overlooks Fifth Avenue and the other, a side street. I see it has started to rain. The rain makes large puddles on the church roof outside, driving away all the pigeons who usually flock there in social gathering. The sky is now almost black, depressing. The air in the office is humid, dampening to the spirit.

At his big desk, the Production Manager, a genial suburbanite, puffs his pipe which protrudes from his natty Victorian mustache. Dale Romano, at least six foot, slightly overweight and very gregarious. Old movies are a big topic of his.....he surrounds himself with nostalgia: Ah, Garbo.....Bogart.....Allyson.....Gable..... He's wonderful. He's harmless. Now Jack, the boss, has gotten through to him, and he's started permitting himself sexual fantasies of ladies in black stockings, though faithful to the flesh of his wife. "Do you ever wear black stockings to bed, Alison?"

He and B.B., one of the editors, are cronies. They go to the same bar for lunch where they've established a credit account. Now they are distracting me by a comparison of the drainage systems of their respective garages, speculating whether the commuter trains will be running on time if the rain keeps up and exchanging episodes which have occurred in the drinking car..... typically domesticated.....and therefore responsible, suburbanite husbands.

What did F. Scott do, I ask you (aside from inspiring Dave to marry me), to deserve that such a blunderer should be drawing his face for a book cover? Yech. This is really a bad job here. This pen stinks. I can't make it do what I want. They don't even provide you with decent pens at Academia but expect you to turn out a presentable job. And when the drawing is finished: "Go back to the typewriter, be a secretary again." Oh, phooey on it all.

Poor handsome F. Scott..... I am dotting up your chin via instructions. Jack, (*el BOSS hombre*), says, "Cut it off at the ear." I ask you, does he deserve to be earless? Just for the sake of design?

.... I'm finished with this. I haven't anymore in me. ....

"Do you think it will do?" I query Dale, disgust evident in every word.

"Take it up front to Jack and see what he thinks." Dale is very aware his thoughts won't count, so he won't say them. If Jack is scathingly critical, Dale may try to encourage me by saying, "It's not so bad, but you know the boss. He has his own ideas......" (*Dale!*)

Jack doesn't like the rendering too well. (I agree with him. It's lousy.) "Maybe you could try doing a regular pen drawing," he suggests.

"With the ear?" I make the return trip to the Production Office. Down the hall, up the hall. To hell with it. I retreat to the Ladies Room to sulk. I throw water on my face and blot it with a paper towel and wash my hands which are full of ink. I don't know how to be neat. A stranger looks back at me from the mirror. I barely recognize myself.....and I don't like my face today. It's good it is buried in the Production Room, instead of being on display at the reception desk.

The Ladies Room is sometimes the only place at work you can find to be alone. It is important not to get lost in your thoughts because you can lose trace of time alone in there...... I repeat to myself that I've got to get back to the work. I've got to......there isn't any choice about it. I need the job.

I rejoin F. Scott Fitzgerald and try again. The pen goes scratch, scratch, scratch. I draw the hair, trying to make lines, which feel like hair. This improves it. The drawing begins to resemble Gregory Peck in *Beloved Infidel.* The period look is there, and at least now it looks human. Close enough. Now to get the lapel of the suit to look like wool.

I'm incompetent at this,.....no real training. But it could be worse. I'm afraid to do any more to it for fear of ruining what I've got. Therefore, I'm finished!

"Don't ask me to do another one," I pray silently as I seek for Jack in the front rooms for the umpteenth time. "I've no more drawing in me today."

Jack is dubious, the goddam perfectionist. He's right, but why expect more of me when I have just told him there is no more today?

"I can try again tomorrow," I add as I squirm with apprehension, waiting for the verdict.

"Well...." Jack considers. "Maybe it will look better on green." I am tuned for criticism in his voice, but he seems rather hopeful the drawing can be made to work. If there is a trick that will do the job, a change of size, placement, Jack will find it. Another book cover. Wow.

"Whatever is the matter with *YOU* today?" he asks me with some astonishment.

"I'm having a *CONFIDENCE CRISIS!*"

"A confidence crisis? In who? In yourself?"

"Well, you don't think I'd be having a confidence crisis in *YOU*," I snap at him. "That would be impossible. And irrational, of course." This pleases me. It pleases him too.

"Get someone to cover your phone, and I'm taking you to lunch..... for your confidence crisis."

"Oh. Fantastic. Sure...." I run for Dianne. "Dianne, can you watch my phone? The boss is taking me to lunch." She agrees. "Thanks, you're a doll...."

* * * * *

Over the egg rolls, Jack narrates the account of when he sang with a big band before World War II as a lead vocalist. I am all big ears. We drift into a debate. Can there be such a thing as a 'competent improvisational approach'? Jack is, more or less, a control and mastery person. So he takes the position that you create the illusion of spontaneity and make it all look as if you are carried away with feeling. According to him, the success in doing so is due to lots of repetition of getting carried away. "It's all a question of practice. It's real."

I am a romantic. I want miracles to happen. I tell him as best I can about the cadenza Leo played for me one night in my apartment..... that never happened before and might never happen again.

I sip my whiskey sour and wave my hands in the air trying to gesture how I felt with it, spiraling into infinity. Jack puts on his 'you've got to grow up' look. Rock and Roll is here to stay, he agrees, but it doesn't move him.

The main dishes arrive. This is a good time to ask him. I twirl my Lo Mein noodles around my chopsticks until I've got an edible shuttle and spit out the words, "Jack, what exactly is a nymphomaniac?"

He stops eating and surveys me thoughtfully. "You have to be careful about all these definitions. A nymphomaniac is someone who can't control themselves. Compulsively fucks around. Anyone." He waits for a reaction. "Which is not the same thing at all, you know, as loving sex and wanting it all the time......

Jack sees I am still fretting with my food and seem to be unresolved.

"A nymphomaniac is just a word. That's all. It's just a word. You could probably find another word, and it might have a different connotation. Be very careful about using other people's definitions. That's what I was getting at. It's a goddam shame. Most people don't allow themselves much pleasure from sex, and lie to themselves all the time about what they want. It's taboo to even think about who and what they really want. And when someone is doing it right in front of their faces, they just get more uptight. I've explained this to you before.....and you can see I'm right."

He puts a piece of roast duck with almonds in his mouth, savors it, and washes it down with Martini. Then he exhales. "Ahhhhhh......"

Watching him eat is like being in the food scene in *Tom Jones*, the movie. Always it looks as if the food is making love to Jack. "Take Bill," he says, in our office, for example."

"Bill? Our straight man, Bill? What about him?"

"Bill," Jack crows with triumph. "Bill doesn't even like eating! Extreme. When you see someone who can't even allow themselves to enjoy food, you're looking at a magnum case of repression. I'm not including dieting. That's when you've enjoyed food too well and have to limit it for a while. No. Bill genuinely doesn't like food. Watch him for a while. It's very peculiar. But observation will prove it to you. It's true." He orders himself another Martini.

"Bill doesn't know what to do with food. It's perhaps too tangible for him. He doesn't know what to do with women either. He goes to those movies, sits alone in the dark.....and it's safe. Nothing can touch him."

Reflection confirms numerous occasions when Bill has been very ill at ease with me..... and I can't understand it because I've always been very friendly to him.

"Bill doesn't know what to do with me either," I tell Jack. "He always looks uncomfortable when I'm around."

Jack chuckles. "Of course, Bill wouldn't know what to do with you, Little Fox. You are so honest and open, just trip through the office being yourself..... Bill doesn't know how to be honest with himself, let alone anyone else....."

I am flattered by what I see in Jack's eyes. He is hot for me in a companionable way, clearly projecting what he'd like to do, were it not for *The Office Rule*. I am made to feel like a delicious, though untouchable, dessert. Thank God, though, for The *Office Rule*. If he hadn't made it up, I would have to keep him at arm's length, and we wouldn't be able to gobble down all this scrumptious gourmet food and talk about half the things we do.

"...........group fuck?"

"Sorry, what did you say?"

Jack wants to know, hypothetically, if he and his wife invite me to come out to their house in New Jersey for a weekend group fuck, what would I do? Would I accept? I feel out of my depth, totally undecided.

"The book I read yesterday." I fill in the time, "separates writings about sex into the haptic-convulsive, the pornographic, and the celebratory. And the author goes on and on about the first two categories. He's not got even one single thing to say about the celebratory part, except to mention it is there." Jack is puzzled. What sort of answer is this?

"Orgies," I continue to confirm my erudition, "began as seasonal festivals in primitive cultures that associated sex with fertility, and....."

"Forget fertility. That's not at all what's going to happen at my house. No fertility!" Jack states emphatically. "It was just a passing thought. You're looking very well these days, and I have a weakness, as you know, for women who look, well, as though they enjoy living..... It's such a temptation to forget *The Office Rule*. But look, we're a half hour late already. We'd better get back."

At the office, Jack decides I must redo the drawing again. What torture. I wasn't up for this project in the first place. Between Jack leaning over my shoulder, purring directions in my ear, and the soothing influence of the whiskey sour, the drawing begins to look more like F. Scott Fitzgerald and less like Gregory Peck. Finally, it has approval.

"If you took art classes," says Jack, "I think this sort of thing would get easier. I can't imagine why you gave up art in the first place. You should think about it." He gives me a look of sincere admonition. "You're much better at drawing than talking.....take my advice. Forget about this book you're writing. Go take art classes!"

* * * * *

Dear Pierre,

My head isn't completely functioning, but electric typewriters are so much easier to tttttranscribe one's thoughts from mixed up head to paper that I'm just letting my fingers trace my wandering mind and waiting for something profound or intriguing to happen along the way.

I calculated today, and as soon as I've paid off the dentist, I ought to be able to start taking drawing classes on Saturdays. It feels like a different mouth, and he hasn't mauled me too much. I'm a terrible coward about it as there is no virtue in pain. I'm extra sensitive, and when I go to the dentist, I try not to be.

These nerves work both ways. When sunlight shines on your bare skin and you can feel your pores opening to suck it into your body and bloodstream, when the texture of what you wear is felt in discreet patterns, the extra dimension of feeling plunges you into such a current of sensation in all its rich subtlety.....but then you go to the dentist. Well, if you get extra bruised, I guess that's how you pay for it.

What a library I am because my nerves store away all the details of experience. Going to the beach, (I do this a lot when I'm at the typewriter in the office....) First grains of sand, their luster, salt everywhere, solar plexus undulating with the waves, an ocean meditation for you if only you relax, buying ice-cream from the vendor because your tongue was so dried out, sand in your bathing suit, uncomfortable when you sat on it. Trying not to have sand in between your toes, the sun blessing you with heat, going home later and showering off to find a sunburned flush and fever because time was left behind at the office.....lemonade and TV and going to sleep wishing five day work weeks didn't have to be.

And any time, a fever can take me back to the beach, or an ice cream cone or a bit of dirt stuck in my shoe..... and all the while my physical body is holding down a job, sitting at a desk, typing someone else's business......

I'm going to take art classes, Pierre. I want to. And yet, I've been so afraid. If I find out I'm no good, I know something perfectly awful will happen. My mind refuses to even explore what that will be.

Chapter 7

INTERLUDE: PETRA AND RUTHY, THE FRIENDS

Our *'ROMANCE RESTAURANT'* is where our symposium of personal affairs, (yes, that is another deliberate pun), is held. A private club, it shifts from friends' house to friends' house or could be celebrated al fresco or sometimes at the local bar and grill where a professional brings your order to you. Sometimes we pick a gourmet landmark.....but always art lovers and friends bring two ingredients to these feasts: their secrets and their loves; discuss secret loves of their own and tell as many of love's secrets as possible. Thus, all is shared, and all leave taking enlightenment with them.

If those assembled truly love each other and respect each other's pure intentions, they will not get indigestion. Indeed, they will enjoy the food so much that they will get together frequently for meals, make better food, dress for the occasion, and the discussions will get higher and higher, until fully satisfied, and euphoric, they go off into the world spreading good thoughts all around.

At the romance restaurant, new elements come into play around the same old theme. The interior may be different, or it may be a picnic.....or there is a different menu.....or the discussion appears to be about something altogether changed.....but one ingredient is there: *NOURISHMENT*.....and the result is *GROWTH*. And when the nourishment is accompanied by *LOVE*.....the growth takes the form of personal creativity   and this is one of the secrets of friendship and also of romance (which adores secrets); also of the food, which lovers know in advance is going to be good and which artists arrange in a beautiful order.

Petra, Ruthy, and I have developed our fantasy symposium.

We share a mental diet of Casablanca chicken marinated in honey and spiced with kif and sesame. Salad Hokusai is served by actors wearing ceremonial Shinto temple kimonos who arrange the raw portions in vegetable compositions which comment on positive and negative space.....and they read your *I Ching* from it.

We romance about our mythical food in Petra's kitchen which is a den of romance in reality. Her cuisine is always accompanied by defining ornamentation: candlelight for Bavarian chicken, rustic woolen tablecloth for sandwiches, and always freshly ground coffee beans, regular grind, (fresh, if poor; special imports from Africa or Russia if wealthy). Petra herself combines the mystery of Hermann Hesse, the Spanification of Bizet, and the edification of a scientist which is considerable. She gives us the rundown on diseases and the true medical facts which most doctors haven't bothered to catch up with yet. I haven't bothered to become a hypochondriac because if anything is wrong, Petra will notice and let me know I should worry. I am too absent minded to keep track.

Ruthy didn't expect me to go all the way into psychedelic madness post-divorce. She herself had stopped at psychedelic mid-Victorian. Ruthy is very moral, and the sight of my morning-after one-night-stands offends her sensibilities.

Given my brave words full of sound and fury, I may yet be something....... *WHAT* none of us know yet. This probability is weighed by Ruthy against my repulsive habit of consorting with men below my station, (*whatever that is*). Ruthy consorts on occasion, but *never* below her station. Ruthy reads my symptoms as follows: "This woman has fallen past reproach, and will end up in hell where she doubtless belongs....." Other times her response is: "This mystic trip is too disgusting for words; you can't expect me to believe that sticky spiritual stuff....." I am furious with her when she goes either of these routes. The first means she has decided I am not worth being a friend to, and thus she has devalued me. The latter means she has no idea who I am.

Greater than my irritation is the gratitude I feel toward Ruthy who has played midwife, helping me out of the old life into the new. And Ruthy manages to get over her attacks of morals and comes back into my life, remembering the word 'loyalty.'

Petra and Ruthy have quarreled because of a man, something they thought could never happen. I don't want to be caught in the middle, yet I'm the next best friend to each. I listen but refuse to arbitrate.

And they inevitably react to the men in my life, particularly the Angel. Petra cannot find Angel attractive yet understands that I should desire what he gives me: *satisfaction*. Ruthy finds him decidedly unattractive, and besides he is married. Never mind my motives, it equals a moral wrongness.

Petra never makes me feel she thinks I am *BAD*. She just holds my hand or says: "I told you so" as if to indicate that I have been impossibly naive but not actually stupid. She accepts the odd denizens of my Vita Nuova, although she does make faces at them. All I have to say to her is 'Tommy.' Petra asks for qualification: "Tommy, the Seven Foot Wonder? *Wonder?* Tommy, the Drip?" "Him." Automatic wince on Petra's face.

Sometimes she actually says, "Excuse me," feeling I should not have to be confronted for her distaste for my food while I am eating it. Petra also pulls faces about actions of mine, which she categorizes as helpless idiocy.

"You're still fighting about the same old thing with your father?" (Petra's face of aggravated pain.) Agonizing over rejection by the 'Ps', (*parents*), never accomplishes anything according to Petra's model of the world; therefore, sensible souls abstain by disengaging.

* * * * *

Not all wives are nonperson, but with time, I realize the many ways I allowed myself to turn into one.....though maybe that was a sort of waiting.....as Gauguin waited before he stopped being a banker and went to live the street life of the poor artist on the left bank.

In any event, now I must live for myself in the West Village, which once was the haunt of artists but now is too prosperous to qualify for true Bohemianism. I am supposed to *BE* something all by myself. Ruthy and Petra expect more of me than just Secretary to the Director of Academia Books.....and it is not the Director they are expecting me to be. I must do something world-shaking as they will do. How they will do it is equally unclear.

Ruthy is a budding Victorian literary critic. Petra is a German language major on the borderline of scientific discovery. Though their direction appears to have merit, they are not sure these are earth-shaking enough professions.

Oh for those moments of rare harmony as a triumvirate.....oh my darling friends.....*TRUE* friends.......the rap sessions, (spiced with grass or pills or exotic tea), taking place on the floor. If a rug exists, on the rug. Cross-legged around the ashtray, which is always the hub of the gathering, we have one of those indoor picnics which include the delights of a stationary stereo system. Trips to and from the refrigerator to provision ourselves.....and, ahhhh, the luxury of music when you're stoned, an avenue to an other-world panorama.

These picnics around the ashtray, symposia flowing ideas like nebulous smoke on its way to the stratosphere, these romance restaurants....... To my friends, suddenly, I pour myself out, being transformed by the ideas that rush into speech for the first time. Visions of myself as a hermit searching for an appropriate mountain cave, having passed through a myriad spiritual disciplines and schools, ready for a cosmic solitude. My hermit spends half her time in her retreat painting and the other half meditating......

Ruthy contributes her Crusader Rabbit, (alias her Jesus Christ fixation), which lasted six months, and her discovery of feminist psychology.

Petra contributes George, an enormous slobbery mutt, over-affectionate and without manners. George, a personality in his own right, insists on drooling on anyone he can reach.....and if you push him away, he stares at you with sick hurt eyes until you get the point: He *LOVES* you. Then he tries to slurp on you once more.

Around the ashtray, we contemplatively compare notes and collectively build the image of the ideal man. Petra mentions hip bones; hip bones are sexy. Ruthy doesn't know. I think the ideal man has long straight red hair reaching to his knees, an ivory complexion, is well over six feet, divinely beautiful, and an inspiration just to see. (I have never seen anyone in the least close to this description, but imagining it is great fun.) But I admit I would happily settle for Andres Segovia; think of living next to that heavenly music.

"He treats me like a human being," I add, feeling a trifle guilty because I left that important qualification for last.

"AHA. Now we're getting somewhere," exults Ruthy. "How important is it to be treated like a human being, and how important is the long red hair?"

"Maybe, just maybe, if he treats me like a human being enough, I can forgo the long red hair. It does mean a lot, being treated like a human being." (Among women this particular phrase seldom has to be elaborated on...... It is accepted at once, understood and related to: 'I relate to that!')

"He's got to be a great lover.....and that's not negotiable," chimes in Petra, "although you could educate someone who is willing to be educated." (Petra tells about the summer she educated a young man on a tour of the villages in the Rhone Valley.....) "But men without feelings cannot be considered, let alone be worth idealization."

"He must shiver when you touch him." I breathe this wish from a romantic haze, redolent with smoke, "and he must be true to himself so as not to shiver if he is not in love."

Petra and Ruthy laugh. This is going too far out for them, although they can sympathize with the fantasy.

"But look, how can you have an ideal lover who doesn't know what it is to love?" I want to know. "Anything else is just exercise, it seems to me." Angel, (and the whole question of love), reminds me of a circus now. What a circus.....a depression flick.....

The bag of potato chips is being reduced to emptiness. The carrots have been crunched, and time to go out for more fuel. Petra, with her luxurious dark hair, dark snapping eyes, nose of refinement, and greedy mouth waiting to feast on life, wants to wash it down with good wine or fresh coffee. Ruthy, with her swelling hips, like an houri of Leon Bakst, patterned blouse with bell sleeves, and peasant hairdo, quivers, catlike.....an aristocrat contemplating the social amenities. And then like the queen visits Africa, majestically delivers speeches imbued with all the native ideals. Here. A bowlful of heartfelt morality. *Snap. Crackle. Pop.*

"The ideal man should be a human being!" (*Exclamation point profundo.*)

Hungry, hungry, starving, insane with lust for more food. Where shall we go? Into Petra's Volvo and down to Chinatown? Open twenty-four hours a day.....to be continued.......

The shared heart-hungers of women friends, familiar theme. Wishing each other were men so we could marry and live happily ever after. Remorseful that we are such vestigial chauvinists that we never do consider it in reality. Refusal to give into the very real pressures toward lesbianism.....the number one pressure being lack of good men.

Waiting for that special man, holding each other's hands, and drying each other's tears. Music is important to me Morals to Ruthy. Style and sensibility to Petra.

Pictures projected in the mind; one after another.....click.....

click.....like a series of still shots.....or flowing continuously like a movie but framed. Between the motion and the passage of time are sandwiched images of these picnics and their chains of conversation.

TWO HIGH PRIESTESSES INITIATE EACH OTHER INTO WOMAN POWER

Petra and Alison take a trip to outer space by leaving New York City and dropping acid in a State Park. They communicate with each other in parallel lines.

ALLISON to PETRA:

The gift of writing is very precious, my mother said to me when I was very young, and I never forgot it. I never forgot, either, that everyone else than herself who knew about her writing said that it was very good. She herself never mentioned it except to say: A great writer must know everything: novels, scientific discoveries, all the languages in the world, art, music, opera history.....you know.....and she really believed all that.....and also that Dostoevsky proved it in *The Idiot*, where he spoke in a language of heavenly madness.....and so she never wrote anything.

She made such a beautiful martyr, a Russian Ikon, resigning the chance to do it all herself to be a wife and mother, and all for the sake of love.....a creative love.....doing good things and never saying a word about them.....keeping her emotions concentrated on her loved ones, and eating herself up inside until she died of cancer.

My mother gave me all I ever had of perfect love. Her entire schedule revolved around my day. Whatever I needed was there in the person of that special human being who cancelled herself out. So.....is it my karma to write a book about the book my mother didn't write? Does that seem the product of chance to you?

PETRA to ALISON:

Listen. The essence of the best style comes from testing reality.....like a scientist. Leonardo, for example, a great artist, was also a great scientist and many of his scientific drawings are great art.....a mixed bag. Besides that he saw into the future. He understood that someday men would fly.

Having gravity act as a human limit would become a provocation because birds defy gravity.....so Leonardo drew a picture of a man with artificial wings, the armature of which resembles the skeleton of a bird. Because he was willing to give man birdlike qualities, he fathered the modern spacecraft. He knew well enough that when his ideo-maps were discovered by scientists of the future, they would cause a lot of excitement. Not only would the beauty of his life be understood, (which he testified to by painting a minimum of beautiful paintings, some of which he never bothered to complete), but the tragedy of it: Leonardo had to write his journal backward in mirror writing to avoid being burned at the stake.....

The scientist of the future looking at the high level of Leonardo's communications with himself would see a timeless being exploring his century single-mindedly. Amazing to absorb and understand the depths of his conclusions about it, which is why Leonardo's greatest art form was his diary.....one of the best submissions in *The Glass Bead Game*, a one man show of culture. (Hermann Hesse.....you have read *Magister Ludi*?)

Yes. Hesse in German is wonderful. You can curl your lips around the words and taste the serious passion of a Dr. Faustus before he lost his soul.

Anyway..... The scientists of the future, meditating on Leonardo, are going to find him such a source of energy that they will figure out how to contact the place beyond time where he has gone and call him back into life again.....

ALISON to PETRA:

Leonardo was called *'Divine'* by artists and poets and writers whose cannons he fixed and their lives thereby made much more secure. Leonardo was called *'Divine'* by the aristocracy who paid him to do anything he felt like it in the privacy of his own mind, (and not often society lets you do that and pays you.........I mean, *THAT'S* genius. Arranging to get paid to do exactly what you like, whether you finish it or not.....) Why is it taking the scientists so long to acknowledge the divinity of Leonardo? Because he is definitely still a living force?

PETRA to ALISON:

They want physical proof for divinity.....the body of Leonardo, living and producing high thoughts. When they see it and touch it, and he talks back to them, they'll believe it. And not before. Wait and see. The scientists will find a way to do it. They'll bring him back. Those that want to believe in life will make the necessary discoveries to save humanity. They'll learn the secret of life itself. I can feel it out there waiting for me, to be discovered.....and if it calls me, it calls other people.....sooner or later we'll get it. Life must be loved scientifically if it is to be preserved.....and you must make your own life worthwhile too, so that misery won't get in the way of you discovering something to make life be longer......

After this conclusion of why being a scientist is a rational decision if you love life, Petra enumerates for me what is necessary to enjoy life, love, and the process of scientific discovery. Every concept is a poem. Petra is lovely. She talks to me in the kind of language about science that a romantic like me can relate to. I can agree about respecting science when she shows me microphotography of little parts of the body, cells and bacteria, seen for the first time and photographed for the first time by scientists.....inspiring the artists thereafter with a different resource material for vision, different ideas about relative size.....vision itself.....you name it.....

PETRA to ALISON:

Scientists are the photographic explorers of the only new territories that are left.....inner and outer space.....bring back proof that all that stuff is really there. Did you ever think about that? (Did I mention that Petra is in love with her camera, a *Nikon F2*?)

PETRA to ALISON: *(with a sigh)*

I'm not sure why I'm a German language major when I like science and photography so much better. It is just that German is so classy.....*The Magic Theatre, The Sorrows of Young Werther,* Sigmund Freud, (who rediscovered sex), Bach fugues, the uncertainty principle and Albert Einstein. German. But when I think about it.....just sitting back and looking at the language they did it in, watching their thoughts is not half so much fun as getting in there and really exploring. I don't know how Ruthy can reduce '*German*' to '*Nazi*' when so many Germans were the opposite......

When she talks like this, I love Petra. It gives me such courage. I'm not sure what the courage is for. I'm not sure what to do with my life. She talks to me as I need to be talked to, believing she can change her own life with a momentary decision, and effectively charging into her new future all brain cells functioning. *PRESTO!* Discoveries will come to her that will make the change worthwhile. She speaks to all the hidden dreams latent in me as if they too were possible. Shyly, various memories creep back into my thinking vocabulary. I realize I have become an illiterate, and that a decade has gone by without my reading anything more than Kazantzakis's *Odyssey Sequel* and meditating on the poem.

Hesitantly, I mention Kazantzakis, a great literary love of mine, a spiritual quick change artist, slipping in and out of the different religions, trying them all out for size and turning them into a literary masterpiece. I grope for words, fearful I won't measure up to the standards of university literary criticism, but hoping that my feelings for the subject might turn out to be better than

a forced term paper written for grades under compulsion......
oh.......my darling friend......

I am seeing gray rectangular geometries bursting in series from concentric blues; moire patterns buzzing all over the damn place.....oh, and now I see faint tints of rainbows...... Life is passing by in black and white, refracted. Life is an oscillating abstract painting. Ohhh.....

PETRA to ALISON:

That's interesting.....but I think I have turned into a hamburger..... this hamburger. I had planned to eat it, but now I'm not sure if I want to bite it or not. On the other hand, I could go ahead, and if I find myself saying *OW*! I can stop, and I'll know I bit *ME*, and if I don't say *OW*! then I know it's not me, and it's okay to go ahead and eat the thing. To bite, or not to bite?

(Knowing Petra's appetite, which is legend, once she gets a real taste of it, there will be no further questions as to that hamburger's destiny.)

ALISON to PETRA:

I wish my door had a lock on it. I am not sure if I mean the door of my room or of my mind or of my emotions..... Artists need a selective kind of privacy to bloom.....supported by collections of seemingly irrelevant stuff, and minds that naturally tend to fragment themselves

I can't make it out in the world. Out there I can only be worldly. Art that is other worldly has to come from a sanctuary......maybe from a school.

The artists of a society control its speed, you know? In some societies, they push forward by making marks that have no sense until technology has caught up enough for the marks to be read as a picture of something. Today I think the artists trying for increased forward motion ultimately explode nuclear weapons and eliminate all existing art in one shot. Don't you think artists should now remind society of the importance of keeping still or even of moving backwards in time a little bit?

PETRA to ALISON:
(listening with great absorption and trying to make sense out of what she is hearing):

It is amazing for someone who talks so well, your writing is so shitty. I have great hope, Alison, that one of these days you will purify yourself of bull-shitting, and that you'll really say something respectable.....like a book or a painting....anything at all.

ALISON to PETRA: *(thinking aloud):*
Artists must remind themselves that once love was an idea...... One way of doing that could be showing what pain today's world causes to innocence. Yes. Yes. Romanticism is a mode that ought to be affected by the artists of today. It is morally appropriate. But the only romanticism I can find in today's literature is a nostalgia for mythology and the search for cosmic enlightenment, *The Lord of the Rings* and Carlos Castaneda. You know what I mean?

PETRA to ALISON:
Yes. But we need women artists now. A new ideal of beauty for women, including intelligence, strength, and willpower as ideal features to be emphasized.

ALISON to PETRA:
Women artists have all of art history to respond to.....their voices, as women, were so rarely heard then.....and there is a whole fiend of feminist humor available. We must take advantage of it.....also feminist romanticism, which is not at all like Madame Bovary. *(Grind your teeth, you Flaubert fan, you.)*

PETRA to ALISON:
No. I'm following you. Feminist romanticism means you are extremely creative, extremely intelligent, a forceful person, and

also extremely *SEXY*. The question: what does the feminist romantic person do about the problem of sex? Men with weak characters are not appealing. Women with strong characters are not men.....and what does that leave? Conflict!

ALISON to PETRA:

Cosi? It takes a special kind of man to fall for a strong woman and not find her mind a threat? Is that what you mean?

PETRA to ALISON:

What am I supposed to do when they can't keep up with me? Pretend I am stupider than I am? Less experienced? Less full of desire? Less imaginative? Anyway, when I find they can't follow me, I get bored. You see the problem.....

(Petra sheds men like a dog wishing to get rid of fleas, impatiently brushing them out of her life, annoyed they have failed to comprehend her significance.)

PETRA to ALISON:

Sometimes I think my mother was relieved when my father died when I was just a baby. She's a businesswoman, you know..... became one at a time when they didn't have many women executives.....brought me up to drive, fix the car, take care of myself, and not to buy cheap clothes.

Most men can't even deal with my driving, which is better than most men's anyway. I've been doing it for a long time and have excellent reflexes.

(This bit about Petra's driving is true. She never makes me nervous in a car. As witness, she can talk a mile a minute, smoke a cigarette, and eat an apple all at the same time as she's taking a curve at high speed.)

ALISON to PETRA:

But think of the mystery of men.....their masculine weaknesses that are so appealing, the football games they seldom play and they watch them with their beer-cans, rooting and acting as if any minute they'll run into the TV, putting down the sports casters and getting excited. It's neat. They're so cute. How can one not love them?

PETRA to ALISON:

I prefer men who run marathons suddenly at age forty, or athletes who give it all up and buy desert islands to settle on.....or businessmen who retire and start rural health food restaurants, or ex-soldiers who find gurus and start meditating.........

ALISON to PETRA:

Those are some pretty good men. Why don't I ever meet any? Oh God, I just ate twice as much as I should have because I thought I was going to stop smoking, and I haven't. Now look what I've done..... Perverse.....

PETRA to ALISON:

That's just like you.

Chapter 8

THE ANGEL

The mail-room is the most comfortable place in the office building where I work. It is the pit -stop for heads, a sanctuary where music can help clean out the small irritations of the working day, restoring you to optimism with reminders of who you really are. The mail-room foreman is a musician, (and dope dealer in his spare time), and so the radio plays well chosen stations with a predilection for Jimi Hendrix and Santana.

The mail-room workers wear 'normal' clothes: dungarees and T-shirts, or hip shirts..... At least they don't wear suits, and you can see that they have real bodies. They look less like business manikins and more like human beings to me. (Pardon me, Jack Livingston, but not all executives can look like fashion plates.)

The hipper secretaries and young dudes who clerk in the offices, (many of them black), find their ways and means to pass through the mail-room. Joints of marijuana are shared in the stairwell, and connections are made when needed. It is a pleasure to socialize without the business personae standing over us with their up-tight alcoholism looking down at our grassy tastes as if we were criminals. We are the 'workers' as opposed to the 'professionals'.....

As I pass over the threshold of the mail-room, I change from a *'broad'* to a *'chick'*. What a relief. It is easier for me to deal with 'chick' expectations than 'broad' expectations. The broad is a 1940s invention of Edward G. Robinson and Humphrey Bogart detective movies. I don't exactly appreciate being seen as a chick, but at least it is within my own time zone.

The mail-room personnel are all of them between twenty-five and thirty, wear leather jackets when it's cold, and all are heads. I discover Angel among them.

Like a glacier, he slowly oozes an icy power that moves his surroundings.....inexorably with primeval force.....chilling movements, so that his work is accomplished almost invisibly. A mountain of large brown cartons is diffused without any exertion, seemingly without depletion.

A cigarette clamped in his mouth, Angel seems more involved in watching the curling blue smoke dance toward the ceiling than in lifting weights. Completing his labors, he sinks into a chair and stretches like a lion before a nap. Then the music takes him, and he freezes..... Only his foot, tapping the ground regularly like a metronome, betrays the fact he is alive.

He sustains the impression of good-natured boredom or absence. His massive body is right there, able to negotiate for him, but his spirit is on deposit in the vault of his own fortress, and nothing essential can be wrested from him except a concession to appearances. What a tantalizing reserve.

Just like a giant clam. I have a curiosity to wrench him open to ascertain whether he is hiding a giant pearl or just a sensitive inner lining. I dive without hesitation, casting a net of remarks.

"We are a country who make holidays out of assassinations, do you realize this?" I ask the mail-room. The voice-over radio news has just reminded us that today is the anniversary of Kennedy's death.

I remember sitting with Dave in his ancient Peugeot heading for the Harvard-Yale game, and the announcer is scooping on the news. Dave and Robbie, (his opposite number at Harvard), have their bets going as always. Robbie is a sportswriter for the *Crimson* so he has gotten us good seats, and we have a flask of Courvoisier to keep out the cold, and blankets with the Yale emblem..... and now we are cancelled out. Game over before it's begun.

Displaced from our native haunts, we are traveling spectators to national grief for a fallen idol.....people crying in the grocery stores where we stop to buy food, at the gas station where we refill the car's empty tank, everywhere. The left sees a CIA plot and the right sees a communist conspiracy......and a mass of college students become soured on the establishment which was beginning to maybe look good.

The mail-room is indifferent to the deceased Kennedy. He was not one of theirs and seems not to be worth consideration. Angel's dark force field does not unbend during this encounter. He's still a clam.

Before using the pliers or a can-opener on him, seduction may be a quicker and easier route. Fan-like, my mind snaps open one hundred and eighty degrees with assorted plans. Like a billiard player looking for a good angle, physics advises me that if I walk in the opposite direction I will ricochet against the wall, and the collision of our meeting will seem to be an accident without intent on my part. I want no connection with broken shells.

I arrange to be sent to Angel as a gift of fortune, special delivery courtesy of the executives at Academia Books, all unsuspecting, even cooperative, and yet impervious to any suggestion that would imply commitment.

"Hello." I reflect the sunbeams of a spring day into his eye. He turns a mirror to me, dousing me with my own friendliness. "Hi there, sweet thing."

"I have a package that must go out this afternoon: Special Delivery. Can you help me?"

"Of course."

I hand over a cube of books, wrapped in corrugated cardboard, neatly sealed with packing tape, and watch over his processing as if my mission included reporting the fate of the parcel. Leaning against a crate, I find his non-attention is a bit overdone. I fan myself with a handful of letters, (stamped), wafting disturbing currents through his atmosphere. Like a Victorian debutante engaging in light flirtation, I try for an ingenuous, helpless femininity, all unsuspecting of the existence of sex.

As I surround him with a mist of airy caresses, I preserve a surface of sheer platonic friendliness.

"You are so helpful.......thank you.....very much."

Angel's nostrils contract as if scenting a trap. He licks his lips swiftly with his tongue, and focuses on my mouth. I smile at him cheerfully. Reaching out, he takes my hand and drops the stamped bundle into it, leaving me holding it. He disengages with a penetrating glance of such ambient salaciousness that I am momentarily stopped in time.....filled with awe. He has bought none of my act.

"Very charming. Ask me anytime," he drawls with a remote and cynical air, as if to suggest I could be slightly less boring than the rest of the environment if I knocked myself out.

"Indeed? So reassuring to know I have a friend in the mail-room." I exit immediately before I can spoil the vignette.

I transact business in the mail-room every day, posting letters and books, and impressions of Angel gradually assemble into an identity that interests me further.

He is capable of making jokes. Silently, dangerously neutral at other times, I pick up on suppressed rage.....ergo: contempt for society and rebellious tendencies. Assorted drugs.....this I know from exchanged accounts of weekend tripping,.....but it seems Angel can always get his hands on any kind of drug he wants; therefore a dealer or a very close friend of a dealer. I trace a street life of irregular hours, with fondness for music and partying, and acceptance of white hippies without making a big deal out of it.

94

Angel is black, though many of his friends are Latin or white. He seems genuinely unprejudiced and indifferent with regard to race. Not that he believes in the *Brotherhood of Man*, but rather because he believes in the lack of brotherhood of man. That's what makes him unprejudiced.

"Who is going to take pride in belonging to one bunch of assholes when it's clear they are just as assy as the rest? It's hardly worthwhile speaking to anybody." Angel makes it clear he's out exclusively for himself and feels no kinship for anyone regardless of skin color.

The withdrawal of soul in the interests of dignity fascinates me. He stands as if built of solid rock, a colossal monument, unaffected while the pollution of New York City deposits the residue of time on his surface. Nothing changes him except drugs, and they don't change him much. And all the time, underneath his nonchalant and sometimes happy-go-lucky masquerade, I sense a hunter waiting for the next attractive game that will unsuspectingly pass by. It could be a woman, or the prospect of making easy money, or a joke that is asking to be played. I observe that, like a good hunter, Angel doesn't go after more than he can take care of. Nothing can be traced back to him exactly.

He is quite good-looking, and a scar on his cheek from a knife fight makes him look like a pirate. I do not think of Angel sexually though. Instead I construct a fantasy, piece by piece, of what his life is all about; roaming the streets of the East Village at night, having adventures. From the things I am not getting told, it is positive that there is more to him than meets the eye. For one thing, it seems that just about every one of Angel's games are illegal. He likes playing without a license..... What I want is a firsthand guided tour of his underworld.

Toward me, Angel begins to unbend, displaying the indulgence of an elderly epicure toward a young hedonist. I am getting at least one joke a day from him. He manifests disinterest in me as a woman. This doesn't challenge me, but I want to know what it is he does on weekends, how to get there, and where to find it.

The essence of 'COOL' seems to be the ability to remain unmoved by all that is happening. Being entire to oneself, impenetrable, never losing one's balance. The philosophy of 'COOL' seems a natural development of life on the streets. Any weakness is quickly spotted. Blankness is cultivated when young, and becomes an art form after it is mastered. The streets are a dirty hard territory full of a never-ending drama, reminding one never to care. Caring for anything very much is the easiest path to self-destruction.

There is reality. The poverty and cheapness are inescapable. The filthy narrow stairways of the walkup railroad flats, (some of the stairs shaky and unreliable), exposed electric wires dangling from hall ceilings, bathrooms with rusting pipes, and peeling paint. Old damaged linoleum or shredded rugs cover the floor. If lucky, there is a color television set: the only window out of this place.

Either you have the choice of participating in the neighborhood and knowing everybody's business and having them know yours, or you can try to be a recluse. But all things can't be hidden. There are spectators who have little else to do than look out the window and listen for the stairs..... Yet there is isolation.

Angel is a product of this life and cares for nothing. He does his day's work in a job that only matters for the money. Then he heads for the quickest way to get stoned.

For acquaintance to become friendship entails ritual. Angel and I commence a waiting game, which both of us enjoy to the full. Points are scored for non-response, solipsism, and general coolness. We demonstrate how we need nothing from each other, are getting it all elsewhere, and how life itself leaves us unmoved. When we have clarified that we are each totally independent souls, a balance is reached that permits getting together outside of work; the purpose ostensibly being the location of a party and good acid for me.

I have enough men in my life who will do what I want. So as I walk with Angel and a group of his friends through the evening streets, I have no intentions.....just going along to see if there is anything new in Angel's world. The streetlights, like beacons on the corners of the streets, are regulating a nonexistent traffic. All the good Judeo-Christians have already gone to bed so they can be early to rise, healthy and wealthy. Now it is the night shift's time. There are fewer of us night owls, most of us not out for work.....just playing around. Even in the dark alleys, I fear nothing. Angel is with me, and if they notice who is coming, people are not going to make trouble for him. He is too large.

We end up in a strange little apartment, a strobe candle spitting flame in the middle of the living room floor.....abandoned by the friends who are stoned out and who have made a gross scene with each other that accelerated into a fight and moved into the street...... and then who knows. And so Angel and I are in the dark, with the candle between us, two nonparticipants preserving good form amidst the insanity of emotions and economizing on expression. Saying nothing in fact.

Left alone together, with the candle moving the room back and forth in its dim light, we study each other. Neither of us spares a word. Angel is completely relaxed as I look at him, impassive, waiting. I am relaxed also, waiting to see what he will do, and inwardly filled with a daredevil recklessness, ready for anything.

Ten minutes elapse. Both of us just comfortably sitting. Angel turns his head and says very politely and dispassionately, "So. Do you want to fuck with me tonight?" as if he had asked do I want to go to the movies. He waits for an answer. Hasn't laid a hand on me. Hasn't shifted from his position. Hasn't made a single remark to heat me up, and hasn't tried to read my palm, (a gambit I detest for initiating the stroking of hands). He also hasn't assumed that dope makes me an easy mark. Hasn't overwhelmed me with sexy looks. I have not felt one single pressure from him, and conclude he is a classy dude. He has taken me at face value.....only to be had according to choice. Apparently Angel understands women, because I do not start affairs without the premise of free choice.

I find myself pleased with him for knowing what I do not like

97

and not doing it. This alone makes going to bed with him worth considering, so I consider. If I say "Non," it's clear he's ready to take me home and no bad feelings. I like that.

Angel gives me all the space I need to examine the proposition. I am curious as I contemplate his body, so large and strong. It may be fun to discompose him. Thanks to the boss and his prescriptions, I have become a competent geisha. Since the divorce, *FRIGID* is the last thing I am. After years of hearing the opposite, I cannot get enough of being told I am good in bed. I write the names of my conquests on paper and add them up. A game of numbers.....so why not Angel?

Very coolly, I look Angel in the face. "You asked for it." This is an assent. We strip slowly, eyes engaged, blandly assessing each other like wrestlers before a match. He reaches out and takes my shoulders in his huge hands, drawing me to his mouth. The first kiss is instant lust, a surprise to both of us. It becomes intercourse, insatiable, which goes on for a long time as we test each other's reflexes, taking pleasure in each other's animality, establishing increasing respect, experimenting........such a long time. I am very, very satisfied. I have been treated as I deserve. Everything is as it should be. I say nothing.

The skin under my hands is a dark brown, hot or cold according to the light. Blue highlights shine from the sculptured limbs. Black hairs curl in the hollow between his pectoral muscles. The jockey shorts of white jersey look inconsistent as if a Greek god were modeling *Fruit of the Loom*. I watch him dress. It is not difficult to imagine Angel in a loincloth or a toga...but the white jockey shorts, though sporty, lack aesthetic grace. They almost proclaim their embarrassment about feeling.....negation.....by a strict conformity with socially agreed on function. At least Angel's sailor pants, which lace up the front, have more nostalgic associations. Men alone on the sea, fighting the elements, they say to me. His navy wool pants speak better for his philosophy. Yes, they do. And his T-shirt is striped like a French Apache dancer. That also is not insensitive, reminds one of the Latin Quarter, Bohemian existentialism. I approve the T-shirt.

I put my own clothes on, and Angel walks me home. In the night air, everything is cold and clean.

"I didn't expect you would be so passionate," Angel admits with a puzzled air as if he should have been able to know in advance.

"That's only natural." I grin at him. "You don't know me at all." I run my hands along his sides and laugh gaily. "You're very good yourself. Thanks for a nice evening." I turn and walk into the lobby of my building, not asking when I will see him again. The doorman gives me his usual look of disdain plus conjectures of what I have been up to. I see him looking past me too out the door to discover with whom now.....

The next day at work, I spent as much time as possible looking out one of the windows in the back offices, telling myself jokes. All morning I did the efficient secretary. I know how to get these jobs done. Got 'em done. My desk is almost clear. Tomorrow is *PADA*, (payday), and we Academians will all make the bank dash, take long lunch hours, and perhaps take off early. (In fact, there has been a discussion of when.)

* * * * *

Yay! It's here. My period is here. I just came out of the bathroom, and there it was, proof positive. *I'M NOT PREGNANT.....AGAIN.* I want to shout aloud with joy. I washed my face and beamed at myself in the mirror. Clean face and soon-to-be-cleaned-out system. How sensible of me to know to bleed during the week. By the weekend, I will be stopped, creamy. I will cream all over the place. I will. I will. Thank God. My period! I'm so happy.

Got to unobtrusively slip back to the bathroom with some Tampax I have stashed in the bottom drawer of my desk. How am I going to manage this without Jack Livingston seeing me? And making some comment, which he would. He's sitting right there at the desk opposite me, (Elaine's desk), large as life.

I have cramps. Right now, I think they're great. I'll lose weight. Great plans.

When I pass through the mail-room, I meet a knowing look of approval from Angel. "What are you doing later on?"

"Oh....." I collect my points of reference. "Have to meet friends..... take care of some business....."

"When do I get to see you?" he asked, certain that I do want to see him. We set a time over the weekend. There is no hurry. And so an affair begins.

Jack came in this morning with a colossal hangover, swearing off the booze. Saying it's not worth it. It costs too much and takes too much energy.

"Why did you bother even to come in if you feel so lousy?"

"Well, you've *GOT TO* come in on those mornings after you've stayed out all night. It's precisely these mornings, part of the code." He looks woozy.

"I know you.....a secret puritan.....the wages of sin.....office work." I tease him. I left the office at five worrying about Jack's navigation. Apparently he went to the Jamaica Inn bar and spent the next three hours drinking up another $25. Jack's capacity amazes me.

* * * * *

My life is full. I have the kid. I deposit and collect her at the day care center. I work. I live two blocks from my office. Some afternoons I take Angel to my apartment for lunch. At night I mother Babette until she is asleep (by 9:00 p.m.) Tommy may drift by and help me put her to bed. Sometimes the Leo and his girlfriend Rosalyn visit along with Tommy. They read stories to the child and neck on my rug. Rosalyn is a beautiful teenager from New Jersey who still lives home with her parents. She is prettier than most models.....and so young. I think she must be a virgin. The Leo treats her like one, very gently as if she were spun glass.

It does seem odd that Leo doesn't have a house.....but I assume he is like Tommy, a floater.

If I have a babysitter, or Dave to watch the child, I go out.

Ruthy and Petra report regularly on developments in their lives. They are now sharing a large apartment in the Bronx. School keeps them busy. But they are watching the transition from housewife to swinging mother and standing by me when I need it.

Once a week at least, the boss takes me to a fancy restaurant. He is intrigued to see me following his plan, sitting over Shanghai shredded beef, satiated and mysterious, lips swollen, neck decorated appropriately with symmetrical bruises, and eyes hazy with lack of sleep. I attract him more than ever.

"I think you have a new lover," he fishes. "You're looking different. I think he's good for you. I hope so?"

"Mmmmmm, oh yes, very. Good food, mmmmmmmmm. Thanks. Oh Yum. More food....."

Angel and I start a new game. He tells me I am not the best lover he's ever had. I refuse to care about it because I'm getting what I want. I remind him he doesn't have to see me.

Then he says I am now the only woman he is seeing, (aside from his wife). Cautiously, I admit he is my favorite man.

"Listen," as I play with his hand. "Certainly you don't expect me to stay alone? You're going to be with your family tomorrow. I never said I would stop seeing other men. I have never told you to stop seeing whatever women you want. And I tell you right out front that I prefer you. You are the favorite. You don't love me. So what do you care?.....You ought to be pleased. You ought to be happy!"

"Hmmm......," Angel hums, perplexed. "I'm not sure I do like it all the same. If I were to get free tomorrow night, would you be here?"

Sexually Angel is making me dissatisfied with other men, and therefore less interested. I am beginning to depend on him; the last thing I want to happen. I try not to let him know it. Give a man like that an inch and he will take a mile. I continue dating other men, even though they don't turn me on..... Some of them are quite interesting people outside of bed.

During the lunch break, I stroll leisurely down to Washington Square Park, wishing there were some way I could be invisible so I could watch everyone at close range without being seen. Dark glasses are all I can do to approximate this condition. The chess players are clustered around the tables, knots of men of all sizes and shapes, all ages, and all walks of life. If I join, I will look out of place. (There are *NO* women.) ....but I love the game......and I draw close.

A middle aged, curly haired man in a white T-shirt is giving a verbal rundown of his plays. He is a near master, and the audience is enthralled as chess strategy, options, historical equivalents for the situation are presented. This man has memorized *ALL* the openings, middle and end games, entire games, variations and theory of the masters. It is his *THINGGGG*.....and so, he is like a chess computer. He functions at least eight times as fast as your normal wood-pushing chess aficionado, thinking ahead eight moves to your average one. His chess-casting commentaries are great fun. The crowd applauds every move, exuberant as basketball spectators and democratically interjecting alternatives. It is a spontaneous learning situation. (I wish I were a man......then I could just move in on the scene and really learn to play without being a freak.)

Smoke from a strong cigar wafts past my nose. Maybe if I smoked cigars, I would qualify. I file a mental note to buy some cigars and experiment at home. My sunglasses are very large. They surely don't obscure themselves as sunglasses, (veritable shields for my entire face), but they certainly do obscure my expressions.

Somehow I maneuver myself into a game. I lose because, as it's explained to me, my opening is too aggressive and full of holes. *(Fuck it!)* Vowing to be more conservative in the next game I play, I walk back to the job, thinking, "These park players, some of them are really good. You can't get away with the same tricks with them as you do playing with preppies."

* * * * *

Angel pulls me into the mail-room as I pass by the door. Angel....... behind the bookcases filled floor to ceiling with complimentary copies, and screened by boxes of office supplies. Like a reflex, his hands go straight for my crotch. I should be at my desk. I don't want to get caught. He is very skillful. My knees go weak, and he laughs as he feels me give in. "You like it.....you like it....." Takes my hand and leads it to his prick, hard as steel under the navy blue wool. I feel very faint. "Baby.....I'll see you tonight."

I wobble back to my desk.......

Chapter 9

Dear Pierre:

Reality is the human element. Fish live in water, and we humans swim through reality. And when you don't know what is real anymore, you flip out like a fish stranded on a beach, out of its element, suffocating and flapping with agony.

Pierre, what a beautiful thing if you can share your reality in exchange for another.....but the danger is.....you could be tossed out of it before you realize it, just like that flipped out fish.

Pierre, my head is a planet revolving on its own axis. Sometimes I see the sun and sometimes I see the moon. Sometimes I see both together, which is confusing, and sometimes I see no light at all, which feels like spending the night in a haunted house. It all depends on whether you believe in ghosts.....what is going to come out of that chaotic nothing of aloneness......

* * * * *

I keen my ears, listening for every sound, trying to make meaning of it. I allow my flesh to serve me as eyes, for I am blind without light.....and my life may depend on it.

I'm still a baby, nursing off memories I'm told I shouldn't be able to remember..... I need the comfort of physical presence just to keep my nights from being haunted. I don't want to starve to death.....

Pierre's answer to everything is another volume of Henry Miller's to read.

Last night I had magnificent dreams. Dreams of good things happening to me. I woke up one time in a sweat, but glowing all over, yelling to myself: "I've made it! I've made it!" What? Immediately lost track of what I had made.

Another dream. I was a large and fragrant gardenia. I liked being one; waxy white petals, soft and perfumed surface..... That was making it in last night's terms. Try being a gardenia while you sleep. You will know what I mean if you succeed.

In the morning, Babette was sick of having her hair in her eyes, so I trimmed her a set of bangs, and she looked charming. She was coughing, a deep-rooted wheeze. I'm beginning to sneeze. I hope the whole family doesn't fall apart before the weekend. I don't want to miss work and use up a sick day. On the weekend we shall stay home, and everything can proceed at a very slow pace, not having to go anywhere.

Saturday night, Lex drops in, towing a dog that resembles an Alaskan Husky. Dog's name is Che. Babette fluttered out of the bathtub where she was supposed to be getting clean to relate to this dog.

Lex, who came to return my poncho to me, was all crackling sparks and small explosions of excitement. Some folks are naturally fluorescent. I was happy she came. We hip-talk to one another, saving time by condensing sentences and mood swings into hieroglyphic epithets.

And so here is Lex, one of the few people I might have expected it to be, although I didn't know she owned a dog.

"It's only my dog for a few days. I'm keeping him for one of my boyfriends."

She came into the bathroom, flashing her greenish eyes behind her glasses, sitting on the sink, busily digging all the news I was laying on her as I swabbed the kid down.

We fantasize about screwing the leather store as a group event. There should be a party and all will remove their clothes and probably sit around just as usual, playing the guitar and drinking apple wine. Then we can screw where and whom we want to. Lex thinks this will improve the store no end. Meantime, she is recovering from inflammation of the womb and having stitches removed from her leg, and I am recovering from another imaginary case of overweight, physical and mental, and from pimples, (undoubtedly due to bad eating, nervous tension, and dwelling in New York City soot.)

The buzzer rings yet again. It is Tommy.

"Great. Come right up."

Lex looks at me with satisfaction. "Tommy? He intrigued me at once the first time I laid eyes on him, if only because he is so tall."

I grin and say, "Yes, he is. Isn't he?"

Anyway, Lex makes it clear she is interested in Tommy and has plans to fuck him. I wonder: will they enjoy each other? Tommy is such a non-malicious person. I hope he can hold his own with Lex. She can be a bitch. He has the habit of falling in love at the least provocation. I know Lex will be very provocative.

I have no right to feel even the tiniest little jealous twinge, because I told Tommy it was inadvisable for him to fall in love with me. We are better off staying good friends. He is ten years younger than me, totally zotzed in the head, and I don't love him as a man. So.....be an observer and watch from the mezzanine as Lex goes into her Svengali act.

"But definitely because I am curious," trills Lex.

"Huh?"

"To find out whether everything about Tommy is in proportion!" *Oh.......*

I dry Babette and put her into her flannel footie pajamas, and she scuttles to the door to give Tommy a gremlin welcome.

"Leo and Rosalyn ought to be here in the next fifteen minutes. They are at the store, buying food." Tommy whips out his guitar, very aware of Lex, and plays a rather intricate piece of acoustic blues, combining rhythm and lead, full of hard-to-execute slides and whines and whatnot. Everything fit interestingly. The rhythm was full of surprises for me, because although every note did work, nothing came where I expected it would. At the end, Lex was asked if she liked it.

"God, yes," she breathes. "Whose is it?"

"Mine," says Tommy as he rises to his feet and heads for the kitchen. I was somewhat taken aback because it had been a charming piece of music, but somehow I don't expect charm from a seven-foot palm tree.....other things, perhaps. Lex follows Tommy into the kitchen.

Babette comes to me with a piece of red construction paper well scrawled on in green and blue crayon; whorls so thick all I distinguish is the motions she went through. I look at it and say with respect: *"A PICTURE!"* This satisfies her. She toddles off, probably now is going to make another, come back, and show it to me. Now she knows what she has made. It is called 'a picture'. She is Babette the girl who can make pictures. She puffs up with accomplishment, feeling bigger. Oh, Mommy's Babette, plucky solid little girl. Next week I'll buy you fancy shoes for your dainty little girl ten toes.

Leo and Rosalyn appear with fried chicken and French fries from the deli, classic young lovers, hungry.....and we settle down for a tranquil evening at home, munching and music-ing, disposed on the floor like islands on the river of the braided rug. Babette is parked on the couch singing to herself with great enthusiasm one of the songs she makes up:

"How do *YOU* do? How do you *DO*? *HOW* do you do? You do?"

"Babette, if you are going to do that, (chalking), please don't do it on the sofa. Do it on the chest." She nods amenably and, surprise, she moves.

"It is almost time for you to go to sleep, Babette. Perhaps you want a story?"

Tommy makes tea for us all and gives out steaming cups. We lean back, and enfolding Babette in my arms, I start making up a little tale.

"You are going to have to assist me if I get stuck. I'm not always good at knowing how to make things up."

Here is the story told to Babette for her Saturday night bedtime by me-Alison, Leo, Lex, and Tommy. Rosalyn is silent. Sometimes I wonder if all she spends her time on is being beautiful.

ALISON:

Once there was a little baby who might have been you. All little babies have parents as you have, unless they are one of these newfangled scientific experiments. This little baby wanted food and entertainment......Bread and Circuses.....so you see, he carried on like an ancient Roman, making a spectacle of himself.....and as he grew he was told he had to make a choice: bread *or* entertainment. He couldn't have both. *(I'm stuck!)*

LEX:

Everybody he knew told him getting bread was most important. If you had bread you could eat, and if you ate, you could go on living. In which case, if you were lucky, you might find entertainment someday. Even if you didn't, you could still go on looking because you were alive, having eaten. Making sure you stay alive comes first.

ALISON:

This wise little baby looked around and was dissatisfied with what the world told him. His parents, his school, everything around him gave him bread, and spent all their time running after bread......waiting for the entertainment to come......but it seldom did.

LEO:

This wise little baby, whose name was Lao King, (this happened in ancient China, you see), felt that if life wasn't entertaining, it wouldn't be worth living. And there was a question nobody had asked him: What kind of life he was supposed to be spending time feeding.

BABETTE:

Mommy, this is a very strange story.

ALISON:

Shhhhh. Just listen.

LEO:

What is there in my life worth it that I should live unless I make some entertainment for myself and all these bread-makers? Ugh.....

TOMMY:

One day, as Lao King was walking in the forest, meditating to himself.....a dragon came up to him. *(Babette looks more hopeful as dragons are familiar characters in fairy tales.)* Fiery and hot tempered, ready to cause a child plenty of trouble.

ALISON:

"If you want to pass through my space," said the dragon, "you have to fight with me because my job here is to make life difficult for everybody." Lao King wondered what to do? Should he offer the dragon some bread? Entertain the dragon by telling it jokes or interesting things or singing and dancing? Or should he just play the game by the dragon's rules, giving in and fighting with the dragon? Of course, he wasn't positive he would win. What do you think Lao King did?

LEO:

"Wait here," Lao King said to the dragon as it breathed orange flames, searing the grass and the flowers. "I'll be right back, after I take a lesson from the Master of Fighting." Lao King had to look in the phone book..... Sorry, I forget. In ancient China, there weren't any phone books..... Lao King went back home and started to work until he could afford to go to a tea house. Over his cup of delicately relaxing, subtly flavored green tea, *(I look at Leo with approval)*, Lao King surveyed the other patrons........seeking for a person who looked as if he would know where the best Fighting Master might be found. Everyone in the tea house looked very peaceful, very gentle.....

TOMMY:

Lao King enjoyed the tea but left disappointed. On his way back home, he was so upset at his failure to find someone who could give him directions, he kicked the stones in the road, the remains of a broken basket, and a dead bird, not that it helped.

ALISON:

"How am I ever going to find out where to go?" bemoaned Lao King to his mother, not with any hope that she would know what he was talking about, being only a woman.....more as a way of getting sympathy.

LEX:

"Just ask," said his mother. This made a lot of sense, although Lao King still didn't think she could tell him where a Master of Fighting could be found. But his mother was a very strong person who stood up for herself. Too much, Lao King's father would remark. "Your mother is a very hard person, getting her way far too often. What can a man do about it? He has to leave the house just to think for himself."

BABETTE:

Just like MY mommy!

ALISON:

Lao King considered the philosophical implications of the proposal, asking for directions. "Who should I ask?" "Someone whose business it is to answer questions....." he heard his mother answer glibly. "Why? What is it you want to know?" Lao King was hoping she wouldn't get too specific.

LEO:

Lao King's mother was called Kwan Yin, after the Goddess of Mercy, although her neighbors who failed to get the better of her in bargaining called her 'That Living Bitch'. Lao King often thought to himself that if his mother was supposed to be merciful, for once in his life, he would like to be spared her attention.

TOMMY:

"I need to know where a good fighting master can be found." Lao King blushed and hoped she would not make fun of him this time. "There is your father," Kwan Yin began, "who is a very good fighter indeed. But you might have trouble learning from him."

LEO:

"No, Mother!" Lao King sighed with frustration. "I need to know where a *REAL* Master of Fighting is, a professional who can give me lessons."

ALISON:

"You can ask the fortune teller. He travels around quite a bit..... or you can ask the merchant. He has to protect his goods when the mule trains bring them from the big city, so he may know where fighters are to be found.....or," said his mother, "you can go to the temple in the mountains and ask the priests. Priests are supposed to be able to answer your questions.....and they also know how to keep the peace themselves.....and God is on their side....." *(Leo gives me an enigmatic glance. We all like this game. He takes up the story.)*

LEO:

> Lao King, thinking over the alternatives, decided the temple was the best place to go. Taking some of his mother's freshly baked bread as a gift to the priests, he spent the long walk into the mountains humming. He enjoyed being surrounded by nature, and his respect for the priests who lived in the temple outside the city gates increased. How clever they were to live close to the happily growing trees, the calm melodies of the birds singing in the sun, and naked animals running around taking care of their business without pretenses or shame.

ALISON:

> I think Babette is asleep..........

> We all have learned something about ourselves and each other tonight. Leo and Tommy fill the remaining time with music. Conversation is all used up.

* * * * *

Nights spent in Wilfred's living room with Angel. Fumes of pot. Decorations of empty gin bottles, rum bottles, vodka bottles, and beer cans. This is the worst section of the Lower East Side. I refuse to come without Angel.

"This is my baby." He introduces me to the gang of petty gangsters and thieves who stop in to collect their cocaine and their heroin.

("Heroin. I don't like it, Angel." "Relax. Just say *NO*. You don't have to do anything you don't want to do. You couldn't handle that anyway." "Are you sure?" "Everyone to their own poison.")

I am the respected property of Angel. No one ever fights with him. He is too big. His biceps are larger than my thighs.....and when anyone around him gets rowdy, he just gives a peaceful sigh and surveys his knuckles. Just this action is enough to stop most quarrels.

Music from the radio obligates the need to consider.....If it is

Friday, I can stay out as late as I want because the kid is at Dave's house.....and if it is Thursday, I have to be home by eleven o'clock, or Dave will be mad. He's with the kid. Which day is it?

I am not trying to do anything, except escape, and I am not trying to be anybody.....so if Angel wants me to be his "*BABY*," I don't bother to deny it. It may be some honorific title where he comes from. He pronounces it in such a way as it is understood: "Hands off this delicious white bird.....which is for my private consumption." Nobody makes a pass.

This stag session seems to enjoy my inclusion and talking with me. Few people of college extraction ever talk to them. They like to describe to me what "real life" is like and to expound their philosophies of existence.

Angel has few words, but is clean and honest with me. His philosophy is very easy. Himself, he is incapable of falling in love. The only two people he has ever loved in this world are his mother and his son. He does not love his wife, although he respects her. She is fine for a wife. He has never loved any of his women or any woman as a woman. He is not going to love me.

"That's wonderful, Angel," I drawl as I rub his hip. "Nothing could be more perfect. So good to be with a man who can control himself so well. This way neither of us can possibly be hurt because, as you know, although you are the coolest thing in town, and I like you more than any of my other men friends, I can't fall in love with you. Love puts a woman at a disadvantage."

"As long as you are my Baby, who needs love? Have some more grass?" He runs his hand up to the hem of my mini-skirt, displaying my legs to his friends, possessing me in public..... amused at any frustration he causes. I am a status symbol.....a free bird, and yet *HIS*. I'm not for any of them.

When there aren't enough chairs, I sit in Angel's enormous lap and lean back against his chest. He is solid beneath me. I never have to be concerned about being too heavy for him. His thighs are black pillars, and between them I can feel his prick, hard. He's too lazy to do anything about it though..... Later, when he gets bored with his friends, he'll take me to Wilfred's bedroom and close the door. I won't mind. That's what I came for.

"I was a pimp, once," says Angel when I question him about his past, "but I gave it up. Too much work. And the women bored me. Once I found out that I could do it.....I'd rather work. That way, nobody bothers me." He has always had several women in his life, even when he first married. By his description, his wife is a real slavey, does all the housework and doesn't suspect that he screws around.

"How could she not know?" I ask in amazement.

"Perhaps she'd rather not know," he replies, massaging my neck. "Her sex drive has worn out, anyway," he adds. "I married her when she was too young. Now she's used up." I can't relate to any of this and am very glad Angel's wife is not my problem. He doesn't love her. She is a woman. And his infidelity started long before my arrival on the scene.

One day I catch sight of Angel's wife. She is lovely. She has a moon face with two long black braids on each side of her head. She looks as if she spends whole days laughing; a plump bosomy womanly figure.

"What is there to turn a man off?" I ask Angel later. He asserts she is a top notch housekeeper, a great cook, a good mother to his son, an ace seamstress, and groovy besides.....but she has no sex drive. Wonderful for a wife. Disastrous for his satisfaction.

"I keep her happy. All she wants is to be screwed once a week, quickly. And that's enough for her," he says.

"Look. It's not really my business why you would want to cheat on your wife....." Angel is not with me for my conversation. All he wants to do is fuck me continuously for hours.

114

"You are a nymphomaniac," says Angel as he holds me down with one hand and fingers my body like a virtuoso with the other. He has me oozing desire.....and he is laughing with gratification.

"Actually you are worse than a nymphomaniac. Your classical nympho wants it all the time but can't orgasm. That's why she's always out there looking. She's trying to get her cookies. *YOU* can't get enough of it but come all the time....."

I have become a continual orgasm, between the acid trip and the appetites Angel has been cultivating. The only change is the level of feeling. I'm a little seasick from it and a lot dizzy, and I can't think very well.

"How do you know I'm a nymphomaniac?" I plead with him. "Be serious....."

"Baby, I *AM* serious. I've seen all kinds of women. I know. That's why you need me. There aren't many men who could satisfy a woman like you. I probably couldn't do it either if I could feel anything. I don't feel very much. That's why I last so long. I get my kicks mostly from seeing you .....from watching you when I please you.....like this....." Fire runs through my body. He is deliberately making me very hot and doing nothing to satisfy me. I'm pinned. Can't pull away. He specifies I have to beg him for it before anything further happens. I'm feverish, tossing from side to side and groaning. This scene is out of a sex magazine.....too ridiculous to be true. Yet Angel wants what he wants.....

"Ask for it, Baby," he urges me with laughter. "Ask for it. You know you want it. And you don't get it until you ask me." He strokes me again and again, gently and expertly, until I'm in tears with frustration.

"You can have all you want. You can have all you need. Just ask me.....nicely.....now....."

I must stretch to accommodate his size, awesome. I have never seen such a big man. I am transfixed on that spike as a butterfly pierced by a pin. When his fingers demanded a climax, and made one for me, I felt as emotionally cheated as an infant given a pacifier instead of a breast. Now he jabs me, hammering me like a metalsmith, pausing to inspect me for dents. Drilling me, filling me, thrilling me, willing me to lose myself.....

"Can't *YOU* feel anything, Angel?"

"Not much. That's the way I am."

"Don't you miss it?"

"Not really. All these poor slobs, falling in love.....woman comes along and messes with their head. The only woman I trust is my mother. I don't trust my wife. I don't trust you. I don't feel anything. I never get hurt. It works for me."

"But surely you can feel this......" As he lies immobile, I caress his tough skin with my hands, my lips, my tongue, looking for a chink in his armor. He lies open-eyed, patiently enduring me with some affection.

"Sure I like it. But nothing moves me much. You can suck me. I like to see you on your knees in front of my cock. But I don't feel it much. It is more watching you doing it than anything I feel." He pushes my head down and I do a job on him. It is like trying to extract emotions from a computer. He enjoys the idea of it more than the sensation. I feel no pulsing response. After a while, he pulls me off him, effortlessly lifting me onto his chest.

"You see, Alison. Give up trying to get a hold on me. It doesn't do that much for me. Nothing does. We're different. You, on the other hand, feel everything.....almost too much.....here....."

He slides his rigid cock into me as he pulls my hips down, raising my shoulders so he can observe my face as he begins to move. It may be primitive and elementary, his art form. It originates in the groin and is painted on women's faces as he replaces their realities with raw sex. It is a transitory art, so Angel has learned how to protract it.

As Angel takes me over, I have an insight. He is out to dominate the strongest-minded woman he can find. A poor man's revenge, who has only his manhood and no other skills, no college degree. He brings all the body skills of a champion athlete who remains in training for a marathon. He has run through his life screwing continuously, accumulating greater endurance and techniques, and picking women with ever stronger minds to blow. Yes.

Mind-blowing is Angel's art form, and sex is his medium. This comes naturally to him. His body is innately tough and gifted with stamina. More absorbed with melting women than getting money by remaining a professional fucker, (whores being no challenge to him anymore), he has retired to amateur status. Now he's doing his number strictly for kicks. And fate has brought him me, a nymphomaniac with a *DIPLOMA*. (It's merely a B.A., but it's the college brand that confers prestige to the possessor.)

I cannot spread my legs wide enough or get enough of Angel. I hurt in my mind from contradictions even while my body asks for more. There has got to be more to life than nymphomania and big pricks. How can I exist so schizophrenically? He is invulnerable, pre-satiated with experiences, and doesn't feel anything. I can only hang on to my independence by refusing to give up seeing other men.

Angel flexes his power over me, messing with me, taking advantage of his strength. I am being reduced to a body. Part of me relishes this, and part of me protests. I like him to be strong, but I don't like to be helpless. As Angels fucks me, I let my mind travel and list the bright notions that seem worth noting:

A. A volume of romantic poetry is to be written in firefly piss for lovers to read in the dark.

B. Obedient children. *(Hah. Contradiction in terms. Oxymoron.)*

C. A God that would save everyone indiscriminately. Thus taking the burden of value judgements off our backs. *(Latent guilt feelings surface here?)*

D. Just because your brother is a candidate for the zoo does not mean you have to be his keeper.

E. My ears have fallen into permanent love with Eric Clapton. I conclude this may be the major event of the year. He's so fine. Where his riffs come from is beyond my knowing, but they are so sonorous, emotionally true, and refined, all at once.

I lie under Angel's body, meditating on Clapton with complete awe and marvelment, saying to myself..... "The guy's a genius. How does he do it?" Clapton is God worshipped by many as divine. I must be insane. *CRAZY* reflects my mental environment. These images of 'What's happening' mirror themselves in my brain.....sheer madness. It really is just a question of stamina, I remind myself, after the original assumptions are made. Dreams and stamina. What you need to become a gourmet chef with food or words or music......or love......

Wilfred's bedroom.....crumbling walls.....old sheets.....wrinkled and soaked with sweat.....mine. Angel's breath reeks with the liquor he's been drinking. His body is scorching. The radio plays soul music. Angel plays my soul through my body. He has a fancy for manipulation, is pleased to force my desire. He likes making me scream so that the sounds carry through the house. He fucks me again and again, inexorably and tirelessly, in every possible position, waiting for me to fall apart. He watches me all the time, overwhelming me with his energy, his determination, his hardness. I am not to be given any rest.

He holds my thighs spread apart, plunges in, moves, pulls out, teasing me. He comes but does not cease handling me, is hard again in minutes, gets back inside. Through all this he wears a friendly but imperturbable mask and seems to hardly be affected by anything.

Everything happening with me is now involuntary. I am rippling lava. My heart feels ready to explode. Eyeless patterns of concentric fireworks sweep my identity away. The orgasm becomes total, all my veins and arteries are throbbing, contracting and releasing.....etching designs of pleasure responses into my sense memory. My brain is pulsating. I am blinded with waves of white light.....incoherent, sobbing, crying, screaming.....

"I love.....your cunt." He repeats softly in my ear, condensing all of my personality into an orifice. My cunt is raw. Hours have gone by, but, miracle: I'm still wet. He's still moving. My heart is sore, exhausted from beating so furiously, no respite allowed. I am being split. I want this, I want it..........part of me hates it.

"It's not fair to be screwing someone if you're fucking someone else in your head," I mumble irrelevantly. Inner dialogue: What are you doing? I am expiating the sins of the world. Where am I going? What am I trying to prove? In order to have the proof, you have to have a hypothesis. "The proof of the pudding is in the eating," Friedrich Engels. Okay. So. But you need a recipe. The stove. Taste buds. You need a stomach. And if you make a mess with the pudding the first time, you have to be able to survive the stomach-ache. I only hope I don't give myself a case of mental ptomaine poisoning. Do they have brain pumps?

The night goes by. The morning light, pale and cold, is a sharp line on the edge of the window blind. Angel is still riding me. I'm still coming and have no will left. I'm shattered. My emotional tissues are in shreds. I have fainted several times and returned to consciousness to find him still inside me moving.

I am so sensitive now, the slightest touch on my neck, on my back, on my thing is enough to stimulate another series of orgasms. He is very pleased with himself and still not tired. He does anything he wants now.

Angel rolls me onto my stomach, slides his hands underneath, sensuously fondling the lips of my sex, lightly circling my clitoris. He leaves a trail of kisses along my neck and then bites it, thrusting his large fingers deep in my vagina. His heavy hips crush me to the mattress as he presses down, violently penetrating my ass with his shaft. There is pain because of his size, but he is master of the situation. He plays with his fingers until I relax, working his mouth on my back and shoulders.....leaving bruises..... I am shaking all over. I feel humiliated, flattened.....

He sheathes his penis in me all the way and is motionless. His hands are in my vagina and on my clitoris. There is no way I can move, but something of him drives into me deeper and I cannot keep still. I am coming.....twisting, and writhing, aching with overuse and stretching, screaming wordlessly. He starts his rhythm again, chanting, "Nymphomaniac, nymphomaniac, you need me.....but that's all right..... That's all right, Baby, because I'm here. I'm here, and I'll take care of you..... Ahhhh, that's good. Isn't it? Sooooooo good.....my little nymphomaniac. That's okay, honey. Little more now. Come on, give it to me......that's right......"

Suddenly, he shifts off me and eases me onto my back. I'm blind now and can't see. I feel him beginning to stroke my body again, brushing his penis back and forth against my sex...... I have no muscular control left. I am slack, except for my hips which follow his motion as if conditioned. I have no voice left. My lips are dry. His mouth covers mine. He holds me so that I cannot move and slides his tongue deep into my throat as he enters me and fucks. He sets me free to thrash around. The soul music is a dim background. I am hysterical, completely submissive, and out of my mind.

"That's the way, Mama," croons Angel. "Sing to me, mmmmm...... I like that.....mmmmmm......give me some sugar now." After forty minutes, he comes. It is morning.

* * * * *

When was it that Angel started to care about me? Was it then? When I began to feel hate for him alongside desire for the way he played on my sexuality, making himself so indispensable. Keeping himself in reserve, he controlled me as a puppet master toying with a marionette. He pulled the strings but gave me no strings of his own in return. Filled with self-loathing for the ease with which he destroyed my composure, I start to lay plots for revenge.

On my sore bottom, aching from a night-long session, I sit in front of the typewriter. Even on the job I am unable to erase the imprints of possession. Casually dressed, Angel walks down the hall, slow, go humored, and sexy as hell. Through the office door and up to my desk, violating class distinctions consciously, smiling. He'd wait in the background if the editors were speaking to me, an enormous black man with a wrestler's build. He found the covert reactions of these middle-class men, (whom he regarded as negligible specimens of masculinity), to be very funny as the rumors and conclusions about me spread in the offices. The only man among the professionals Angel conceded any show of respect to was Jack who was as large and vital as himself.

And the boss, seeing Angel next to my desk, narrowed his eyes, looked me up and down, and grinned at the both of us, saying to himself, "So.....that's it." Down the hall he marches to challenge all takers to a game of darts and enjoy the editorial discomfiture to the full.

Chapter 10

I must get Babette from the Daycare Center. Why does this process wear me out so much? Is it the walking down the street alone and getting stared at? The person reflected back to me is such an unrecognizable stranger. Why me? Why do men look at me, comment about me, follow me? There are many more attractive women who don't seem to face such a daily gauntlet. Is this paranoia on my part? I am suspicious of my own observations. No. It's definitely real. When every day you are shadowed by an inescapable stream of walking noises, words, and whispered suggestions, you come to grips with the fact that sickness has picked up on your presence. I am such a coward, having to ignore and/or flee. I wish I knew karate. I'd beat up half the men in New York City. I am full of rage and end up yelling inside myself:

> "Go fuck the Statue of Liberty! She's the size of your
> ego and believes in '*free love.*' Go find someone else.
> You pervert. You have *NO* imagination! Just stand on
> a street corner saying the same old things. Why do
> you think *ANY* woman would have *ANYTHING* to do
> with you? Please leave me alone. I've had enough of
> this. Just shut up. *DON'T* look at me. I just want to
> be left in peace. I haven't hurt you. I haven't looked
> at you. I don't want to know you. Leave me alone!"

Some days I feel strong, and it doesn't bother me so much. Then I realize the creeps do it to everybody that is female under seventy and not crippled.

Babette gives me a long lecture on the way home. She is *NO* doggie, nor a pussycat, nor a puppy, nor a kittennnnnnnn, and she has no tail in back of her. Proof! She is not anything. She is just *BABBBBBETTTTE*. "Don't you talk to me about nothing!"

I slap her on the back and tell her that is the best thing in the world for her to be: Go right ahead, kid!

We cleaned the house, mostly to placate my father's sense of neatness. My body goes through the motions, piloting the vacuum around the house, hunting down clumps of dust. Why is it that cleaning alienates me so? I shrug the question off in early sleep.

Midnight and the buzzer rings. It is Pierre and Howie back from California, wanting to know "Is it cool for us to come upstairs?" And, God, was I glad to see them.

Both were fresh and glowing, beaming California, and had been to Big Sur and Sausalito. I hadn't even known they were gone. I tell them shyly that I have started art classes.....and they say I look as if I have been to California myself. Color in my cheeks.

Saturdays are now *DRAWING DAYS*, I recount. I have signed up at The Art Students League. The teacher gives me special attention as he does to two other talents in the class. We go out for lunch, recognizing each other as a separate breed. My brain is emerging from hibernation and I am drawing the figure. I can't tell Angel about any of this. He will not care and will not want to care.

Pierre, Howie, and I coffee and tea at the table. I throw my old poems at them and say: "See, it is just as you said might happen, Pierre. Think of it. I am writing....." They are pleased. Howie is going to be in a band, drumming. Pierre is thinking of communizing so he can live in a big house with lots of people there all the time. Howie tripped on a mountain in California. They are considering copping some acid and doing it again together in a few days.

The subject turns to '*FREEDOM*'. Pierre thinks you aren't really free if you haven't got a place of your own because then you are always at the mercy of your host. He thinks it is unfree to float.

"How's your marriage doing?" I inquire politely.

Pierre goes into a rap about Maryann, how she hasn't done his laundry and what this means to him. Then says Maryann and he have agreed not to be jealous of each other and can now experience other people, should they run across people they want to experience.

"This was always so," I say.

"Yes, but now it's official and authorized. I think I dig her even more now," he tells us, "for being so understanding. Marriage is groovy. It's *HER* I want to live with. If I love anyone, it has got to be Maryann.....yes.....it's her all right. But it can limit you. Now I'm no longer limited, but we can grow even more....."

Howie is just about to get his divorce and cynical. He gives me a phone number which I scribble on a postcard lying on the table. Petra sent it to me from her California vacation with her name on it, and one word: *ZAP.*

The laundry was a disaster. The dryer on my floor was broken. You put money in, and it made a whirring noise and left the clothes damp. The weather too was damp. By the time I discovered the dryer was malfunctioning, Babette was asleep. I couldn't leave to go search for a dryer on another floor of the apartment building. I took the laundry back to the apartment She had to wear mismatched socks, which didn't make me feel like any great success as a mom. Nor did the decoration of my house with faded underwear and children's polo shirts afford any joyous party feeling in me. It was still all wet. I had to leave it there. The sheets festooning the shower rod in the bathroom made it impossible to shower without taking them down..... (and since they still weren't dry, having to hang them back up again.)

This laundry session has been a resounding defeat. By now, it doesn't even smell clean to me. This may be carrying it to psychosomatic extremes. My nose can't be happy with the laundry after all the vexation it has caused.

Laundry is the bane of my existence. You are supposed to open the dryer and have soft, fluffy, fresh clothes that will qualify you as a *HOUSEWIFE FIRST CLASS*. But I open the dryer and what do I find? A load of limp, damp, heavy clothes and nowhere really to put them.

Jack passes my desk, flashes me a charming smile. "Your boyfriend's out there in the hall, Alison. He looks like he wants something....." He heads for the accounting office, ignoring the misery of the suburbanites with total unconcern and to have his daily go at the dart board.

When the coast is clear, Angel bends over me. Angel. Jack. What do they care about laundry?

"Howya doin', Baby?" he slurs in a mellow tone. "Can I see you tonight?"

"Not tonight, Angel." I play my defense for all its worth. "I asked Charles. I like Charles. He's very nice.....and I couldn't possibly hurt his feelings by cancelling out." Angel doesn't flinch or protest. I finger the neckline of my knitted top fretfully. "Later in the week, maybe?"

Angel drops his eyes to my breasts until they blush into visible peaks. "I'll meet you by the elevator at noon. If I can't see you tonight, I can have you for lunch."

I lower my face to conceal my chagrin. He reaches out a paw and lifts my chin.

"Be there!" His eyes burn with intensity. He walks away before I can answer.

* * * * *

Dear Pierre:

I have finished SEXUS and am returning it with this letter. Henry

Miller's a great writer, I agree.....but he's an anarchist. A lot of his attitudes bother me.

He seems to imply a fuck is a fuck. If you can't call a fuck a 'fuck' you aren't properly lusty. You fuck a woman and make her come, and then you come, and that's all there is to it. Anything more you dump on it is self-deception. Your own needs for other things to happen to you: imaginary!

Isn't there anything else? What about love? What about making love? Isn't there any difference?

I don't want to be a hypnotized disciple all my life, following some man or some idea around as if I was in a trance.

My kid is a gas. She gives me a new political translation of the world: The workers are all MEN. And the students, (her pronunciation: stoo-dee-ants), are all WOMEN. Together they will make a new world called SOCIALISM. (Strains of Stravinsky's Rites of Spring.) Let it be. The kid at least has a vision.

* * * * *

At noon, Angel appears at the elevator and looks my way, summoning me. I get my coat and join him. We ride the elevator in silence. On the street, he takes me firmly by the arm and walks me to my apartment. He isn't hurrying but isn't wasting any time.

I unlock the door. He pushes me inside and draws me into his arms. "Mama, I can't wait to get my hands on you."

He doesn't. He pulls my skirt up and underpants down, presses me against the wall, fingers working, kisses me. I can't help myself. I start moaning and my knees give way. He carries me to the couch, rips my clothes off and somehow manages to strip. Immediately, he's on top of me with all his weight, thrusting his hot dick into me as hard as he can.

He's not gentle now. This isn't making love; it is a deliberate

126

exhibition of sexual dominance. The initiative and power are all his and the response all mine. He will use all necessary means to extract submission from me.

"You like it when I fuck you like this, don't you?" he insists. "You like it, you want it, and you need it....." A catechism pounded into my flesh. When I refuse to answer him, he abruptly withdraws from my body. I have almost peaked, and I want to climax, and I am in pain, and he knows it.

"Do you want me to stop? I will.....unless you ask me for it....." I look up at him. "Oh Angel, please....."

He is not going to settle for that. "Please, what?"

"Oh please.....fuck me, Angel. Fuck me, fuck me, Angel....." He laughs with pleasure. Inwardly I am disgusted. Why all these petty little games? He runs his mouth all over my body, kissing and biting me and leaving a map of bruises. He pins my thighs and dives in, driving into me like a hammer. We climax together, I screaming and he laughing.

He lies heavy on me for a few minutes and then rolls off. "You can play all you want to with your little Charles," he says softly, "but you're not kidding either of us. He can't satisfy you the way I do. We both know that. And if you let him fuck with you tonight, all you'll feel is the difference. You are going to be thinking about me, wishing it was me, the whole time. You and I, Baby, are a whole lot alike."

Angel stretches and starts dressing. My clothes are ruined. I'll need different ones. Everyone at Academia Books is bound to notice and put two and two together. Nothing will cover the marks on my neck.

Angel is singing to himself as we walk back to work:
"*R - E - S - P - E - C - T.* All I want is a little respect sometimes....."

He is correct. Charles isn't going to be any use to me now. If

Angel can use me like this, there has got to be something I can do to him......and I'll find it. I won't have any pity. He's going to regret the way he went about this someday, I swear it. I swear it.

I arrive back at the office so weak I can barely control my fingers in order to type. Order of the day, thankfully, has me out delivering packages. I put on sunglasses. I don't want to have to look anyone straight in the eye. From behind the glasses, I spy on the street traffic, people passing each other in formal designs as if a choreographer had designed their paths. Bands of color float by according to the varying speeds of pacing feet. Women weave by in mini-skirts, Nylon legs in scissoring motions; one-two, left-right. Sloop shouldered intellectuals with liberated beards, blacks crowned with enormous Afros digging on their private grooviness. Girls with straight long hair lyrically waft by looking as if they'd stepped out of the Middle Ages. Old people stiffly make their way toward the park, timorously scanning the street. Children inspect the world with eager eyes, ready for surprises.....as if all surprises are good.

I cannot help being aware of men. I feel the tallness of walking men and the width of their thighs as if I were handling them. Hard legs stride by with sold trunks growing out of their joining. A sea of crotches on legs walks by, and I am walking in the other direction trying not to encounter faces.

Where do I fit? I am irrelevantly trapped in my identity. If I was still a 'housewife,' I'd be in a safe little world. I'd never have found out I was a 'nympho.' And I'd still be 'frigid.'

No longer invisible on the street. Must be broadcasting something. Not half a block passes without a leer, a gesture, or a proposition.

I wish for a talisman, an amulet.....

* * * * *

Jack wants company after work. He takes me to his regular bar, an Italian restaurant. Jack and the bartender Rocky know each other very well. Under the influence, Jack becomes megalomaniac. For example: every topic, every person, every achievement, he has to put it down. He does this in such an interesting, apparently logical, fashion. But why should he have to?

"It's all shit! Everything in this whole world, it's all bullshit." And then excuses himself to go to the bathroom.

Jack, that's half my trip. The other half is to write it all down anyway. Who am I to judge which part of it is shit and which is the other part and what *THAT* is? I write in my notebook:

> *Bullshit, bullshit all around,*
> *Our writers sell it by the pound.*
> *In every book it will be found.*

Jack reappears and takes over my pen: "*Why think it is so profound?*"

"Aha," he says. "Scatology. Shit. What is it anyway? What do we mean by it? It's wastage. It is what is left over. We burn everything else. Shit is what remains, flammable, eternal." He glows with Martini, not his first. More like his eighth or ninth of the day.

"Good compost for new living food," continues Jack. "Shit. We talk about it with contempt. The Hindus have a better regard for it. They burn it to keep warm. That inflammable shit. If the body won't burn it, they'll find some other way. A shitless culture, theirs....."

Here's a bar full of businessmen, getting bombed and talking about their salaries and their investments. I just want to be me, and I wish I was at home in the shower. I'm too funky to be comfortable. Got to get out of here.

"What are you doing?" Jack questions me. "What do you want to do with yourself?" He is full of alcoholic affection, muddled.

"I just want to find myself. I want to be sure of what I want to do.....I'm not sure now." Jack calls this bullshit too and an evasion of the question.

The man with no name smiles across the bar. He is on *MY* side, whatever that is. He tries to establish a conspiracy between obviously sober me and himself versus the equally obviously drunk Jack. I don't need his support.

"*ME*?" asks Jack, trying in his head to 'pin her down' and 'make her get to the nitty-gritty.' "What is *ME* worth? What am I getting when I pay for *ME*?"

"*ME* isn't for sale and can't be bought." I reply. "There is no $30,000 *ME* that would be worth it enough for me to spend my life just trying to achieve that. I don't sneeze at money.....but look at the prices some people are willing to pay for it."

Dianne, our copy editor, is leaving the job and going to Europe to live. Jack comments that Dianne is the kind of person who will never be happy. At which point, I ask him if he is happy and he says, "No."

Jack catches sight of the man playing eye-games. Oh, oh. Jack is easily provoked when he's drunk. He lunges at him, growling various imprecations.

"Jack. Jack." I tug at his sleeve, half embracing him, to distract him from his rampage. Got to get out of here. Gracefully. Got to get Jack out of here before there is a scene and cops. Before he punches the nameless one in the nose. The nameless man doesn't know Jack gets into blind-mad fits when he's drunk. He's courting extinction.

"Don't leave without me," whispers Jack, partially restored to himself. "I'm worried I might take that guy apart. Did you *HEAR* what he said?....."

"Easy, Jack. Let's go now then. My babysitter has a sinus problem and has to go home....."

Elaine, Jack's A/A, says he is the most insecure person she has ever met. The extent of his drinking is just beginning to really sink in. Elaine says Jack has made many enemies, which he is aware of, and which bothers him. She says she loves him too.

* * * * *

Here I am at my kitchen table, typing away after typing in the office all day long, and it is a night I've sworn only to rest. Why do I bother? I must be a lunatic. What does it all mean? I was trying to make sense of it during my walk home with Babette. I'm not writing for publication. Do I even dream of publication.....honestly, now?

When I see the way manuscripts get treated, I am almost certain I never want my writing to enter a publishing house. Besides, I can compare only to myself, and even then I can clearly see.....*IT'S NOT GOOD!* As people talk, I listen, trying to understand what lies beneath, around and interwoven with the words. I look at the scenery around me selectively. Someday I will reconstruct this world I see on paper; an edifice of words.

I read an author, and he says: "Like this is how it is." And I feel like having a verbal jam session because I feel: "No, really. It goes like *THIS*." All I have so far are *feelings*.....and the ammunition I need is *thoughts*.

Half the best rap sessions I have are with dead authors, who left their words behind as a legacy for whomever would claim it. Somehow, when I read Kazantzakis or Maxim Gorky or Laurence Durrell, I feel that all I need to do is start.....

This writing process has got to be like learning to dance. You have to learn how to walk first. Some babies get up one day and *WALK*. I've seen it. But those have been sitting, experimenting in their thoughts. And all their falling has been done in their heads. Other babies fall thousands of times before they learn how to run. They all seem to be driven to walking and running in the end. And to dance means flexibility and a sense of style.....

So if all this writing I'm doing is crap, (and I can see for myself it is certainly nothing better), it doesn't matter as long as I keep on doing it. There is a goal at the end, shaping ideas.....and someday I'll have papers with words, lots of them, which I can hold in my hand, waving them at the world: "See, I've got it----right here."

All I want are some ideas of my own; interesting enough to prevent me from being bored; happy and optimistic enough to keep me from feeling sad; and enough to make me happy by contemplating the depths of which I am capable.

I want to read all this and recognize it as the work of my equal. My equal? The equal to the me that only exists in my imagination.

I feel this person there, but the only contact I have with her is in dreams or in ability to respond to life with emotion. I wonder if it is true, that genius is related to sexual capacity? God.....I hope so. That way, I'm sure I've got a chance. Maybe if I screw around enough something will happen to me someday, and the words and the paintings will be good instead of miserable failures. But how?

My fingers whiz on the keys of the typewriter, and I feel a vitality in me demanding powerful expressions. Power. Classical feminine attributes make me suspicious. I think they are invented by men to insert into the minds of women to enslave them; that way, women will be no competition.

Since the end of my marriage, it is not enough to be only a secondary compliment to some man. For one thing, there was the trauma of ending something that was supposed to be *FOREVER*. Now I know that forever is a gross lie, and the marriage wasn't good for my growth anyway.

A man who requires support of his importance by putting the woman down is not worth myself who have learned to stand alone. I'm not talking about partnership or collaboration in life with a man. I'm talking about the kind of men who require their women be 'feminized,' eternally childlike, with ivory soap complexions, devitalized.....secondary at doing everything but knitting or cooking. Those men who find foot-binding women 'cute' and who remove a woman's sting and render her ineffectual and nonthreatening. (High heels = Twentieth Century foot-binding. Not very good for running away. Not very good for defending oneself.)

African tribes, some of them, operate on their women as part of the rites of maturation, removing the lips of their vaginas and their clitorises so they will be passive and will not want to have sex with anyone but their husbands. And what kind of cultures have subjected women to such horrors? Unconcerned about their feelings, treating them like childbearing animals.....removing even their access to physical pleasure?

When I imagine such an operation being done to me as the price of inclusion in society, I know I'd rather live in the forest and maybe die. I read *The Female Eunuch*. All I know is that it isn't passionate enough. I don't only want to be a full 'woman' equal to men. I need to be allowed to be better than they are, if that is what I naturally am. To write and paint, I have to be free of conformation to all social laws that reduce vitality.

I have finished paying my dues. I don't want to cook or knit anymore or spend any time in the beauty parlor, or have anxiety about whether I am pretty or not.

That is one of the good things Angel has given me. Whereas every other personage in my life is waiting for me to complete myself by being 'somebody,' Angel acts as if I am already what I am supposed to be. This attitude makes him the perfect companion for relaxation.

It's quite a new experience being treated as the ideal present for the man who has everything—a luxurious sex toy or sex pet. (I don't have to cook or sew or clean.)

Angel never stops appraising the other women who pass by when he takes me out, but it is only a friendly habit. He has found his queen: *ME*. And why? I suit his needs, such as they are. The hotter women look, the harder they strive to fit the image of society's idea sexpot, the funnier Angel finds the contrast. He's been in bed with hundreds of women who look like that already, and they bore him. Lately, I am what turns him on.

Even my appearance has become charged with electricity for Angel. He cannot look at me with indifference any longer. I have ceased to envy Sophia Loren, Marilyn Monroe, and Raquel Welch. Whatever size I am is obviously the right size, and whatever face I present to the day or night is agreeable. There is a lot to be said for the results of acceptance by a professional lover.

As Angel's friend, I am a part of life behind the back of polite society. In the pool halls, getting drunk with a bunch of men who talk freely in front of me, I don't care much what I say. I answer back. This, the answering back, which they would have beaten out of me if I had the bad luck to be their wives, they find very attractive in an unattached woman. It's the hunters' instinct they have. Women who have thoughts of their own, (as opposed to parroting their men's thoughts), are meant to be 'taught a lesson,' domesticated, broken like wild horses.

Angel's buddies are no doubt wondering when he will teach a lesson to me. But he just laughs, feels me all over in public, and lets me say and do as I please.

Amid all these thoughts, I write eleven pages. They read fast but perhaps that is only because I am interested in myself. Would anyone else be interested?

* * * * *

Petra calls in the middle of all my questions. I tell her, "Look, I'm going to write and rewrite.....and all this takes time, and then there is the time I spend working in the office and on the kid. But this bitch of a book, I <u>will</u> work on it at least until it is a finished *'thing'*!"

Petra, who always knows what a friend should do in my case, is the perfect friend for me. What more can be said? She knows when to call on the telephone to save me from collapse, mental, physical, or emotional. If the collapse is physical, she can prescribe for me better than a doctor, (most of the time). No. Disloyal of me. All the time! Petra understands the intangible portion of my being that is my will power. She knows how much I can be expected to endure and when my flip-outs must be countered to prevent the dysfunction of the Alison machine.

"Alison, you're not as crazy as you're making out," is one of the necessary remedies she applies to me. She says this to me now.

Thank God. Petra wants so much for herself, she understands my wild schemes for grabbing at life. She listens to the strange plot of the book as I tell it to her, expecting her to know what importance this has, though I have never written a book before. She does not for one moment suggest in her listening that the book isn't real. This act of faith she performs for me fills me with gratitude to whatever divine intervention that supplies Petra to my life. She doesn't scold me in advance for taking risks, and never limits the courage with which I face my life.

How can I repay her in kind? Anyone can see that Petra is gifted with the faculty of doing anything and being whatever she chooses. It is only the question of choice, necessary commitment, and time.

Petra is a living synonym for loyalty in human beings. I never question her. I always know she's there.

Ruthy also is there strongly for me, but her moral sense creates intense refusal to confront some basic facts about me and about herself.....and about Petra. We don't always know what makes her tick off our side from time to time, but there is a cycle that ends by her rejection. After a while, she returns, able to deal with us again. But she hurts us so much when she cuts us out. It is hard to repose one hundred percent of one's confidence in her. Ruthy is so brainy, so eloquent, so charismatic, that she retains our love even when she has these lapses.

Ruthy and Petra are *NOT HAVING* an affair. They are actively choosing not to be lesbians; though they admit the possibility is there. They accept lesbianism as a healthy alternative but prefer not to engage.....hoping that looking for men will make the men happen.

I don't consider affairs with women at all. I don't know why. Certainly they are beautiful. I think it is a predilection for penises. (Petra and Ruthy question whether this makes me at heart a male chauvinist, especially when I add that only large ones are suitable for a lady my size. It is true, a nice man should be attached.....)

Petra has all the qualities necessary to make me fall in love..... and if she were a man, undoubtedly, I would be after her. But she is a woman.....therefore, we can love each other platonically, like Damon and Pythias. I cannot understand why I don't want to make love to her. I like showing off for her.

We discuss this. Petra and Ruthy both say they have felt desire for other women. Desire? I desire their company. I like them to dress up and look pretty..... but I have never felt desire for a woman. Strange. I wonder if I'm repressing something. Hope not. I don't approve of repression. Maybe I'm just an extreme case: nymphomaniac.....tough for me.

But being with Petra is a moment-to-moment education in how to provide the finer things in life, notice them..... She is a walking expression of delicate sensibility.

For example, the quintessential pair of shoes, as an art form, is one of Petra's secrets. Nothing so common as a *shoe fetish*. Each of her select footgear expresses a defined philosophy toward the world and its function, a blend of foot comfort, subtle coloration, elegant cut, and fine material. Perhaps a trace of historicity; a faint resemblance to Art Deco. Exquisite shoes and boots have the capacity of being an art form. So much for Petra and her shoes.

Petra = apt name......the Red Rose City.....the Red Rock.....native land of Vashti, Queen of Queens, the most beautiful woman in the world.....or Petra, a modern Petronius.....a female avatar.

Someday Petra will write a *Satyricon* of her own: a Byronic epic, no doubt, amoral, and filled with aesthetic raptures, perhaps too artistic for a primetime-television audience but filled with sensuality and mystery.

"What can I expect from a first book?" I ask Petra before getting off the phone.

"Henry Miller says if you ask too much of one, you will be a monstrosity if you succeed," Petra answers.

"So if I fail, under Henry's terms, I've only proven I'm not a monster?"

"That's right," she says cheerfully.

"Good deal!" (*Small comfort.*) We hang up, promising to make contact later in the week.

My little girl is appropriate to her circumstance. In the morning, I will wake her by asking does she want cereal for breakfast, and she will command to have it "Right now!" She gives me a task at which I can be a complete success, that of filling a bowl with dry cereal from a box and adding milk from a container.

* * * * *

Tommy was a very bad boy. He needed a place to roost and I left him in my apartment. He had the keys, so he could lock up when he left. Angel showed up for lunch while I was out having one of the luxury meals I get with the boss. So far, so good. Angel and Tommy know each other. Tommy is polite to any of my friends. Angel accepts Tommy as my watch dog. But Tommy is mischievous. He has turned Angel on with a mixture of Orange Sunshine and other psychedelic goodies.

137

I am at my office battle station, the front desk. Tommy innocently materializes in seven-foot glory, (albeit in his tattered shirt and rags dungarees), executes a medieval bow and virtuously slaps the keys down on my desk with a flourish.

"So this is where you work." He scans the office with curiosity and astonishment as if he has never been inside a business place before.

Editors and production people cannot believe their eyes. What is this hippy-giant doing in their safe little office? I begin to think I should get Tommy out fast.

"I don't think you should be here," I hiss at him. "It may get me in trouble, having personal friends....."

"Oh. Sorry." He apologizes like a small child. "I just wanted to see where you were all day....." Then with a courtly gesture, he takes my hand and kisses it. The world shall see he is capable of fine manners. I am as embarrassed as hell.

"Before I go, there is one thing I should tell you....."

* * * * *

As soon as I can make time, I rush for the mail-room. Angel is seated in a swivel chair, listening to rock and roll and idly spinning back and forth across the floor.

He grins at me beatifically.

"Mama, where were you?" he complains.

"I went to lunch with the boss."

"I know you went to a restaurant. I was at your house. Your 'brother' was there."

"I know." He is very dizzy and softer than usual around his eyes.

138

Angel grabs me onto his lap and spins the two of us in his chair as if the mail-room were an amusement park.

"Mama," he declares with inspiration. "Get yourself a babysitter. I'm going to take you out on the town tonight. We'll go eating, and we'll go dancing, and we'll see Wilfred and his lady, and then we'll go to your place."

The prospect of going out appeals to me. I agree to make the arrangements.

As I return through the halls, I am already in my night persona, dreaming incandescently.

Jack is playing darts with the copy editors, betting and winning.

"Who was that large person at your desk before?" asks Benny. "He is the most grotesque human being I have ever seen."

* * * * *

I take a slow bath. Babette has been consigned to the care of her father. For the night at least, I am a free lady. I pour in bubble bath, take the radio into the bathroom along with a paperback novel, a cigar and a joint. I linger an hour in the water, reading and puffing and allowing the wage-slave to dissolve thoroughly before leaving the tub.

I dress carefully. A wine colored dress with a decoration of sparkling beads around the neckline; the hemline = short. I brush my hair out and fluff it. I've washed it in orange shampoo, and it glows tawny and blond like an animal's mane. I never set it, and I cut it myself. I want hair to look wild and untamed as if I were surrounded by the elements, undomesticated, natural, primal. *(It generally does.)*

My reflection poses at me in the mirror, making faces. The pudgy housewife of a year before is unrecognizable. I look like a star. I apply mascara carefully to my lashes and gaze into my eyes to see the effect. They are blue intensity, blue whirlpools. I could drown in them.....good! I work on my mouth, drawing it smoothly; the lipstick must not look like paint. My lipstick is Italian. They know what is sexy. I wipe it off several times, then my lips are correct. My mouth mustn't clash with my dress. Aha! I open and shut my mouth. The lips are as full as ripe fruit. I race for the kitchen and rub vanilla extract on my neck and the backs of my wrists. Angel likes vanilla. And he'll get hungry and salivate. And he won't know why. *(Pavlovian stratagem.....subliminal conditioning.)*

I drape a necklace of red crystal around my neck as a good luck charm. The beads catch the light, translucent as drops of wine. I am ready for war. Maliciously, I prepare for my allotted place as Psyche on a pedestal. Festooned with beads and expensive rags, I combine the sleepiness and false bravado of an 8th Street hooker with the crafty mind-stopping humor of surrealism.

Just to look at me is a jarring experience, let alone if you are tripping. My clear complexion testifies to innocence and ivory soap..... *(A great disguise.)*

* * * * *

Angel looks unfamiliar in evening clothes. His skin blends into the dimness of the bar. He is still floating in the clouds.

A lethargic waitress with dyed platinum hair swabs at the bar with a rag, collecting empty glasses as she goes along, a vacant expression on her face. She is a quintessence of macho fantasies; blonde, glossy-lipped, her curvaceous buttocks glimmer in pink satin hot pants. As she turns away from the customers and leans over the sink, she flashes intimacies and inner thighs. Angel's eyes staring from the shadows are jet.

"Angel, my dear ole fella," turning to him and tugging on his jacket. "How many drinks did you have before you collected me?"

"Well now, Baby," he counts to himself with the satisfaction of having outmaneuvered me. "I just stopped in at the local pool hall for about an hour....."

"OK. I can see that just to talk with you, I shall have to do some catching up."

Determined that he shall *NOT* have the advantage of a head start, I flag down the bartender, gesturing thirst. The bar, which is classical Western saloon, is decorated with the predictable nude lady in an ornate gilded hand-carved wood frame and with the bartender. Dapper and neat in a red and white striped shirt and black bow tie, he comes to my service, heartily offering assistance.

"What can I do for you folks tonight?"

Angel orders himself another straight scotch.

"Six whiskey sours, with cherries, please." I bat my eyelashes at the bartender with exaggerated ingenuity.

The bartender counts Angel.....and myself.....and is somewhat at a loss. "All at once?"

Sparing him the deductive process and the mathematical conundrums because that would take too long, I clue him in. "This is called *CATCHING UP*," pointing to Angel. "Feel free to watch."

"Baby, I hope you know what you're doing," Angel says, squeezing my waist.

"I know that I'm not going to let you keep a lead on me when it comes to drinking..... Hang loose. You'll see." Seven whiskey sours, liberally decorated with Maraschino cherries, line up on the counter in front of me as if on parade.

"Yes, there is an extra one," says the bartender, smiling under his small mustache. "That's from me, contribution of the house. Can't have you just catching up, you have to pass him and take the lead."

Calmly, I down the contents of each glass, munching the fruit as a chaser and going on to the next.

"Say goodbye to your head start, Angel dear. *(toasting him)*. Well, off to see the wizard, *(one down)*. Christ! That cherry is all riiiight! And CHEERS, *(two down.)* Dahling, I hope you notice, *(three down)*, *m*mmmmm.....this one is for you. Health! *(four down)*. To all Scorpio women who have trouble adjusting, *(five down)*, and all Aquarian men who are not allergic to the Scorpio ladies......*(Angel is an Aquaria......six down)."*

"This one is for you." I pay homage to the barkeep's generosity, raising the last glass to him, "and may the sugar-frosted-flake fairy remember you to the sender of just desserts."

Angel gives me points at once for the conception, style and execution of the whiskey sour vignette. "Now let me see, can you hold it?"

"Aw, Angel. Can't you see me flying?" I spread sweet smiles on the sandwich.....and walk out of the bar carefully lining my feet up parallel, drawing a straight line with my walk to assert my mastery of space.

Angel suavely follows, resplendent in evening dress; white dinner jacket and spotless black pants. His shirt even has cuff links.

"Bet you didn't think I could shine like a star." He chuckles over his successful usurpation of the international playboy role. "Too much effort to get up like this all the time."

We find ourselves a table in the nightclub. Candles shining through transparent rosy globes with scalloped edges casting warm flickering lights across the white tablecloths. Stucco-ed arches surround the dance floor. The band is Latin.....friends of Wilfred. He drums with another Latin band when he isn't dealing or stealing. Wilfred joins us with his lady, a small pretty woman with fashionably teased dark hair. She looks like a bird.

Angel sits close to me, keeping one hand on me all the time as if to keep my attention on himself. It is over my shoulder, around my waist. There is little conversation, only drinking.

Under the tablecloth, Angel grips my leg. "Look at me." Straightening up, I turn, keeping my face bland. I signal him by glaring that I don't want to be handled in public.

His eyes are melting, but his hand starts traveling up my leg. "Baby....." he starts to arouse me. I keep still, refusing to register any passion, wishing he would stop.

"Please, Angel. Let's dance."

He offers me his arm and leads me onto the dance floor. He glides us around unconcernedly as formally as if this was the grand ballroom of a palace and the floor is cleared for the reigning monarch.

"You wild and crazy man. I know I've met you before." I break from his hold and shake my shoulders at him, gliding away. Angel swings me back.

I accede to his rhythm but persist, "Where was it?"

"Where was what?"

"I said: Haven't we met before? What's your name?"

Angel looks at me puzzled. He was expecting Ginger Rogers but is getting Gwen Verdon, (Lola in *Damn Yankees*), La Meri, and Isadora.....slipping out of his arms at intervals, performing a jazzy ethnic freeform counterpoint around his formal correctness and perfect rhythm. Dancing gaily around him, I continue teasing: "What's the matter? Why are you looking at me that way? Have I ever gone to bed with you? Did we make love? I could swear I know you."

Beginning to catch the drift of my fantasy, Angel smiles. He captures me easily, taking my hand and pulling me into his arms.

Making a display of docile submission, I subside into a follower, melting onto him like dripping wax. "Why are you playing so hard to get? At least give me your phone number?"

I stamp my feet like a Flamenco dancer and haughtily start moving away from Angel. He stalks me across the dance floor with a cool laid back shuffle.

I let him catch me and put my arms around his neck. "Don't be shy, Baby..... I won't do you no harm." I deck his face with kisses. "Just give me your phone number and I'll call and wake you up when you need it the most."

"You're insane, woman."

He wants a swan to glide serenely in his wake on the current of the music. I arch against his arms, slowly curving my neck, acting out the perfect compliment. "Why won't you tell me where we've met? In a previous life? I even feel as if we've made love before."

"Never!!!" groans Angel. He pulls me tightly against himself. "I've never seen you look like this." He cannot get over it. "You're beautiful. I've never seen anything so beautiful. Why are you different? It isn't just the clothes." I see he means it, and fail to remind him he is on acid. Not only is he tripping, but he is getting very drunk. The only sign is a blurring and tangling of his speech.

"I got to get out of here. Let's go." We collect Wilfred and his lady, Gloria, and leave the club. I sniff the air. It is cold and late at night. There aren't too many people out on the streets, which is good. Angel is fully intoxicated, which is scary...... As we cross the streets, I see the shattered glass of wine bottles and whiskey bottles lying in the gutters.

By the time we are in my elevator, Angel has started a quarrel with Wilfred, accusing him of looking at me the wrong way. It is absurd. He has imagined the whole thing. Wilfred is his best friend and has a lady of his own. Drunk and snarling, Angel doesn't hear a word we say. When we reach my floor, he goes for Wilfred.

Like a dope, I try to get in between them. My reputation is bad enough in this building. I don't need all the neighbors at their peepholes. I don't need the police to come.....

Angel pushes me very lightly aside; he doesn't even see me. I go sliding down the hall floor at a velocity I don't appreciate. Red glass beads scatter like pomegranate seeds as the necklace rips.

"How dare he do this to me? They can kill each other for all I care," I complain to myself as I collect my beads from the floor, ignoring the fight.

"I can't deal with it. I just can't deal with it." I reach my door and unlock it. Wilfred and Gloria cram Angel into my apartment. How they have managed to remain unhurt is amazing.

"Here. Take him, such as he is," and slamming the door. Angel is an alcoholic monster. I am really frightened. He has no brain at all left, and could kill me with one blow by accident. Oh, why do I get myself into these situations?

Angel beats on the door, "Let me out. Let me out." He has forgotten how to open doors and also why he wants to get out. I soothe him over to the couch where he passes out, dead drunk.

"Damn. My beads. Ruined."

I have a hard time sleeping. I move the heavy limbs off me and crawl my way out of bed. Fortunately, Angel is a heavy sleeper. I turn on a soft light, wrap a sheet around myself. When he sleeps, he is at my mercy. I can make anything out of him I want to. I get my sketch pad and start drawing.

I work on the portrait trying to recreate the essence of sleep. The pencil moves across the paper, analyzing structure, deciding about proportion. I am in control now. Fairly happy, I blend into the activity of drawing so that myself disappears and all that remains is the dance between the pencil and the paper. The pencil has eyes with which to see the sleeping Angel and is relaying that information to the paper.....and that is all.

Angel wakes, sees what I am doing and thinks it is a fine joke. He summons me to bed to get fucked. To him the artwork is only a hobby; my real purpose in life is to be at his disposal.

It is clear Angel is still tripping, although not as intensely as before. I start talking to him since he won't allow me any moves of my own; talking into his eyes, refusing to allow him to retreat into his own world. I chant anything at him that comes to mind, casting a net of words over him, injecting my thoughts into his brain.

"Always agree with a man.....very important.....stab him in the back later maybe, yes.....but say yes to his face.....especially if he's large and mmmmmmm.....distracting. Why waste time arguing, man? ......Mmmmmm, all the time you could be Mmmmmmm.....and of course you're crazy too. Don't move. Freeze. Stay right there. You can't feel this? Open your eyes, man. Well, if you can't feel it, just relax and let *ME* play. I won't hurt you. I know it's not your trip, man, but stop arguing and do as I say. You don't want me to be frustrated? A fine thing that would do to your reputation in this town. Mmmmmmmm.....just lie there.....you won't feel anything, but it will be relaxing.....and a good time will be had by all."

Like an egg hatching a chick, I see cracks in Angel's shell, but not enough. At least he is paying attention.

"Hey, don't act so remote.....like I was a thief waiting to steal your heart. You don't have one.....so how can I rip you off? All I do is ask for some kind of reaction, and suddenly, you are the ice man."

This double entendre makes Angel laugh, (the blue association, Big Bill Broonzy..... "I don't want no Ice Man, always hanging around.....")

146

But I get other ideas from it. "Not that kind of Ice Man,.....Man of Ice. Let's fight ice with ice. Wait here." I dismount from Angel's body and go to my stereo, looking through my record collection. I reject Ravel's *Bolero* and Aretha Franklin and settle for the Rolling Stones *Let it Bleed*. That's wild, raw, rebellious..... I light candles and incense and a joint, which I insert in Angel's mouth, insisting he smoke it. As he puffs, I fumble in the refrigerator, returning with a ceramic bowl filled with ice cubes and a washcloth.....the product of inspiration.

I make Angel hard again, which doesn't take long, and sit astride him, holding an ice cube in my hand and caressing his body to the music, drawing on each limb at a time, running ice up and down his body, eliciting a series of flinches.

"Good!" I exclaim. "Finally!.....an honest reaction!"

Writing my name on his chest with ice, I sway back and forth to the music, tightening pelvic muscles around Angel as I feel him jump with each contact with the ice cube.

"This is fun....." I rub the ice on the back of his neck, crooning, "Let go, Angel. Let go. Sometimes everybody has to let go. Don't be so tight, man..... Give yourself something real..... Why not?"

I pass the ice back and forth over his left breast, circling the area where I think his heart might be. "Let go, Angel..... Let go....." I search him for pressure points, anything that will arouse an involuntary reaction.....chanting: "Let go," and I feel a difference starting to happen. Angel is no longer impassive.

I refuse to disconnect from the first evidence of vulnerability I have found. I call his name, unlocking his control with words, calling his mind back into his body from wherever it normally goes during intercourse..... I talk and talk, demanding he be there, laying aside the ice now, fingering him with my hands, and as he takes my body, I talk to his mind, and it is mine.

Angel is tired and confused, feeling unfamiliar to himself, and falls asleep again. I creep back to my drawing in triumph. No longer a victim.

I confront myself in the mirror, so directly that I bump. I am not entirely displeased with what I have to look at, but it just isn't the glorified vision I've been nursing all these years hoping I will fall in love with it. This person I see is finally so deromanticized as to be insulting to my imagination. There is more strength and power in her than I ever thought possible, but where is true love? I remember when I thought love was of importance. I consider what Jack Livingston would tell me now.....some existential words over a bowl of soup..... I guess I'm too blue to do anything. I retire for the night.

* * * * *

*MIASMA OF DREAM.....DREAM AGAIN.....*a country road and Ruthy and me crowded into the front of Petra's little car. The leather store companions end up in the same spot. It is a mountain climbing expedition, and we're all going straight to the top. We eat later.

Ringo Starr and George Harrison are poised on the stony crags playing electric guitar and drums. The music floats into empty space over ravines. They remind me of the Statue of Liberty.....only made contemporary and adequate for our times.

Slithering and grasping and groping, somehow we do all reach the top of the mountain. It is the afternoon. There is a food committee of four people of whom I am one. We eat.

The group begins the descent. I am selected to make a solitary expedition to retrieve some food left back at the picnic site. It is growing dark, and I am afraid of a solitary adventure.....but I go anyway.

Spirits of the First People who used to picnic on this mountain and play music on the mountain tops, thousand year old spirits, come to see me. They are transparent and incorporeal, but I can see them and speak with them. Occasionally they appear to people,

(I am instructed), to let them know there is some continuum. This is a beautiful revelation but all the same......*FREAKY.*

When I return to the group, they are seated on the rocks, gazing across a river, seeing the scenery on the other side. There are strange trees with golden fruit. None of us know what these are for. A mountain spirit whispers to me that these are oranges and that one day a person will come along and discover they are for eating. My friends and I look at the trees in blankness, not knowing what to do with them other than to appreciate their beauty. I hold an orange in my hand and peel it open, and like a genie from a bottle, there is Lady Arcana standing before me.......

* * * * *

I wake up to a large meaty man, soggy with booze and alien to me in every way. He will not understand anything, except my body, and it is a waste of time talking about anything because he isn't really interested. I look at my drawings and I am dissatisfied.

Angel is changing. He still appears the same, large, casual, dangerous. He is no longer in control of himself. He is drinking more than I've seen him, sometimes reeling into my apartment only to fall asleep.

Instead of only dealing drugs, he has taken to snorting heroin..... and so most of the time I see him he is in a stupor, his black fire dulled.

In bed he turns to me, desperately shaking me. "What do you want from me?"

"I don't know." I am as frank with him as I can be.

He takes my throat in his hands. "You don't love me, so what is it you want from me?"

"Maybe I want you to love me. How should I know? It's hard to be sure of anything. You're so drunk nowadays when I see you that all you do is sleep."

He almost cries. "You scare me, lady. You scare me."

"That makes two of us."

When he takes me now, Angel's face is no longer a blank. Sometimes he looks so angry and handles me with too much force as if he would knock me into compliance. When he hurts me, I swear to myself never to bed with him again.

"Bitch. You Bitch," he moans as he fucks me. "What have you done to me?" He informs me as if it was my fault that he can't even make it with his wife anymore unless he thinks of me. As if I have put a spell on him. I don't know what to believe.

Angel is not what I want, and I want him. I am busy contradicting myself with sense memories from inside my body which conflict with rational planning. I hate Angel afresh each time he says the wrong thing. He never used to say the wrong thing, only the right thing. Now he always says the wrong thing.

I wish I had money. Lots of money. Enough money to travel and keep busy and not think about how there is no one I really want that much. My gyrations interest me. I am a trapped mouse running brainlessly in circles on a treadmill and also a detached historian standing by making a chronicle of it.

Saturdays are now filled with art classes. I and the two other talents in the class get special attention from the instructor, but he is very, very polite and gentle to all his students, patiently explaining anatomy. I find his explanations helpful, and grow a respect. During lunch break, we start having coffee together at the nearest luncheonette.....high strung, nervous, but talking and dreaming.

My brain is emerging from a deeply frozen sleep and wants to claim its rightful place in the world. I might be worth something after all. Believing that can drive a person to really do the work.

Chapter 11

INTERLUDE: CONVERSATIONS WITH PIERRE INSPIRED BY GOOD COLUMBIAN AND DILUTED WITH WINE

Pierre and I sit in a corner of one of the Village's ubiquitous Italian diners, a little apart from the gang. The magnetism between us is in full force, and we are animated with words, lots and lots of words, which emerge from our mouths when we are not snarfing down the spaghetti. We have splurged and ordered ourselves two bottles of white wine.

"I tell you, you ought to give him up," Pierre argues. "There are other men in the world, though you may not believe that right now."

I look at him with affection and amusement. I am sitting with another man right now. How absurd to think I forget other men.

"I know it. I know it. I know it." I grunt through a mouthful of food.

"It is too bad for him. People like that aren't given many chances. Crime and sex, the only permissible arts.....that's too bad." Leather clad in his Plains Indian shirt of deerskin, Pierre's dark eyes are covered by perfectly spherical eyelids like a Flemish painting. How odd.

PIERRE: Isn't it true, really, that he's not good for anything but sex?

ALISON: Yes.

PIERRE: Does he take an interest in your art work? In your poetry?

ALISON: No.

PIERRE: Can you talk to him about *anything*?

ALISON: Not anymore.

PIERRE: And you say he's on the hard drugs now?

ALISON: Yes. He's half asleep most of the time we're together.

"And you don't love him, you say?" Pierre scratches his head. "You know what you ought to do. I know it. I'll give you the advice," he exclaims, "but I don't expect you'll follow it. I think you're too weak. *BREAK "WITH HIM!"*

Pierre and I sneak off by ourselves, ending up on the waterbed in the back of the leather store. We keep the lights off, wanting the darkness to take us out of our normal surroundings, letting the waterbed slosh softly. We do not touch, but ethereal voices float in the air, like balloons, filled with gassy thoughts.

INTERLUDE: TWO PROSPECTIVE
AUTHORS DEBATE FORMALITIES:
PIERRE AND ALISON IN THE DARK,
TURNED ON AND TRYING TO CREATE MEANING.

LOOK, I WISH YOU WOULDN'T TELL ANYBODY WHAT I JUST SAID.
> Even if I only wrote what I thought you said, privacy would be maintained. Is it so important if nothing matters?

WORK BY ITS DEFINITION IS WITHIN A SYSTEM.
> No system is your system. Alas, pretty darling, do not cry. The words are not mine.

AS LONG AS THEY WORK.
> How can words do work? Is form work for words? What is freestyle in words? Does nothing matter, or does everything have meaning?

NO DIFFERENCE BETWEEN THINGS THAT MATTER AND THINGS THAT DON'T.
That is a Koan. Koan is only one word. What does it mean?

WHY DON'T YOU JUST BE THERE?
Don't tell anybody about this, and don't try..... It won't help them, and it won't help you.

Is there such a thing as me according to your system?

IF THERE IS, IT DOESN'T MATTER.
It doesn't hurt.

IF IT DOES, IT DOESN'T MATTER.
It is only a game fixing itself on one moving.....

DON'T SAY IT......

ALISON: Point of view, mine.....claiming the space and time, labeling everything with my own words, making everything that matters tangible to me, you see, creating value. Making something is changing the world, making something good is bringing good into the world...... making truth is good, if truth is good, if something is really going on to write about.....if it matters.

PIERRE: Alison, can there be such a thing as a Zen writer if language is just another system and Zen is beyond systems? Or is there a special game Zen people play when they are writing that is more Zen than writing? How do you catch it?"

ALISON: Oh, I think Zen is probably just another art, as writing is an art, and probably all the arts are synonymous in some dimension beyond language.....don't you see the progression of this dialogue.....it could go on into infinity.....it is all fiction......a rose is a rose.....fiction is a rose.....a rose is fiction.....the fictitious rose divorced from its name is also divorced from its smell.....but the real rose is fragrant no matter what you call it.

PIERRE: Put it all in the mouth of a character in a book, and it will mean something, you say?

ALISON: No. Everything is the same. Even the name of the author doesn't matter. Every book is the same. Every word in every book is just a word. All the same. Ultimately, it will all be of no importance. Even Henry Miller, when he dies, will not feel anything.....and so ultimately, it will be of no importance to him what he felt.

PIERRE: Are you saying everything is just there?

ALISON: I'm saying it doesn't matter if it is.

PIERRE: Are you saying that your book doesn't matter?

ALISON: It doesn't matter at all.

PIERRE: Then why are you writing it?

ALISON: Reading, writing, it's all the same.....the novel form..... attach some names and PRESTO: you've got a novel.....without the names it is just loose thoughts and ideas, wandering around in dark detachment.....like our conversation.....

PIERRE: It is an invention of society.....the novel.....and you are writing in order to get recognition.....otherwise you wouldn't confine your writing into the novel form.....

ALISON: What do you mean? Is this more of your grouchiness? or are you saying something?

PIERRE: A novel is a book, *(in soothing tones, lilting),* which is acceptable to a publisher because it can fit in between two covers, *(like lovers in between sheets—shut up),* and be reproduced in identical copies, which the publisher can sell and make a profit. A novel is a book which people will buy to read it, or because it has a pretty name or pretty cover, or because all their friends are talking about it, so it is important for the book to live in their house...... Consider it all, old girl, and see how seriously you can take it. You are writing in a novel form......but if you get published, you don't seriously expect that the publisher will not change it into his idea of a novel?

ALISON: Yeah, I know.....where you are headed, and his idea of a novel is what he thinks the public's idea of a novel is, expressed by what they pay money for..... I see that every day on my job.

PIERRE: Alison, I didn't mean to put you down. If you're writing ideas down for yourself, well and good. But if you are expecting to sell them, you have already been sucked into the system.....selling and money have automatically thought of other people and shaped your writing into an acceptability.....so you see, the writing didn't matter to you for itself.

ALISON: It *HURTS* enough! Here you are telling me how things are not, and my writing doesn't matter, (it can or can't be), and that I am not going to understand what you are thinking, let alone telling me.....and you are thinking of time all along, how many minutes are in your life, because you are sure it's all going to end when you die.....and you are counting the time because it is limited and spending your days not caring and advising other people not to care.....and if I write about you, you tell me to be sure to use another name, although you don't care..... I'm sorry, Pierre. I care about you.....about myself, about my writing.....everything.

PIERRE: What happened between us is a very personal and private matter. It can never be discussed in a public way. That only brings pain, don't you see?

ALISON: No, I don't. I think I know what you're saying. But I don't want you to be saying what I think you're saying. It sounds like a cowardly rabbit.

PIERRE: I know you don't understand, but look: everything that happens should be quiet and non-caring and nonpersonal.....not attached. I don't care how you feel, that doesn't matter. Only about how I feel, which is my business, but that doesn't matter to me either. Nothing matters.

ALISON: Pierre, I hope you're only going through a phase. I care. That I care matters to me. It is crucial. Do you understand? I care about everything. Everything I do, all the pasts I ever lived, are always there in me, summing up a caring from my whole life.....to what is happening. Pierre, I don't know how you expect to write if you don't care.

Chapter 12

How lovely to go to a New Year's Eve party in costume. I've always wanted to celebrate the coming of a new era in the company of fantasies. The party is being given by a friend of mine, Jill, and her husband, Roger. Once she was a housewife too, but now Jill is a fashion designer with her own line of clothes. He makes his living as a drug rehabilitation agency director, but really, he is an abstract artist. Also, he has the most expensive stereo system of all the people I know. Two thousand dollar speakers and a fantastic collection of special tapes..... He has interior decorated his apartment with all the spatial and textural considerations of an abstract artist, and his wife has added spider plants and fabric works.

Furthermore, Roger is a fish freak. His dining room is lined with large aquariums, wall to wall, floor to ceiling, in which swim a priceless collection of tropical fish, the hard-to-get kinds, rare specimens, and prehistoric replicas. His living room has his easel, the plants, the stereo system and speakers, one personally designed chair, and more fish tanks.

The perfect environment for a ripping good time. His friends are all artists, singers, actors, poets, and somehow me, from when we swapped children in the old neighborhood as fellow parents in the children's play group and babysitting co-op. (Jill and Roger have also moved away from the old neighborhood to better housing.)

I am greatly excited by the entire scene and start planning my appearance for this event. I will go as myself. Who I *really* am. This takes some consideration.....what is essential? The most classic of my regalia is selected: a skirt from thirties, mid-calf length, plainly cut from an extra heavy black satin material; my sheer black blouse with the gold embroidery and gold spangles. (I have never worn it without a vest to cover the transparency.....a flesh-colored brassiere attends to the needs of my modesty. Contrary to what you may think, myself has never been an exhibitionist in the sense of flasher.) Gold slippers from *Capezio* that were rejects from an Off-Broadway musical will adorn my feet and in my ears, a pair of Indian earrings with lavish tassels, layer upon layer of dangling gold filigree. They ring softly as they sway with the motion of my head, like temple chimes whispering in the wind.

Checking the assemblage on the night of the party, I have never looked so well in all my life. My skin is clear like a child's and with wonder I perceive that I *AM* beautiful. So fleeting.....beauty. I have never looked really beautiful to myself, and here I am, given this instant to treasure because I may never look like this again, and New Year's Eve is the perfect night.....to go out and mingle with people, hoping for an unknown adventure to complete this occasion. I have set up for this unknown whatever is coming, bringing to it my best efforts.....rising to the occasion, and now I must find out what I have roused from the depths of fate.

I have left Angel out of my plans. He has his family on holidays and I am already thinking beyond him.

"If you want to see me, you can show up at my apartment at about 2:00 a.m. I probably won't be home until then. It's all artists and writers.....you know, they talk a lot. You wouldn't enjoy it."

Angel agrees he would not and says he'll probably go to the local pool hall with Wilfred and gang and spend the night drinking.

Before I leave my apartment, I open the top drawer of my dresser. There in a small wooden box, inlaid with decorative geometric designs in mother of pearl, lies a little green pill, which I maneuvered from Tommy. I have saved it for three months, waiting for a special occasion.....this night.

Tommy offered to share this pill *WITH* me one day when he was clearly smitten with lust. The expectations in his face as he looked at me, hoping I'd take it right away, have led me to conclude: powerful.....*POWERFUL*.....*A-P-H-R-O-D-E-S-I-A-C*. Yum, yum. I didn't want to deal with an aphrodisiac and Tommy at the same time. That could and probably would be the ruination of our sweet friendship and mutual support system. But if the pill was so hot, I wanted it for *LATER*.

"I'll buy it from you. I can't do it now.....things. Be a friend. You've already had some, and you said you don't want me to miss it......" Having offered the pill to me, Tommy couldn't refuse to sell it. The honor of the cosmically attuned head was at stake.....and so he grudgingly agreed, telling me offhand that it was great stuff, whatever it was, and he had dropped eight of the same already that day, and that God was happening.

I now remove the pill from its hiding place and considering all of Tommy's remarks, I cut off a little section, about an eighth of the whole. It is an unidentified pill, (except for its effects, which have already been demonstrated on Tommy), and I am a cautious and responsible person. It is wrong to get into situations I cannot handle. Right? Therefore a preliminary testing of this pill should be made, preparatory to dropping the rest. Limited experimentation with small quantity.....the scientific method.....good.

Holding the small piece of tablet in the palm of my hand, I head for the faucet, place it on the middle of my tongue, and wash it down with a handful of tap-water. If it lives up to my expectations, I will share the rest with Angel when we meet---a consolation prize for him---may restore him to a semblance of life.

Ready now to leave for the party. Everything's in preparation; pocketbook with Kleenex, money for cab ride home if it gets late. (It may very easily.) Even remembered lip gloss for repair of mouth shine.....hairbrush for removing excess wind from the curling hair.....

Upon exiting my apartment, I lock the door, carefully tucking my keys away in the zippered compartment of my purse where they will not get lost. Now I can safely forget about them. Before I ring for the elevator, I already dig in my wallet for bus fare. Now all that remains is for the feet to walk to the bus stop.

I waft airily to the bus stop. What a fine evening it is. The bus comes exactly when I reach the stop. I get on it, drop the money into the change collecting machine.....no waiting, no hitches...... everything is smooth and easy as if I were expected.

There are many seats on the bus. I pick a seat near the back door and as it heads uptown to the West Seventies choirs of angels singing Hallelujah choruses start singing to me. This does not surprise me, nor do I notice it as anything out of the ordinary, so much a part of the special occasion does it seem.

When the bus reaches the corner of my friend's street, I get off with no problems. I float down the sidewalk seeing aureoles of rosy light circling the street lamps, and this also I accept as necessary to the evening. Invisibly dancing while appearing to walk and feeling good all over, I traverse the distance to my friend's apartment building, ringing her bell as I arrive. "Voila! Here I am."

"Wow" Jill, my hostess, exclaims at the sight of me. "Great costume.....a gypsy, are you?"

"Farrrrrr out!" yells Roger, her husband, my artist buddy. "The Thirties have arrived....."

Nobody seems to notice I am 'myself.' They say groovy, and the word 'beautiful' is mentioned, but no one realizes this is *ME*. I am a little disappointed and sadly think to myself, "Guess I'll have to go on hiding it."

Comfort is the first thing to look for at a party, so I direct myself to the wine. As I walk down the hall, passing the paintings, large canvases, wall size.....the spectrum of pure colors weave in and out in designs that expand and contract in space. Stoned. The paintings are dancing along with my trip. They have probably always been this active if I had only stopped to look.

"He (Roger) is a trip-head," I reason to myself. "Tripping is necessary to be able to know that paintings should move like this....... Dummy! Should have noticed it before."

The dining room table is clustered with flasks of Sangria spiked with all kinds of goodies. Large canisters of weed are being passed around. Also lit joints with hashish blended in them. All these wild looking people in makeup and costumes are standing around like mannequins grooving on each other's disguises.

There is an Indian with a bare broad chest and a fur loincloth. His hair is cut as a Mohawk, an eagle feather dangling from his scalp lock. War paint makes him look fiercely ceremonial. A flapper in authentic beaded gauze is fiddling with a velvet fuchsia rose tucked into her gold headband. "En garde." D'Artagnan charges from a doorway, complete with musketeer boots, cap, and rapier poised to thrust. I dodge. There is a walking box of detergent, a ballerina, a harlequin, and a large rabbit with an enormous carrot which it carries around everywhere. I can't decide if it is a man or a woman. Also, there is me.

Everybody continues to assume I am in costume and invent new identities who I am supposed to be, from silent movie queen to prohibition socialite. Hard to deal with this lack of recognition.....and I have tried my absolute best.

The aphrodisiac part of the pill takes effect rather abruptly, and I move to my friends' bedroom. I lie down in the dark by myself, waiting to become accustomed to the sensations. As I recline, listening to the music, my physical awareness of everything is heightened, from the paintings shimmering from the dim walls to Jill's paraphernalia of hats, ostrich feathers and belts, knick-knacks and sundries.

And the music. It is Janis Joplin singing *Summertime* and Jimi Hendrix singing *Little Wing*. Various jazz groups whose names I don't remember are playing various pieces of music which I do remember, although I forget the names. Full blast through these bonanza speakers, the music carries me *A*-way.....and I stay in the music until I feel that something else can happen.

Emerging from the bedroom, I see that dancing has started. Several pairs of very good dancers are flipping out in wild improvisations on the floor. (License.....to barge in and do anything you want as long as you do it good.....*OK*.)

I don't have to tap my foot for more than a few seconds when a monk in a brown friar's frock with a cowl hood asks me to dance. He is a handsome creature and reveals his profession to be a singer..... like singer in a choir.....religious music. (*The Messiah* for Christmas and Bach for special occasions.....Great.....) As we boogie, I make a mental note that sometime it might be nice to take this attractive creativity to bed.

But damn.....everyone masculine in the room is a turn-on. My next partner is the next-door neighbor, an actor, the one dressed like a Mohawk. He is the spitting image of Yul Brynner. I am told too that he was once a cat burglar, for real.....but after working out that part of his karma, he has metamorphosized into a music therapist who works with children. So much I can understand over the music, which is loud. The Mohawk too is very sexy.

Games are played on the dance floor such as you might expect from an Indian who is an actor and involved with music and a lady determined to be herself.

I am so entranced by the power of movement. I dance with all my heart and soul...... laughing with joyous exhilaration, leaping into the air, no longer a clumsy housewife looking for nonexistent steps. I'm here......It's really *ME*. I'm *ME*, at last.......

I can see my partner thinks I'm pretty flipped out, so high on some drug I don't know what I'm doing. He thinks it is *HE*, by virtue of his actor's magnetism, who has evoked this unrestrained manifestation from a hitherto reserved persona.....masculine vanity..... They are all babies, these men. The Indian thinks I don't *KNOW* he's thinking he's playing me. Winks are being exchanged between the Mohawk and Roger, my host.....stag looks, man to man. "The lady is hypnotized. Well, see what you can make her do next." I catch this byplay from my peripheral vision but broadcast no reaction.....go right on dancing as I please.

As I pass Roger, I whisper in his ear, "Boys have their little tricks, and when they are allowed to play them to the full.....women find out just what the little boys are thinking. Very interesting." A shocked face is left behind me.....pondering, "What the???"

At the end of the tune, I make an elaborate court curtsey to my Indian brave and gurgle at him, "What a delightful little play. But you really should have come as Svengali, don't you think?" Astounded that I have caught him up to mischief, he bursts into laughter.

"It's all a friendly game."

I think I ought to go home now while I'm still ahead. "I'm going," I say to Jill and her painter. "Got to go. Bye bye."

"Going home *ALONE*?"

What does *THAT* mean? Am I supposed to go home with someone? *(Who?)* Do they think I'm in an unfit condition to travel? *(Why?)* Perhaps I am disappointing someone I flirted with? *(Too bad.)* Why, why do they say it like that? ....Going home.....alone.......

"Is there any reason why not?" I ask.

"No." "No." "No."

"Well, all right then."

I walk down the hall and feel my stomach telling me that if I don't want to vomit in the hall, I'd better make tracks to the bathroom, quick. I hasten, not wanting to make a mess in a strange place. How odd it is that I haven't noticed myself getting so drunk until now.....

I expect that when I've barfed, as always, I will feel better, clear headed, and then I can find myself a taxi. But nothing of the sort happens. I barf and flush the regurgitated Sangria away. Dizzy, very dizzy, I sink to the floor of the bathroom and just sit there, contemplating the white tile and waiting for the whirling head to stop spinning so I can leave.

Jill sticks her head in the bathroom door. "Are you all right?"

"Yes. Just a little overly high.....maybe someone had better see me to a taxi.....and then the taxi driver can tell my doorman to stuff me in my apartment.....if I pass out."

I have never passed out in my life, but suddenly I feel I am going to.

"Just a minute." Jill closes the door on me, probably going to find a helpful man to escort me to a cab. I remember getting to my feet, slowly.....and then a physical impossibility......levitating until I am in a horizontal position, floating about four feet above the bathroom floor. All around me, the air is buoying me up and then very slowly lowering me to the tiles.....sinking gradually.....down..... down.....depositing me full length on my back. And my head is whirling, whirling in a white fog. Enveloped by white fog, utterly at rest, fully relaxed, my body starts throbbing with an orgasm so total that I am separated from my soul. My brain is on fire with pleasure. Every nerve is singing. Every cell is vibrating. Every particle of my flesh is stirring with love of being alive. Incredibly sweet, ravishingly piercing, but just an introduction.

The mist parts revealing in a shaft of light the most beautiful woman I have ever seen. Haloed by flashing light bulbs like a disco queen, wreathed with white roses like a bride, and barefoot like a Greek goddess, her white dress is a velvet richness of Michelangelesque folds. Her face is white like a mime, and like a geisha, her eyebrows are minimal slashes. Her sweet, sweet lips are painted delicately in glowing vermillion.

Soul choruses of blue ecstasy, cosmic jazz, with saxophone solos and electric guitar leads accompany her movements. She seems the quintessence of all wonderfulness, magical, the incarnation of total understanding and tenderness.

She sits on a director's chair of carved ivory and white wool needlepoint, *(Bargello),* on a stairway inlaid with white on white mosaic patterns, between white marble columns, fluted with Romanesque capitals, resting on a bed of cumulus clouds.

This celestial apparition emanates pure love.....spiritual, physical, essence of love. She is too young to be my mother, and yet I feel from her that same maternal love as my mother gave me when I ran to her in need.....but this vision is the totality of *LOVE*: concentrated communication of *LOVE*.....just by her being, by her revealing her glory to my sight. I feel my eyes stretching to let in more of her and more.

She speaks to me in the most melodious voice imaginable, like a master harper running her fingers along golden harp strings. The sound of her speech vibrates in my heart as if she were playing on my heart strings.....tuning me to understanding.

"My name is Lady Arcana."

I disappear into the beatitude of attention, waiting for further enlightenment.

"Someday, Alison, you will know me as *THE FOOL*, the spirit of all searching women. I am everything and can become anything. All that the world has denied you will come to you through me. Everything the world has given you has been my work. As you find me within yourself, you will know who you are, and you will have the power to make inner peace within yourself. You will have the power to do good when you understand me.....if you believe in me.....if you call for help.....if you listen to my advice......"

Arcana's face is surrounded by a whirling rainbow, all the colors in the world merging into whiteness. Behind her all the voices in the world are singing harmoniously in a music that swells into a unity of one anthem of peace and glory......and it is all Lady Arcana's voice.

"I am Lady Arcana. Your dreams have come true now, Alison, and will continue to come true if you chase after them with perfect love and commitment, knowing that they are real....."

Arcana lightly strokes the top of my head and takes me into her arms. I am my mother holding myself and myself holding Babette, a continuum of love, an infinite process, simultaneously all at once. I let go of everything in perfect safety and blend into the white light that is all colors, all the sounds and the silence. I inhale the experience which is everything until breath goes on into infinity, letting everything in, and it carries me into a motionless motion beyond all yet including everything that has ever happened to me. This is the most perfect feeling I have ever felt, and I want to remain forever with Arcana, in her arms, in this place of total happiness and fulfillment.

My life will never offer me an ending better than this wonderful crest...white foam on the tip of a wave.....frozen and flowing. I yearn to stay.

I feel a life I have known before tugging me back to a self I have been before and I am anguished. I hurt in every retreat from perfection and protest with all my life's accumulated sorrows at being returned to my existence as Alison Greaves.

Gathering all my strength to lunge into a permanent remaining with her, the beautiful voice of Arcana soothes me lovingly as a parent sending a child off to school for the second time.

"You have unfinished work to do, Alison. None of this would mean anything unless you go back and discover the meanings..... let the meanings happen. Let your experiences have a purpose, be landmarks..... I will come back to you in the end---as you will come back to me."

I cannot argue with her, though it is pain to be returning to myself.

The separation hurts so badly. I need her, that loving universe, as an infant needs its mother.....for everything. And yet Babette needs me the same way. Of course, I must go back. Arcana is getting hazy; her roses blurring in rim lighting as the electric bulbs of her halo start to dim. Her face mingles with cobwebs of light, receding into a gray mist.

"Arcana," cries the voice of all my soul. "Stay....." Like a ghost's whisper, a voice speaks in my inner ear, not in words but in a vibration of sound waves, the meaning of which is "Remember, I love you always......."

* * * * *

I am absent-minded. I am in despair, knowing I may forget. There is nothing I can clutch to myself, no souvenir except myself. Nothing to hold on to. My heart is pounding. A heart attack is immanent if I don't give it all my attention and quiet it down.

A ring of concerned faces circles me as my eyes admit the reality of before. My hostess, her headdress slightly askew, asks with a pale face, "Are you all right?" My host, the fish-freak-artist-drug-rehabilitator looks anxious, and his actor-cat-burglar-music-therapist friend looks as if he is expecting me to die any minute.

"I have overdosed, I guess," I hasten to reassure them. "But if I can rest in a quiet place, and come down without too much of a fuss, I will be all right."

The music and pot fumes from the party are too overwhelming for a soft landing, so they carefully move me into the next apartment which belongs to the cat burglar that was. He is a wonderful dude, remains holding my hand, telling me he understands and has been there himself.

The lights are dim. I let myself fade out, and my mind trips wildly through a series of cartoon images and art photography in glorious living color, like Monty Python, only better.....more sarcastic and pointed, more poetic and fantastical. When I come back to awareness, he's still there, the actor man, sitting with me patiently, more tolerant than I deserve.

After a time, I rise to my feet and say, "I can handle it now. Thanks. And I had best get home." Taken and inserted into a taxi, I rode home in meditative intoxication, navigated somehow to my apartment, and laid my body down in all its clothes.

At 2:00 a.m., Angel stumbled in, incapacitated by booze and dope. He passes out in bed and is no further trouble to me. Giving him the pill has been scrapped as a dangerous plan. I don't want to give him my attention. Better that he should sleep. I want to let my mind rest in its dreams.

All the night through, half waking and half asleep, the most beautiful movies, stories, ballets, operas, musicals, play through my mind. I know I will never be able to recapture the memories of these experiences, so I am a pure spectator, at rest, enjoying the show since there is nothing I can do to arrest it.

Come the morning, I mechanically satisfy the Angel who is still not all there, and send him back to his family. I wait for a decent hour to phone, and in mid-afternoon, I call Roger who is in drug rehab, realizing that stuff may have happened to my body while my mind was otherwise. I want to discover exactly what has taken place and is there anything I should be doing about it.

"What was in that pill?" Roger interrogates me.

"I don't know."

"Must have been powerful stuff.....maybe strychnine....."

"I don't know. A friend gave it to me."

"Hmpfh. I wouldn't take any more of those chemical psychedelics if I were you," he counsels me. "Stick to the organic stuff if you *HAVE* to get high: grass....hash.....mushrooms.....like we do."

"But.....what happened?"

"Well, you passed out."

"I know that," signaling him my apology with my voice.

"But you passed out twice."

"Oh." Dimly, I recollect rising to the surface and seeing Jill's face.....her saying to me, "Wait here."

"Well, What then?"

"Then," Roger's voice shook a little with the memory, "you had convulsions of the brain..... a sort of epileptic fit..... the divine madness, you know, like Caesar..... only you burn out your brain cells that way.....gone for good. Less brain. Alison, you should see the condition people are in when they come to our clinic for therapy after O.D.s from acid. All their teeth fall out, some of them."

My gums clench. No way I'm going to let go of my teeth. I can see them falling on the table like dice.....but I don't want to gamble with my future Shrimp Teriyaki.

"All right. All right. So. I keep off the pills.....Is that all?"

"No. That was just for openers. Then you went into a trance."

I try to identify the words 'fit' and 'trance' with my vision.

"Your whole body became rigid, stiff-like. Your skin turned sheet white, like a ghost, no blood. The pupils of your eyes dilated completely, black holes all the iris gone, stretched open." Roger chokes a little. "Do you know this happens to people a few seconds before they're going to die? We were ready to take you to the hospital, and all of us lay our careers on the line......"

"Ahh," I breathe into the phone, amalgamating his physical description of the event with my illuminating apparition and her bestowal of rapture.

"Do you know, Alison.....you could have been dead? Are you listening to me?" He waits for a response. I am still tabulating the risks involved, the meaning of the trip, and feeling relief I need not go there again. Repetition is meaningless. That way is closed to me until ending catches up with me.

"Alison, are you there? We all thought you were going to die on us any minute. Do you know how lucky you were to have this happen in a house where people know what to do about it? You could have screwed up your whole life. Don't fuck around with these chemicals," the receiver says with extra emphasis drilling my ear, "because this was a very narrow escape. You should thank God for it."

"Don't worry about me. I'll be cool. I'll quit everything. If I feel the need to get stoned, I'll stick to pot. Yes. I understand what you're saying. Thanks, Rogg....you've been a pal. Sorry to make a mess in your house....."

"That's OK," he assures me. "It's just that we don't want to have to worry about you."

"Don't worry about me, man. I promise. I don't have to do it again, honest. It was the peaks....." And that is all I feel able to communicate with Roger about my end of the experience. Lady Arcana can never be real for him as she is for me. Maybe he has a trip of his own--maybe he has been *'there.'* But few human beings have looked Arcana in the face and lived to tell of it. This I know with the physical evidence of presence and the aching descent back into a body that had been overused in every possible way.

Now what am I supposed to do with myself? Not only Ruthy and

Petra and my father and the boss but Arcana herself expects me to justify my existence. That ultimate trip is waiting in reserve not to be given into my possession until I have earned it.

"Shit. It's too heavy a burden to carry."

My overtaxed mind replays my life and sundry bad trips over the next few months as a crash from that apex. I take myself to the hospital for an electroencephalogram, waiting to see the divergent lines of insanity on the graph tape.....but the EEG reads *NORMAL*. Brain cells all functioning as average brain should function. No indications of disturbance. Normal.....normal.....normal.

Damn. No disability to use as a cop-out. I've got to do something after all. What is it though? The fulfilling of Arcana's instructions, the thing that was so important I had to come back and finish it before I could be let out?

I cannot talk to any of my friends about Arcana. I cannot allow disbelief to profane her mystery. She must never be approached with doubt.

I do not question "Why me?" to explain why Arcana chose to reveal herself to me. I know. It is because I have needed her, and with an open soul waiting for love, there were no barriers to keep her out.

* * * * *

Angel and I go out. We make the scene---the bars, the pool hall, the Wilfred's house. It is a deadly bore. On the way home, he stops at Nathan's on Eight Street and buys egg rolls, fried shrimps, and seafood. We eat them in bed. He is probably feeding me so I won't want or expect him to fuck me. Angel knows I don't like making love on a full stomach. He is drunk. Too drunk to do anything, as he always is these days. We go to sleep saving fucking for the morning. Blew another one of Mommy's precious nights of freedom. Bad.

I really want to be nice to the Angel, but what can I do? Tell him not to drink? That's absurd. He'd laugh in my face.

He doesn't want to be anything that he is not already. Doesn't want to make art or poems.....or write or even play any sport except pool.

If I explained Arcana to him, he wouldn't even hear what I was saying. Not that he would think I was crazy. He'd find a way to make it have been a story.....not real or find a way not to hear the sound coming out of my mouth.....like being too drunk to hear.

Spending time with Angel is becoming a waste. We don't do anything interesting at all. There is nothing to share but bed, and less of that all the time. I know he has begun to care for me in some nonverbal way, but this only makes me feel guilty. He isn't using my presence in his life to accomplish anything.

Resentfully, I appraise Angel as he snores, loose-mouthed and dulled past recognition with heroin. His flesh is dissipated. I am repelled by the boring stupefaction Angel has let himself turn into. And he and his buddies laugh about WOMEN letting themselves go. It is such a down head he has on these days.

He wakes..... "Please," he begs me in confusion......he doesn't even know how to end a sentence. He senses me slipping away from him, filled with pity not unmixed with fear. The only answer he can find is to filter new problems with alcohol and hard drugs.

Never does he offer me booze or any drug more potent than grass. In his way, Angel is protective. I have been raised to a pedestal, and he won't drag me under.....but we are moving farther apart all the time.

He looks bitterly down at the purple brown obelisk of his penis, rising perpendicularly from his body.....

"That's all you want from me—--SEX," he snaps with despair. "What do you stay with me for?"

He passes his hands along my nakedness as if searching for something tangible. I twist away from him, rising to my knees, closing my thighs.....I don't want any more of this self-pity. Angel flips out. Denials before were child's play, but now they are a threat. Balefully, he grabs my shoulders and shakes me to a froth, screaming, *"BITCH!"* With no preparation, he throws me on my back, parts my legs with his hands and pins them by kneeling on them.

"You're hurting me......."

"You'll get what you want....." He stabs me with his prick.....the punishing jabs are painful, but I am well trained. I yield to him, flowing like water, arching to lessen the pounding..... I am afraid. Dropping all his weight, he rips into me easing his pain with mine.....

"You think I'm just an animal," he groans, "an animal......"

"Angel, no! That's not true. You're imagining things....." Yet it *IS* the truth, and he is more honest than I am. I just want to escape.

Forcing me to my hands and knees, he slaps my ass until I am positioned for him. Paying no attention to my crying, he rams me as cruelly as he can, exacting a grim propitiation from my screams. I don't understand men. No resemblance to seduction this time; this is punishment; you could say *RAPE.* I am supposed to be fond of him for this? He's never coming in my apartment again! Looking over my shoulder, I see Angel's eyes filled with tears.

"I'll give it to you, Bitch!"

Why does no one write of the orgasm that turns against itself, the return trip from pleasure, aching with memories, wringing out the heart and cunt with grief like a washcloth.....and just as limp afterward.....life tasting like brackish indigestion.....a crash-total-state-of-being as opposed to a total-state-of-being-in-ecstasy? Just as a pleasure orgasm is a void of erasing all except pleasure, now my insides are rattling with total badness, jolting all the bad memories to the surface in paranoid distrust of everything.

The lack of connection between Angel and anything meaningful in my life is galling. Even the fact that a man like him can make me orgasm hurts me. He can't make me like the fact that I respond to him this way. I am losing more and more of myself and getting nothing in return.....and now it is utter badness, physical pain. I think Angel is transforming into a sadist. Funny, I never thought of that when we started making it together.

My head is a whirlpool-washer-full of pain orgasms, trusting in nothing, feeling the death of my brain..... Filled with hate and never........

And the man who brought this on me is heading out the door whistling to himself, pleased and eased, having settled the situation. He has dismissed me as a consideration until the next time he is horny. We aren't even friends anymore.

Angel and nymphomania have become synonymous to me, painful associations fettering me to a physical existence which has been reduced to acrobatics or degradation.

My drawing classes are much more exciting. I can see my progress every week. I examine a series of paintings I have been working on at home and realize they are variations on the female organs in assorted flesh tones. (Homage to Judy Chicago? A private 'Dinner Party'?) There it is. A vaginal universe reflecting what my world has become. Painting doesn't lie. Symptoms of the disease: nymphomania..... The subject matter is not particularly profound, isolated as it is from all the rest of life.

I've got to end this affair and get out of this life. I feel a post nasal drip crusting the back of my nose and throat. They feel raw and germy. The familiar virus feeling is coming on. I will probably get sick. That is what happens to you when you make life gross and inescapable......except by being sick. It can't last forever, (horrified thought). I'm going to lick this bug..... Who in the office can I call? One should be responsible and call. They surely can do without me there, but it will not be good to let them realize it. I get away with murder at Academia, which is why I work there. They haven't fired me.

After being sick for a suitable time, I break with Angel. I go to find him in the mail room, waiting for him to be alone.

"I want us to stop." I speak the words from the doorway, ready to run away. "You are married. I am taking art classes now. I want a man who is all my own. I can't deal with drinking anymore. You don't love me anyway..... If we keep on there will be no chance for me."

No surprise, no disappointment is visible. "There is somebody else," he says in a whisper.

"Angel, I don't like being hurt. Maybe you don't remember the last time we spent together as unpleasant, but I do. I don't want that anymore. I'm not even going to chance it."

"There's somebody else," Angel repeats morosely.

"All right. I do have a crush on this art teacher. It probably doesn't mean anything.....but he's very attractive and helps me do what I want......and I see what I'm missing with you."

"You think you're in love with him?" he raps out contemptuously.

"I'm interested. Which I can't be anymore in anything we have going. It is no good for me anymore. I'm not happy with you anymore. I *NEED* us to stop."

No more argument from Angel. He just flatly says, "All right."

That weekend I have so much more energy than usual to spend on my drawing. Elated, I rush straight to Pierre and Maryann. "I did it. I did it. I broke with him."

Pierre, the HM apostle, admonishes me: "I still think you will probably get back together with that man. And I'm warning you, he will do you no good at all. I don't believe you when you say you will never see him again. What would you do if he called you up when you got home tonight?" Pierre sets up these straw dogs..... It is true. I have become accustomed to compatible sex. Well........

At lunch times Angel passes me. Now that we are disconnected, each time I see him I mentally exclaim, "What a fantastic back..... What haunches, full of intricate muscles, supple, smooth and hard..... What biceps....." just as if I were admiring a horse. But in general, we don't want to fuck horses just because they look beautiful. That is a good thought. From now on, I divorce Angel from his status as a human and consider him as an aesthetically remote experience, like a horse. I hopefully repeat the prayers for the dead, reflecting on my dead illusion which could not coexist with reality. I'd rather live by myself with the ghost of Arcana's visitation. Meaningless men are out.

Chapter 13

I'm back on my celibacy campaign. Surprisingly, the boss is the only one at Academia Books who can understand.

"So. You overextended yourself," says Jack, patting my hand. "Just promise me you won't get emotionally involved with anyone for the next few months. That's your problem. You go to bed, and: *BINGO*! .....rush into an emotional involvement. It doesn't have to be so complicated."

I try to explain that love had nothing whatever to do with the relationship I ended.

"You'll snap out of the celibacy bit when you're ready to. You aren't worried about pregnancy, are you? because....."

"No..." I interrupt him as we enjoy egg-lemon soup with meat balls at our favorite and very expensive Greek restaurant. "I'm not emotionally involved. I'm not pregnant. I'm not worried. I need time off..... to think..... I've even quit smoking."

"A purification ritual?" inquires Jack.

"Who wants to turn nature into an ashtray? Only pop artists. It finally got to me....."

"The Japanese have a good attitude toward nature. Let it grow..... but *TRIM* it."

Jack orders himself his usual, and we spend the time over dessert collaborating on limericks. Swirling the ice in our drinks, digesting the food, trading lines.

ALISON: *An entrepreneur from the Bourse.....*

JACK: *Had a wife who asked for a divorce.*

ALISON: *Monsieur, he said: NO! Unless you give me some dough.*

JACK: *In which case I'll do it, of course.*

* * * * *

Festering in my daily miseries of repetitive typing, I wait, very hurt and impatiently for a signal of what to do with my life. The job, nice though Jack is, means hours of stiff neck transacting other people's business. Sympathetic, Jack tries to arrange for me to transcribe some manuscripts.....but that is no fun either. The manuscripts have been squeezed dry of humor, and are only statistical presentations of facts for the digestion of students who are serving time waiting for their degrees.

"I pity the students who have to read our books," I tell Jack.

"By and by, you'll find out what you want to do. Everything is not as dramatic as you make it. It doesn't have to be."

Back at the office, I empty my *IN*-box as fast as I can and then sit behind the typewriter looking like I'm working. ("Preserve the image," Jack has requested. "Look like you are working at least. Then no one can complain to me.")

I am alone. There are no men who spend the night. I pass the time drawing and writing. Sometimes I'm very uncomfortable..... withdrawal from sex amounts to an agony.....but I'm no longer willing to settle for only a physical act.....and I refuse to submit to a label: *NYMPHOMANIAC.*

Sometimes I dream of Angel, and when I do, I rebel. "No more nympho." Even if it is true, I can do something about it. I can refuse..... refuse.....refuse.

178

The phone rings. A very drunk Angel says, "Lemme come over, Baby. I wanna see you."

"No, Angel. Not anymore."

"I want you, Baby." He slurs the words of insistence.

"I'm sorry. It's over. I can't see you."

He threatens he'll break down my door. I say I will call the police and warn the doorman. He absorbs the finality of my refusal. Then he speaks distinctly into the silence, *"I'LL KILL YOU!"* I remind Angel of his family, of his son. "I wouldn't be thinking about them just right then. If you're not mine, you'll never be anybody else's."

"Angel," I try to calm him. "If you care about me, just leave me alone to find myself. Trying to force me into seeing you doesn't show you care for me."

He is intransigent. Insists I will *"GET IT"* if I continue to deny him. He will put out a contract on me through his friends, reminding me ominously that he knows people who would be delighted to kill for less than $100. I may as well expect to be dead soon. As to where and when it will happen, who knows. I can't expect to stay indoors forever.

He is serious. Wilfred's friends have discussed all kinds of petty crimes, stores, hotels..... They have 'brotherhood' connections also. If Angel really wants me dead, he has easy access to the means of arranging it.

My heart thumps like a drum with fear. My stomach knots and I am bathed in cold sweat.

"NO," I say. *"NO."* I'm not a slave. My body, recalling Angel's violence the last time he used me, refuses to repeat the scene. I don't enjoy pain. I won't be forced. There's nothing nice about this. *"NO."* Clearly, I shape the word into the phone. *"NO. NO.* Goodbye,

Angel. I hope you care enough to leave me alive......" Hang up the phone, then shivering, walk unsteadily to the bathroom and throw up into the toilet. Hands and feet like ice.....heart exhausted.

"Adrenaline reaction," I reassure myself. Images of walking onto the cold gray streets in the morning with Babette. When am I going to *'GET IT'*? It doesn't bear thinking about. Either I am free or I am a slave. There was no other choice. The price of freedom now is *fear.* If Arcana has a mission for me, perhaps she will intervene and save my life. But I have no expectations, only insecurity.

I remain awake the whole night, too distracted to read or do anything. In the morning, Babette and I leave for the day care center. I sweep the street with my eyes. Nothing happens.

Angel is not even at his job. Two weeks later, he is fired for not being on time, not showing up, and other forms of unreliability. I am very sorry and very relieved I will not have to see him. Once or twice thereafter, he calls me on the phone to abuse me drunkenly, but that is all. I am apparently released.

* * * * *

My crush on the drawing teacher disappears and I realize too that weekends alone won't make me into an artist. I have talent but no time. I drop the classes.

The faithful Tommy takes me to Central Park on my weekend off from Babette. We spend the day crying on each other's shoulders. His affair with Lex is finished, and he is depressed. He found himself a Cherokee girlfriend, tall like himself, with the face of a cover girl and hair like wheat. Surely heaven arranged this love for him.....and then that too ended. Tommy is now convinced he is meant to be a martyr and suffer loneliness all his life.

Tommy, Leo, and Rosalyn come regularly to play music and party on my floor. After Babette's bedtime, we sit around like a family, and I am the matriarch. As I look at the young faces of Leo and Rosalyn, suffused with innocent romance, I feel nostalgia, dry experience setting me apart from hopes and dreams. But the music is like a transfusion, restoring me to a plateau where emotions dance and for a few moments are believable.

Tommy squires me through the Village as I seek a red shawl with macrame fringes. The idea of such a shawl has possessed me for a month now. In and out of the shops I go. Everything looks great in the window, but when I get close up inside and inspect it, it turns out to be coarse and shoddily made and greatly overpriced.

One day I am in a more western section of the Village than usual, and walk into an antique store where I find my shawl hanging from the rafters. I know I'll never be able to afford it. It is flame red antique silk with hand-embroidered red roses and hand-knotted fringes of intricate latticework. But miracles happen. When the storekeeper sees me with the shawl, he drops the price to an affordable $50. Later I discover it is worth $300. Miracles of compassion still do happen.

At night, when the telephone rings and no one speaks, I think of the death threats over me, how hard it is not to let one's heart beat itself to death. Slow it down. Easy. Quiet breathing and fight fear. Arcana wouldn't like you to make yourself suffer. Think about her. Have *FAITH*.

Like a sex-a-holic, I go through withdrawal, nauseated and dizzy, literally starving from an impersonal desire that I no longer will grant rights over my actions. Large pricks, like Hindu phallic monuments, (Indian women worship by draping them with garlands), float through space, tantalizing me with visions of masculine potency. I curse Angel for having conditioned me to such a big appetite. I remain closeted in my apartment and out of reach until I am positive he will no longer call me.

Why do I feel so unequipped for being alone? There is writing, drawing, and reading. There is Babette and her needs. Tommy is a regular member of the family. That's it.

I think of Ruthy and Petra but do not call them. I feel so hurt that they have been ignoring me, I am unable to make a move towards them. Is it pride? All I know is I had rather be alone than go begging for friendship.

I'm not like Jack Livingston, it seems. I'd rather die of horniness than end up in bed with another beautiful animal with no mind. I have proved myself at fucking. Jack, I'm now beyond the call of duty.....and it is all an illusion. Now I'm dying through lack of being made love to and being able to make love in return to somebody..... another word for this condition is loneliness. Except for Arcana, I don't even know what 'making love' is.

Fucking wouldn't remedy this condition; it would only make it worse. Having sex with a stranger is hardly a solution; it is like watching yourself in a mirror, another form of narcissism. How you go through the motions, and they prove you're a woman or a man..... and all the time you are operating on a physical level, just a body..... and later it is all as if it had never happened. One is supposed to spend one's life, as *Playboy* suggests, running after these isolated fucks? Making sure there are no strings. Falsifying your name, your address, your past? And remembering later that you were.....'good'. How many times must one be good at fucking to forget about doing it altogether? How superficial are we now in our sex-crazy world? Women in hot pants lying all over this year's new cars, caressing them and panting.

The eclipse of a fuck isn't worth all the self-appeasing lies I would have to use to rationalize the impersonality of it.

* * * * *

Petra and Ruthy come to see me of their own accord. They are the avant-garde of gourmets, always discovering the best Chinese restaurants in advance of their reputations while they are still cheap and have the best food in New York. Now they want me to go to Hing-Hong or something like that. It would be useless for me to remember the name. The restaurants instantly go downhill as soon as people discover them, and the more stars they get, the more expensive the food becomes, and the nastier and less mellow it tastes.

As for our mythical romance restaurant, each of us brings a detail vital to its fabrication. Petra orders Shanghai steamed dumplings. Ruthy, while showing me how to mix vinegar and soy sauce for a dip, insists they be accompanied by choruses from the *Mikado*, (Gilbert and Sullivan). I substitute unaccompanied Zen flute meditations, haiku by Alan Watts, and titling the dish Dragon-Balls. So we build a secret meeting place even in a public restaurant.

Taking them back to my house, I sing for them a blues for the departed Angel:

LIBERATED WOMAN BLUES (Ahem.....)

> *Gonna find a replacement for you, Babe.*
> *There are plenty of good lovers in this town.*
> *I have no intention of staying at home*
> *While you are out playing around.*
>
> *You chase all the women who let you,*
> *And when I want the same kind of fun,*
> *You dump a lot of evil names on me*
> *And say you're going to be my only one.*
>
> *You think you rate special treatment*
> *Because you know your way around a bed.*
> *I never thought I was so bad myself, Babe,*
> *But I never let it go to my head.*
>
> *If I did, I'd have one man to do my dirty dishes*
> *And another one to polish my floor,*
> *And a third to babysit with my children*
> *While I go out and make time with more.*
>
> *You can stop calling me your old lady.*
> *You've had your notice: We're through.*

You've thought all I was good for was fucking with.....
Now I think the same about you too.

"I like what it says," Petra tells me kindly, "but I have the feeling it's been done before." Then we have one of our blowing-it-out conversations, agreeing on subjects for passion: movies, photography, the entrancement of a performance by a famous dancer, a passage by a literary titan..... Why was it so great? Taking it all to pieces to find out.

The ashtray is the hub as usual and we are the spokes. I am understood by my friends. I have spent $80 of a secretary's salary on one outrageous hand-embroidered Romanian blouse. But I am understood. I have invested $60 in three art books. But that qualifies as *'reasonable.'* I have purchased an antique necklace, which I couldn't live without......and I can't even confess the price.....

Tommy visits by himself now. Leo has broken with Rosalyn and disappeared. Tommy misses him. No one has seen him. It is as though Leo never existed. The lack of his music is regrettable. Tommy slips further into speed.

One night I let him stay with me. (Lex had asked: "Aren't you at all curious? Seven feet tall? What it could feel like if he is proportional?") It is a memorable occasion. In the morning, Tommy looks at me worshipfully and says, "You look just like the Virgin Mary!" Immediately, I have an attack of paranoia. What have I done? Tommy is already making love noises. He is so susceptible. And I don't care for him in that way and can't support him. Having him around *ALL* the time wouldn't be good for me or Babette. It would just be Angel all over again, and I can't do that to Tommy. I banish him for a month.....explaining, "We've got to forget all this and go back to before."

Tommy is patient and gentle and feels it is only his fate; what's always bound to happen. He goes. I find a note the next week tucked under my door. It is on yellow lined paper folded in quarters:

Dear Alison,

I'm givin' you this letter because I can't talk to you about a certain subject. Don't get me wrong. It's just that lately I have been getting confused when I rap with anybody, so dig!

I guess you want us to stop meeting each other on a lover basis? Well, I don't know. I am really just a little upset about it. I'm gonna miss our past intimacies. I refuse to get overly upset because that would probably, (oh, fuck it, you know what word I mean), get you upset too. I don't want to cause you any hassles. Anyway, I still feel very affectionate toward you, but if you wish I shall keep my place. However, it shall be hard, I think, not to see you for a while because, you see, you're one of the few people that I know that really are alive. I'd hate to lose your affections and your friendship. I would still like to see you very often, (if possible), and rap, goof, have good times too. Etc., etc., etc., okay?

I still would like to be your friend. I feel pretty sure you would like me to be your friend too. I hope this letter doesn't confuse you or anything but rather that it makes you feel better. I remember your past affairs and their hang-ups, so I wanted you to come away from our night happy and with fond memories and with us still friends.

Your bro, Thomas

I am sickened with a remorse for him that I should have taken care of his feelings and not caused him pain. I am also surprised at how well written the letter was, all things considered. The punctuation in the right places, spelling.....Who would have thought it? I turn the paper over, and on the back I see:

LOVE POEM

*You took me
    by the right hand,*

*Then ya shook me,
    making me more of a man.*

*You made me cry,
    sometimes I was so sad.*

*There was a while for me to sigh..
    I guess I'll love what I had.*

THOMAS RIVERS

It is so direct, and so Tommy. I am unsure whether to laugh or cry. I feel ashamed of myself.

After Lady Arcana showed herself to me in that chemically inspired vision, my attitude is changing every day. I have broken with Angel and messed up with Tommy, and I think it would be better if I just live with my dream lady's memory.

* * * * *

Now I am very vulnerable. God could appear around every street corner. It is necessary to be prepared to greet God's appearance with enthusiasm, as one might greet a lover.....so accordingly, my clothing gets more and more festive. People look at me as I pass by with open mouths, unbelieving and sometimes no remarks, even. It is the blitz.

I feel so 'groovy' in my antiques, my vest with tinsel patterns embroidered crustily on it, my Greek blouse with gold spangles worked into the cross-stitching and big airy sleeves. Plus, wearing necklaces has become an art form.

I pose it to Petra: "How many necklaces is it possible to wear at one time? All of them adding to one another and none of them detracting? There must be different lengths and chains and pendants, different luminosities; metallic, transparent, textural, color differentiation.....etc. etc. It is a variant on abstract art. You see?" She immediately does.

Through experimentation we discover what an expensive art form the 'Multiple Necklaces' assignment can be. Also, the maximum number one's neck can support with any comfort is ten. *OK*, the "*TEN NECKLACE CLUB*." They have to match one's shirt or blouse. We start our collections: metal chains, beads of wood dyed with colors, assorted stones, amber, turquoise, coral, etc. Even Ruthy turns herself on to five strands. Seeing us on the bus together, we look like a sect of female ecstatics hunting for Krishna.

Wearing my philosophy around my neck as I walk to and from work, from the house to the day care center, wherever, I wait for the moment of encounter. If not God, perhaps a kindred assemblage of sensitivities will appear walking toward me from the horizon.....but it doesn't happen. I am not disappointed when God doesn't show up because I am having too good a time waiting, and I know, deep in my heart, I *KNOW*.....sooner or later, heh, heh, heh, heh. *IT'S BOUND TO HAPPEN!*

The waiting is prolonged through days and weeks.....months. I work at Academia, and am mostly celibate with a few lapses on the spur of the moment. Nothing important, nothing you could really say anything about. Almost you could say: "Nothing happened." Insignificant one night forgettables.....not men who were a mistake. One remembers those. Just men who weren't anything.....seems to be the general order of the world. *(Alas.)* I give up finally on men altogether, draping my body with all the ornaments I can bear the weight of: vests, beads, broaches, rings, ribbons, and other fancies. I hum to myself little ditties, rhyming good-humored comic little verses with nursery melodies. Sometimes I write them in my journal. Sometimes I let them slip away.

I keep off the stuff, occasionally taking discreet puffs from someone else's joint. I don't keep anything in my house, only Basho and Babette. I have sowed enough wild oats. Now I want to get down to real farming. Life is a great supermarket. I go and shop, bringing it all home and putting it in the cupboard of my journal, seeds for a garden. Writing becomes a mirror.....more than a sheet of glass backed with mercury. I honestly want to get a grip on my thoughts.

Painting. I still want to and am afraid to blow it. Roger, the artist-drug-rehabilitator, calls to check on me. He blasted me over the phone for not painting.

"Alison, you have *IT*. Why are you just letting it go?" It seemed to me that I had been recognized and judged and felt more guilty about not painting than anything else. But I have a hard time figuring out what stops me from working at it..... That is a biggie.

Last night I scared myself. I had the worst thought I ever had. I was in bed after a night's writing and trying to draw, and my eyes hurt. They itched, and I was rubbing at them.....and suddenly a voice said to me: "Why don't you just rub them out? Go ahead. Get rid of them.....then the pain will stop."

"What?" I looked for the voice, and there was nobody. But the thought had been implanted, and my eyes itched more than ever. Something in me said, "Leave this thought alone. Don't think about it anymore and go to sleep right away because you can't handle what might happen if you go on thinking this way."

Blindness would be worse than death to me, coming as it would in the middle of my uncompleted life. A suicide of the personality..... abdication of the unfinished painting and writing. I must really hate myself or think I deserve major punishment for this kind of episode to occur.

But I couldn't sleep. And the voice returned and said: "Go ahead. You can get rid of all your problems fast. Rub your eyes. First gently, and then a little harder. It could be so easy."

I freaked. Classical schizophrenic symptom.....hearing voices. "The Devil!" I thought to myself with amazement, "I've really heard my own personal devil. No wonder the Devil is called a *MASTER OF TEMPTATION*. Really knows how to twist the knife in your private wounds....."

It was fairly clear that no one else was in the apartment and that the voice had to come from inside my mind. But I had *HEARD* it as an external voice. I had alienated it. Schizoid as hell. But what good does it do to name the disease if it doesn't shut off the voices?

I lay in my bed, hands pinned under my rear so that they wouldn't do anything involuntary, and tried to calculate the best way to lay this spirit to rest. I tried to imagine how Arcana would advise me, trusting in her to speak when I needed her.

A melodious whisper in my ear came to my rescue. "Get your eyes checked tomorrow, Stoopid. You probably need glasses."

Incredible. The impeccable solution to the problem. How can you argue with that? I can certainly hold out for one night.

"Go away," I tell my devil voice, "I'm going to sleep. Don't bother me anymore. I'm getting glasses in the morning. Furthermore, I'm under protection. You won't get anywhere with me."

All these years, vanity has stood in the way of my wearing glasses.....but now I'm ready to wear them. I want to save my eyes the pain. This noon, on my lunch hour, I shall collect my new glasses from the optometrist. I shelled out forty-five smackers, (in order to have frames that wouldn't be so horrific that I would never be caught behind them).

The fantastic commitment for me to get glasses.....it is like going to a shrink. To have decided to bring my vision into a correspondence, a conformity, with the world everybody else sees.....that clarity in vision is preferable to vagueness.....a reaching for sanity. A hell of a lot to dump on glasses, but I have always enjoyed having my own unique vision. If it weren't for my devil finding a weak point in my defenses, I wouldn't be getting them now.

I had to confront sticking a regular shape, the glasses, on an irregular shape, *(my face).* The human face is assumed to be symmetrical, but in fact, it never is. But superimposing the symmetry of glasses on my face made me look cockeyed to myself. I couldn't get used to that no matter which frames I tried on.

The optometrist was annoyed with me. He certainly wasn't the most helpful person I've met. And then I had a problem with my eyebrows sticking out of the tops of the glasses, looking untidy, and irregular as everything else.

Finally I found the frames that would do. They are out of gold wire, rectangles with glass, inside of circles. I am hoping that anyone who sees me in them will be so busy trying to decide what shape the glasses are, *(rectangles or circles),* that they will overlook the contradiction of the regularity of the glasses with my irregular face.

Glasses as functional objects.....and also conceptual art.

Chapter 14

Will the split shards that were me ever marry each other again? Or is this divorce permanent? Schizophrenia is bewildering because each alternative profile is real and completely in opposition to the last. As witness, Durrell's symphony about this in four volumes. He writes a masterfully devised mesh of interconnecting, mutually reactive fragments, straining the web that binds them together. Such a sensual process. And turning different facets to the spectator, revolving.

If life would just run smoothly like a spool of thread in a sewing machine.....but no. These snarls of lifelines intertwined into knots.....

Another emotional session with my father. We have them every time I see him without bringing Babette along as a deterrent. He tells me it is all in my own head---that I feel like a failure. (He doesn't guess at what I feel I can be, what I should be. He is not inside me, feeling my potential self-stretching, requesting liberation, feeling no height in this world is beyond me, even if I am over thirty.)

According to him, I have done a number of unforgivable things, though it should be understood: *HE* forgives me. But I should not forgive myself. Face it. He hasn't forgiven me.

I went home and interrupted Babette's dinner which Dave was feeding her. Went into the bathroom and washed my face which looked bleary and repulsive from crying Spent fifteen worried minutes on a small blackhead in my nose that suddenly seemed larger to me. Ultimately decided that skin care was all well and good but in direct conflict with living in ye goode olde New York City air. What product can cancel smog?

I went out again. It was my free night. My mind began to do arpeggios, warming up. Talking to myself again. If I could only be a good listener, maybe could learn something.

What if it means a choice? I have to stop loving myself or stop loving Dad? His version of who I am is driving me to a point where it is either his truth of who I am or mine. While Mother was alive, parents only said good things. Even until Dad remarried, mostly good things were said. I can't even be sure his version of me belongs to him. Maybe it was implanted, (by Ida, wife #2.) And his version of me is *CRAPULENCE*.

It is in my head that I am a failure. But, too, I am unforgivable. What a bummer. Maybe Arcana should have come to my father instead of me. I can almost hear her saying, "You have to deal with this one yourself, girl."

I am just about ready. Steadiness. I feel it coming on and want to scrap everything. God! I'm almost excited. I *WANT* to paint.

I am ready to resume. I think I can stand looking at myself again. Words are not my greatest specialty and at bottom seem untrustworthy. Why does one resort to visual art in the first place but as a guide to objectifying reality? And if the reality is not to your taste, why.....change it. In a painting, you can do that without hurting anybody else.

Gone is the need to display. I want to keep it safe in the closet. I don't want to make the revolution on a canvas......only in my own head.....that I have a right to my own vision and my own paintings. Paintings are an act of prophecy. The hell with anyone who dislikes them. I won't show mine to anybody.....so it won't matter if they are bad at first. I guess I should be prepared for that. It is an exam I will have to pass in terms of self-discipline.....being bad at first. But I think I have the perseverance now to cope with it.

I really <u>don't</u> have to show my paintings to <u>anybody</u>. That's it. The mental rivet, quite unseen by me, that has made it impossible to work for all these years. It hasn't been me.....it has been everybody else in the world not liking it.....and me worrying about their likes in advance.

I haven't studied anatomy or light sources for months now. Should I have a system? Or just *patchka* at first with the paint? I don't know. I only know I want to start.

I don't care if I waste $10 on a 5' x 4' canvas and just destroy it. I can set this $10 aside for my own pleasure every week. My money = my time and they are my own to waste.....and I can put the waste in the garbage and dispose of it before anybody has a chance to see what it was.

Now I get it. I feel like a dam that has been destroyed by a flood. It doesn't matter how many paintings I ruin. I am no longer scared to dare.....which means I can probe..... I was clenching, tantamount to creative frigidity—frigidity of the paintbrush.

I've got to be selfish about this for it to work. Fuck labels and critics and formalistic words..... Selfishness in painting is a positive virtue. How else can I achieve honesty? I have been a million bottled-up impulses.....but no longer.

Bullshit? Chi sa? I will see what gives me pleasure to pain, and that is what I will paint.

I start by painting a symbol of beatitude that partially resembles Babette, my mother, traces of Lady Arcana, and the infant Jesus.

The clock is ticking, and there are sounds of trucks outside. But Babette and Basho and the entire block is asleep. No voices, just ticking, ticking. Painting in the night hours; time running by lightly touching me like moth's wings.

Moths don't wait to search for the light. The light calls for them, and they give themselves to it. What would it be like to be a moth who had been given electric shock treatment and told that light was bad? Wouldn't there be a pulling apart, a separation of the vertebrae of the personality?

And that is what has happened to me and my painting. I was told it was bad by indifference, by having it ignored, and outright statements: "It's bad." "It's Bourgeoise." "It's no good." "It's uninteresting." "It's out of style." "It isn't our painting," (from nonobjective artists for my representational work). "Can't tell what it is," (from those who like photographic realism".)

But now I see it so clearly.....my painting is *MINE*. It is supposed to work for me first and then for everybody else. Otherwise, why do it? For money? That's not painting. It's something close to prostitution. Money and truth have a hard time mixing. At least I have never wanted to be a rich painter.....(rich having the priority in that marriage).

Light fractures into a zillion color sensitive dots.....I love it. It's better than acid. A thousand times better. Acid makes my skin break out.

I put myself to sleep with a face plastered with Noxzema, expecting to wake up beautiful to a painting that has just started being born.

Even more than before, I am waiting for God.....but instead, I receive a voicemail from Leo. I haven't seen him in months and am glad to find out he's still alive. He wants to see me, and after hesitating, (because I had planned to spend the evening alone painting), I said, "Please do come." Because it was the first time Leo had felt like seeing me by himself. I have invited him to visit before, but he has never come without Tommy or Rosalyn.

Leo is lots of fun to be with because he always has a twinkle behind his eyes.....but the rest of his face stays in a deadpan mask. That enigmatic self-sufficiency is still on his face whenever I see him.

"Where have you been hiding, Leo?" I ask.

"Just had to get away for a while. Besides, it's cold on the streets in the winter. Now it's Spring! Doesn't it feel marvelous? Can you dig it?"

He turns me on to a joint and asks to listen to John Mayall. I study his face as the record fills the space between us with expert guitar licks. Leo has a particularly naked face, a peculiar observation when I have already described him as inscrutable. But his inscrutability is his own blankness. Leo isn't an immediately flashy dude until he breathes or moves. Then I pick up emotional verity, raw essence of humanity, everything firsthand and direct. He hardly even copies himself.

Leo seems to float through the time we spend in silence, not talking, allowing the record full attention. He doesn't seem to plan reactions and waits until time calls for a move from him. The record finishes.

"I've been a lot by myself lately," I confide. "Every so often I have wandered the neighborhood, checking out the leather store, the Feenjon, or Cruisan's house, (a basement crash pad where Tommy and Leo are sometimes to be found). I'm beginning to feel different, changing.....so I haven't been going out very much." Leo relives a drug experience he has recently had, and I space out while he is describing it. I relate some of the periphery of the Arcana vision without actually committing myself to what the central feature was.

Leo understands *O.D.* Makes noises to the effect of, yes, he has been there.....but does not go into detail either. Somehow I believe him; that he has had a revelation of his own, that it wasn't a simple matter of excess electricity but accompanied by visions and life-changing inscapes.

"May I play for you?" He takes his guitar on his lap.

"Oh, yes. Please."

The relief of silence when you have run out of things to say to a new friend. Leo sings, and I hear wonderful things. He's better than when I first heard him several months ago. That is the first thing that impresses me. He sounds even more real. Yet there is a reserve which confines his emotions to a good-mannered 'laid-back-ness' so that what I hear is an obscured version of feeling behind a veil of hesitancy. Never allows himself to do anything vocally that he is not in full control of, in front of me, anyway.

Despite this, when he sings, I hear tremendous power, a forecast of what someday he may be, one day when his shell cracks open, and he is ready to let himself go completely.

A drama teacher, one of Academia's authors, once told me that the hardest thing he had to teach his students was how to be lousy. That the greatest tragedy was staying in the perimeters of what you already knew you could perform well: the safe path. You'd never grow that way.

"They come to me," he said, "fresh out of high school where they've been the star.....the best in their school. And they're used to it. And here they are in college, where everyone else in their class has been used to being a star in high school, and the competition is rougher.....and they need to be *GOOD*. But what I need to get from them is to lose it."

"That's fascinating. Give me an example?"

"You see, emotion has to regress to the formlessness of infant tantrums, to screaming hysteria. They have to flip out and be sloppy all over the place.....letting it all loose. And they're terrible,.....just awful. But *THEN*..... Then they can learn how to control all that diffuse energy, how to channel it. But if they don't let themselves go, to the point where they lose control, they are cutting themselves off from their full range. And there is no way to be good at it in the beginning. So I have to teach them it is *OK* to be bad. Am I making sense to you?"

This conversation comes back to me as Leo sings. And there it

196

is, in plain sight, enormous capacity for emotion, harnessed behind good manners. Someday it will unleash itself, be organized and tapped. And yet it is already apparent.....the potential to be more than just good.

I am so tired of seeing and listening to secondhand versions of Hollywood stars, to a million second and thirdhand imitations of rock personalities and their mannerisms.....not to mention a plethora of clones of their parents. Leo is *REAL*; no one but himself.

He is shy and very polite. I can hardly say I *KNOW* him.....yet I do know him. Parts of him, revealed in music, his genuine capacity to feelings. He sings his youth and idealism, his belief in love and peace, (as if someday we could have them on this earth). He sings his compassion for the poor immigrant, for Lady Madonna, the tactility of a rose in a fisted glove, the brilliance of Lucy in the sky of his universe. He sings with the passion he could bring to a woman.....

The range of feelings is archetypal: sadness, happiness, gaiety, anger, pain, ecstasy.....but to each he brings his own multidimensional personalization......the naked complexity of totally experiencing with a feeling mind.

Leo believes everything he sings to me, at least while he is singing it. In spite of my cynicism, my college-bred elitism, political theories which deny, or soulless encounters with would-be Don Juans..... I believe Leo while he is singing.

I am grateful to Leo for his gift of faith. Though it is transitory, it is contagious. And I forget to ask him where he is staying. And there was another question, too, that I forgot to ask.

We exchange a few more words, very abstract, nothing personal..... and then he leaves, disappears again.

I summarize his visit to myself: "Wow. He's a good singer. Going to be a <u>very</u> good singer someday," and then remember I wanted to ask him something about his smiling. I haven't yet found the right words to frame the question.

Cleaning up the house, I discover a green covered pocket notebook with Leo's name on it. Must have fallen out of his guitar case or his jacket. I leaf through it. Most of the pages are lyrics for popular songs, but on one page I read:

> *How can I live for you*
> *when you are killing me*
> *this way—why do you*
> *take me for such a fool?*

> ## *LEON GLASS*

No indication of who inspired this quatrain of emotion. Somehow I find it disturbing. Leo looks so young.....a teenager almost.....but these are not the words of an inexperienced boy.

I tuck the notebook away in a drawer where it lies for several months, waiting for Leo's reappearance. But he is gone again.

* * * * *

Summer has come. The Village now is a bustling traffic jam of tourists. Street fairs and art fairs draw them. The cafes' night life burgeons.

I visit antique stores and import shops on the Lower West Side looking out for rare necklaces at low prices.....hard to find. To maintain variety in the art form of necklace assemblage, an inflow of new materials must be sustained. I've accumulated an assortment of strings of cheap shells and wooden beads. I rummage in the bead stores for unusual beads I can string myself. What I'd really like to own would be a few antique pieces.....but I don't have enough money.

One weekend, while window shopping, a collar of stamped Syrian

198

coins draws me into an import store on a side street. The young man at the cash register is the spitting image of Durer's unfinished portrait of Christ that hangs at the Met museum. From a center part, red gold hair cascades in symmetrical rivulets down each side of his head to a little below his shoulders. He wears a colorfully printed Indian shirt and a string of plain silver beads around his neck.

I point to my selection and make hungry noises..... "Must have it......this one.....how much?"

The hip personage gives me a sharp look from a remarkably serene countenance. After purchase is arranged, small conversation takes place.

The weather is mutually agreeable, and so is rock music, and his name is Kirk, and he was once a drummer...... and do I like Ravi Shankar's drummer?

"Yes."

Kirk is one of those people responsible for bringing Swami Satchidananda to this country, and knows him; also was once a member of a band whose record never got past the demo phase, (but they will try again next year); and was part of *The Brotherhood*, an underground distribution system for free Orange Sunshine...... turned on half of New York several years ago.

"That was in the past. Now there's no more need for acid....."

These facts are charming, but they do not integrate into any particular significance for me at the time. I am invited to return for chatting. Between the peaceful friendliness of Kirk and the high quality of the jewelry, the store becomes one of my regular stopping-off places as I make my Village rounds.

I decide to buy a second necklace.....but cannot afford it. I got into a peculiar agony of not being able to have...... Kirk gives me a strange look. He already is apprised that I am a secretary at Academia. Probably has concluded I am a spendthrift..... Too true.

"I'm leaving New York next weekend. Going up to Provincetown with the goods....." says Kirk. "Come here at closing time, some night next week, and we'll have a real talk before I go." I'm open. Kirk is one of the most interesting and attractive men I have met recently..... whatever he has in mind.

The night before Kirk's departure, I meet him at the antique store. He is busy packing up the merchandise. He's really going. No more store.

"Yes. I'm leaving." Motioning towards the jewelry case, Kirk looks at me. "Help yourself. Take anything you want. Gift."

A fortune in antique necklaces lies on the dark velvet. I am sure I haven't heard correctly. "What was that you said?"

"You have a thing for jewelry. I have noticed. It's all right. Take anything you want."

I am to have free choice—expense no bar—it sinks in. I take the antique Persian pendant I have been wanting and could never afford and look questioningly at Kirk. "This one?"

"Fine. Do you want anything else? Take anything you want."

Of course, this can't really be happening. The offer seems unlimited, except for my greed for necklaces, which is undergoing a distinct lessening. It's very strange, taking something for nothing. I'm not used to it.

"Take whatever you want. Go ahead," encourages Kirk, and he leaves me alone to ponder while he folds tapestries into a cardboard carton.

I select a string of large amber beads and hold them up to the light. They glow with a golden translucence. "This?"

"Fine. Take anything you want." Shame at my attachment for material things immobilizes me. I have never been confronted by it directly.

"Look here. Take some more. Anything you want."

I pick up a Celtic broach, gold and silverwork surround a large red stone. I feel as if I had just overeaten, my stomach shaky, and my desire for necklaces.....stopped.

"That's all."

"Just be sure about it," advises Kirk. "I'm leaving tomorrow. Are you sure you have enough? It doesn't matter to me. Take some more if there is anything you still want."

"No. No, thank you. Thanks a lot. No one's ever just given me stuff, just like that....."

"I can't be too bothered keeping track of things," says Kirk carelessly. "People give me things, and I give them away. They come and go. You'll see."

He closes up the store. "Come with me."

We walk to his apartment in the Lower East Side. As I cross the threshold, I feel as if I'm stepping into another time. Kirk's attic, which is what his railroad flat looks like, is only two empty rooms with a kitchen. The wall has been chopped out to make one large room, and the walls are painted black. The only furniture is a hammock hung from the ceiling on chains, a large wooden spool that used to hold electric cables that was left on the street and has now been rescued and employed as a coffee-table, and a large square cushion. The floor is filled with what seems to be the debris of art collectors who have had too much of a good thing......

"Things people gave me," he remarks. This residue of paintings, sculptures, objets d'art, books, fabrics lies in disorganization, a romantic garbage heap.

A black Great Dane rises to his feet from beneath the hammock, licks at Kirk's hand, and retires back to sleep.

"Take the hammock," advises Kirk as he lights some incense, makes tea, and rolls us a joint.

I rock in the hammock staring into the black ceiling. Kirk finishes his chores and comes to sit opposite me on the cushion in a lotus position.

"You are so attached to things..... to feelings. I used to be like that..... but then I changed." Scented Russian musk lends these ethereal thoughts a sensuality even with their declaration of dispassion. We sit in silence for approximately five hours. Kirk doesn't make a move towards me but rests companionably silent, withdrawing into his own thoughts.

All I can think of is that I don't want necklaces anymore. Maybe I never did. Maybe I wanted *LOVE*. Maybe I wanted God. Whatever I wanted, Kirk isn't giving it out. Himself, for example. All he is giving out is necklaces.....exactly what I have been chasing and asking for. I feel like an idiot.

Though there is no physical contact or communication in words, I am lulled to peace by the harmony of the environment. The sharing of time seems to be enough of a gesture of affection and acceptance. I'd be greedy to ask for more.

After Kirk takes me home, I never see him again. But my necklace obsession is gone......and slowly I reconnect the facts..... the friendship with Swami Satchitananda, the communal settlement in New Mexico.....the detachment from material things.....the serenity of Kirk's face as he said: "Take all you want."

Chapter 15

GOD IS COMING.

All I have to do is wait. After Arcana's revelation and the guru of the necklaces, I feel positive that something is due to happen. Something has to be done about the house. It feels stale. Too many events have happened here which I'd prefer to forget. It reflects them every time I look around it; and it doesn't reflect *ME*, not the me I am trying to be.

If I'm going to have an important guest, whoever it is going to be, I can't receive them in a humdrum place like this.....no, no. My house needs a rearrangement. Some planning

Item #1 on the list is a personal home model waterbed. I get myself a magnum, king-sized bed, the social kind. Fits six bodies lying side by side, or twelve sitting cross-legged, or one restless sleeper, or perhaps a couple that desire to float away.

The next move is a cover for the waterbed. I commence sewing. I find in a secondhand store, (whose profits go to the rehabilitation of those who need salvation), some oriental fabric. I sew a bedspread and pillow covers. Horizontal comfort has been guaranteed.

Now for lighting. I add to my collection of mirrors, craftily rigging a system so that if a lit candle is placed in a key spot, it is reflected from mirror to mirror and the entire room will be illuminated......just from one candle. I lay in a stock of perfumed candles, and for good measure I buy a nice candlestick.

Now for taking care of smell. Incense. Lots of it. I go shopping for the nose. I test samples at home and return for quantity: Sandalwood, Passionflower, Lily of the Valley.....

Lastly, I invest in a few bottles of Rose', Lancers. If a guest comes, I should be able to offer them something to drink.

Now my room is transformed into a lush den of sweet iniquities. My jewelry is suspended on the wall behind my bed where I can play with it. Bottles and vases filled with ostrich and peacock feathers are advantageously placed to please the eye. My red shawl, its long fringes filtering the light, is draped over a three panel screen. The stereo has been moved so the sound is aimed at the bed.

Completion. My nest. My playroom. My little palace. My imagination no longer has to operate on the external environment to make it tolerable. Now it has been liberated for better employment.

Petra and Ruthy arrive to appraise the changes. They prompt me to name my bed. They name everything, cars, beds, bistros, people.....everything has a private name. I title the bed: *OASIS*.

And now my father is coming. Let's face it, I am nervous. Babette is fretful, probably tired from her day at the day care center. I gather up after her in her room and order her into the bath. I lather her all over with a face brush.....and she glows all over, clean-smelling. She looks for a pile of dust to roll on, just like a puppy. But I catch her.....and put her into a dress.....combing out her curls. There she is: Shirley Temple. All ready for Grandpa.

Of course from the minute he arrived in my house, he started picking on me.

"The place stinks. Do you always have to have it smelling of incense? It is too sweet. What about the child? Have you no consideration? Are you trying to turn your house into a nightclub?" Then he tries to make me feel guilty about the price of incense, and whether it isn't morally incorrect to have it burning in my house, considering there is a young child.

"A waterbed? Why did you have to buy a waterbed?"

I try to explain that #1: It is *MY* house, which I have to live in and he doesn't. I like incense. *How* does he know Babette doesn't? She probably does. Probably only *HE* doesn't like incense.

#2: It's *MY* bed, and I lie in it. He doesn't. He has a bed of his own. So what's the problem?

The first skirmish completed, my father, from his self-defined heaven, opens the next. My budgeting is my affair. I can starve myself and spend my money on some dopey item if I want to.....

We're in the car on our way to visit Aunt and Uncle. "I don't like this conversation," Babette tells us. I absolutely agree with her. There is a silence. *NEVER AGAIN.* Never again will expose myself to an evening with this man and his philosophy of noble suffering. He has been a participant in nearly driving me to a nervous breakdown. He still doesn't admit to the mental cruelty he and his wife exercised..... unconscious in his case perhaps.....but still having that effect.

All he wants to do is flagellate me about my behavior. From the puritan code he legislates for me, you would construe anything I enjoy is *BAD*.

We have to stop at a diner to feed Babette, who looks like a little angel in a picture book. Not one smudge to mark her as a real child who lives and breathes. But she reads the vibes clearly enough. The adults lack a solid front and the sky is now the limit for what she can get away with. She runs wild, jumping up and down and wriggling, yelling and 'misbehaving.' I am starting to get paranoid.

"Please! Don't talk in such a loud voice....." Then my father looks at me, and I can see his brain ticking out: "What kind of a mother *ARE* you? Look at your child. *NO* manners." He has visions of himself arriving at Aunt's with a clean grandchild because Aunt has a sanitation fetish. So he shushes Babette and orders her not to slob.

"Sit down! Babette, don't *DO* that. Don't do this. Be *QUIET!*" I snap at her, feeling myself to be on trial.

My tone of voice contains annoyance, and Dad tells me to stop using that tone of voice....the exact same tone of voice *HE* has been using ever since we've been in the diner. I tried to point this out. He was entirely impervious to seeing himself that way. I didn't like his attitude. I didn't like myself either because kids will get noisy, but that was our fault for letting Babette sense she could play us off against one another. So I got up and calmly swatted Babette to demonstrate I was hip to what she was doing. After which she quieted down. My father glared at me for causing a public scene.

It is so painful just to be around him. He is creating tension about such minor things just to punish us.....so out of proportion.....what a pusher-around-er.

Then I had a blinding thought. Here am I, weathering the storm, the first time I haven't let Dad drive me into a rage or a fit of hysterical tears.....I am handling it. I suggest he see a shrink.

Naturally, he thought he should be insulted instead of seeing it as the last resort of a dying love. "I'm not saying you're insane," I try to ex plain, "just our relationship seems to cause you so much pain..... and it isn't good to live with pain. So why not go see a doctor? I've done all I can. I am holding down my 9 to 5 job, taking care of the kid, and I'm healthier.....and you don't like the clothes I wear, maybe, or the smell of my house. But to get so miserable over it is *SICK*, and I can't take the responsibility for this, Dad. I see no other alternative to saving our relationship at all. Go see a shrink, please."

He started bellowing: "*WHAT? DO YOU THINK THE VALUES THAT HAVE CARRIED ME THIS FAR THROUGH LIFE.....*" He can't take the role reversal. During my winter of bad flip-outs, exacerbated by Ida's suggestions of nervous breakdown and Dad's rejections, he abdicated and sent *ME* to a shrink.....and now, when he is the disturbed party, I mention a shrink and he flies into a temper.

206

Babette completes this disastrous scene by smearing her face with vanilla custard. She runs to me asking to be lifted up. "Yech!" I say, daubing at her face with an insufficient napkin. Dad is glaring at me with disgust, as if I've finally reached the epitome of incompetence as a mother. Each time I see him, we get further alienated and I lose a little more of my childhood.

All the same, my father proposes to do me a favor. He and Ida will take Babette to Connecticut for two weeks, during my vacation from work. That way I can have a real vacation, rest up, and be prepared for another year of working and mothering. He does try to live up to his ideal of grandparenthood. I know Babette will have clear air, a lake to swim in, and a pair of willing slaves to most of her demands. I can definitely use the break from the routine of childcare. I agree to his proposal gratefully.

Chapter 16

INTERLUDE: PETRA, RUTHY AND ALISON TAKE A THREE DAY CAMPING TRIP IN NEW HAMPSHIRE

ALISON: Look at the campfire. A religious symbol, can you see it? You can observe the flames, but they aren't material. They can touch you and burn you, but you still can't hold them in your hand. Fire is like the essence of religion. No wonder primitive cultures worshipped *IT*..... that which is perceivable is not.....yet there is a testable effect on all it comes into contact with.

RUTHY: (Ignoring all mention of religion with distaste:) Read a simply terrible article by Dr. Joyce Brothers the other day. In *Good Housekeeping Magazine.* About exhibitionism in relationship to choice of clothing. She didn't talk about the clothing, whether it was beautiful or not, and shied away from the question of whether sexy clothes were good. (She assumed not, I think.) She did say 'attractive' clothes were good making a distinction between attractive and sexy.

PETRA: Hurrah for Dr. Joyce, the All-American Housewife. She's still playing the girl who grew up next door. The marrying kind of woman..... Men are truly peculiar. They want their wives not to wear makeup and then go to the movies and have fantasies about Raquel Welch......

ALISON: I've figured out now where I stand with relationship to men. I'm ready to defend my feelings at the price of theirs.....

PETRA: Finally! So you're no longer an ass kisser. Great.

ALISON: Nope. Finished with being an ass kisser.....or going around with a do-gooder earth-mother complex. I've committed grave and fundamental sins against my body. Since I could not close my ears, I closed my skin.....and since I could not close my eyes, I shut my heart tightly like a mud-fish trying to survive a heat-wave. My nerves grew fists instead of tongues.....the negativism of defeats.....

RUTHY: That's getting a bit mystical, don't you think?

PETRA: Listen, we had to put up with *YOU* when you went through your Jesus Christ fixation.

RUTHY: All right. All right.

ALISON: The senses must be nourished or die of atrophy. You don't want your senses to decline into vestigial remnants of abandoned potential? The eternal question can't be resolved by the mind alone.....the mind sits in the house of flesh.....but how does one make a house a home?

RUTHY: Very artistic.

ALISON: I should have said in advance .....I am not an artist. I'm only a person who seems to myself less smart than I thought......but a lot more real, thank God.

PETRA: Did you hear the Stones are coming to New York?

RUTHY: Tell Alison your Mick Jagger story.

ALISON: Do you have a Mick Jagger story, Petra?

PETRA: Uh huh. It goes like this: Once there was a girl who was in love with Mick Jagger. She wanted more than anything

else to go to bed with him.....had fantasies about it.....
but she knew she would never meet him. Anyway, she
went through a long succession of affairs, and each
morning she would wake up and say to herself: "That
was a really great time. And that guy was OK. But he
wasn't Mick Jagger." And each time she met a new fella
and went to bed, she would say to herself: "He's very
far out. But he isn't Mick Jagger."

Finally, one day she met Mick Jagger on the street
entirely by accident. So she said: "Hi, Mick, Baby.
How are you?" And they started to rap. And she being
attractive and definitely friendly, the two of them ended
up in her pad, and so her dream came true after all. And
in the morning she woke up and said to herself: "That
was really great! It was out of this world. But it wasn't
Mick Jagger!"

We are all quiet for a time, mulling over the consequences
of star-chasing.

ALISON: Did I ever tell you what happened between me and
Pierre?

PETRA: No.

ALISON: You know he is a Henry Miller freak, don't you? So we're
in this cafe, and it is late at night, dim lights, and you
know......the grand intellectual 1930s passions of Paris
transplanted to the West Village. And we're talking.....
and Pierre conceives that the script includes his duty
as a true-blue Henry Miller acolyte to fuck me and find
out what I am really all about.....and to prove to me in
the process that he really digs sex.

We wouldn't even have been sitting there if he hadn't
been someone I was very fond of.....so I figured, what
the hell, and told him: "Don't worry about it.....when

210

the time is right....." So we ended up in my apartment, having decided the time *WAS* right to fuck.....and you know, it had never occurred to me but Pierre is a little short guy, and he was *TINY*.....and there wasn't much length to him either.

And it was a parody.....he was making up for being small by being a really speedy fuck, in and out, in and out, fast-like being uninhibited and showing how he loved fucking, heart and soul. I wasn't sure exactly what hit me.....because his speed jolted my nerves. Anyway, like I wasn't dazzled and I wasn't satisfied.....and I knew I wasn't going to be either because nothing he could do would make me feel filled up, no matter how good he was. So I just lay back, split off from my body, and made it as good as I could for him. He was a *FRIEND*, after all.....and he *loved* it and wanted to fuck all over the house..... like in H's books, so I figured: What the hell. I let him start this. He might as well have a good time. Why puncture another human being's ego? Told him he was great.

Life is such a farce...... Here is Pierre, I mean, he is a beautiful guy. He has a great brain and he's pretty gutsy and visceral in his own way.....and why should providence have visited him with such a small prick? I mean....it sadly gets in the way of his playing Henry Miller. It is a paradox.

And I was hoping he *WOULD* turn me on.....because if anyone deserves to be able to make it as a good lover, it is Pierre. It's central to his philosophy.

RUTHY: You just can't always have what you want.....

PETRA: I can't always have what I want......but I generally manage to get what I need.

ALISON: Yeah..... If you can only make yourself aware that you <u>need</u> something, it generally comes and finds you.

* * * * *

I have a strong desire to talk to Leo and start hunting all over town for him as soon as I return from my camping trip. What I want to ask him, now I've got the words, is: "About the question of God, what do you think?" He must have been doing a lot of thinking about this subject lately. I know that he's got some answers for me.....about something important. If only I can get him alone again and talk to him for a while.....maybe I can get the nerve to ask him.....maybe he will be willing to tell me something.

Before Arcana's visit, I was a sort of atheist, a hangover from my life as a Marxist-Leninist.....but now I have an open mind. I remember when I denied the existence of God, failing to find organized religion anything other than a collective mouthing of long familiar words written by people long ago, and chanted to familiar melodies on specially designated days of the week, (hardly an appropriate investment for human energy.)

I remember the day I discovered the bomb. I was in school at the time, my very first day in first grade, in fact. My parents had let my grandmother teach me to believe in God. And I did, without any questions, as I believed in Santa Claus.

I was only a child. I had been cushioned against shocks in every possible way by the love of a stable family. Everyone gave me their time and shared their excitements with me fully. I was never taken any place bad, and precautions were taken to prevent accidental conflicts without my being aware of it..... so as not to break my spirit of adventure or curiosity. When I managed something original...a thought of my own.....it was applauded and interacted with as much as possible. I was presented with the means to explore: paint-boxes, books, toys.....a rifle..... No one ever made me parrot meaningless words. It was so obvious I was busy with my little mind grasping at life. Nobody ever lied to me.

And then school came,..... and I could see immediately that teachers there didn't worship God as grandmother did.....or explain about history the way my father did.

I loved 'people' so much already that when the teacher said some countries were better than others, I was disgusted with the whole mess right there and realized *LIARS* existed. And then I found out about the bomb because we were instructed we had to have shelter drills in case it fell.....and wear metal dog tags, ugly and cold, in case we got lost. We had to crouch under our desks in silence or line up to reassemble in the school basement where it was cold without our coats.

But the teacher said that we also had a bomb which proved that the men in Washington were smart (!!!) and looking out for us. All I thought was that *ANYONE* who built bombs to cancel out human life, (including mine, which I liked), had to be absolutely evil.

I asked my father about this bomb when I got home. Why would anyone be crazy enough to build and stockpile bombs if even one was powerful enough to blow up the building, the neighborhood, even the city? Dad then explained to me about the war machine. (He didn't call it that.) He said some greedy people made money making weapons, (an aspect of *CAPITALISM*, prioritizing profits). Other people bought these weapons and made wars.....and required more and more powerful weapons to win these wars, which manufacturers were happy to invent and provide. The end result of this contest for power was the evolution of the nuclear bomb.

At once, although I'd not been conscious of politics before, understanding this information resulted in distaste for governments, for all philosophies that could justify money if it culminated in a bomb, feeling betrayed by God that he could permit a nuclear bomb to be made, and a hatred of all people who were willing to make their money at the price of human lives.....leaning back in their armchairs in safety.

As for respecting school, I dropped out emotionally right then, at the beginning of first grade, because they made me swear allegiance to the flag of a government that made bombs. As for prayers, all the children were made to say them in unison by the same teachers who led them as they recited their patriotic catechisms. Religion fell into the same category: institutional. No real God! What they worshipped, judging by behaviors, was *MONEY*!

All these assumptions remained unchanged until the appearance of Lady Arcana. The experience of Arcana..... I feel pretty much the same about institutions but now I am entertaining all kinds of thoughts about divinity.

So I am hunting for Leo because I feel intuitively he has the answers for me.....even though it is hard to say what the questions are.

I keep finding Leo several times that week, always with Tommy. Tommy clings like a leech, never leaving us alone, and the conversation I want to have with Leo won't happen in the presence of others. Tommy hardly allows any words at all. He claims his head is befuddled. ("All fuuuuucked up!") "I can't talk now, Alison, unless it is really important. Do you mind if I play my guitar?" Never before have I been impatient with music.

When guitar playing is exhausted, Tommy gets up and puts on a record without even asking, always too loudly. The drugs have made him harder of hearing, a weird condition for a musician.

And so the talk that was meant to be is squeezed out of existence. I look at Leo helplessly and take out my sketch pad. Leo looks at me, smiles, and says nothing.

Each time I see him, I know he is the one I have to talk to.....and each time, he is with Tommy and there is no opportunity. Tommy is not leaving us alone, not for a moment. When we move around from house to house, the three of us on the street, Tommy takes my arm possessively. I look over my shoulder at Leo, not wanting to be a possession of Tommy's, very angry at him for implying by that gesture that I am personal property. There is no way to escape. And

Leo is just floating, wearing a khaki army shirt from Australia, singing marvelously whenever we make a landing around a local ashtray..... and being unavailable for talking to.

I'm also finding it very hard to get the words out to him. The more I want to see him, the less I can talk to him. It is a vicious circle, and my vacation is almost gone. Soon it will be time to return to Academia, Jack Livingston's orations about free love, and Babette's back and forth trips to the day care center. I feel pressured and frustrated and very resentful of Tommy for getting in the way. It is almost as if he were doing it on purpose.

One night Tommy takes me to Cruisan's house, and there, as if he were waiting, is Leo, tripped out on acid, playing along with a record, glowing like a torch.

"Wait here, Alison," Tommy says. "I have to go out and deliver something to somebody. I'll be back very soon." And he leaves.

Leo and I look at each other. The minutes are disappearing, and the conversation is waiting along with a bottle of Rose' back in my house. I am scared to ask him in case he turns me down. I am not used to asking a man for anything. They are supposed to do the asking, and I don't know the way of it.

I reproached myself for being a coward, and I spoke. The chance was slipping away and might never come again.

"There is a bottle of wine at my house. Why don't we go over there and talk?" Leo smiled and rose. As it turned out, he was scared to ask me if he could come over. So we beat it out of there before Tommy could catch up with us. Neither of us had any idea what we were doing.

We ran through the streets almost as if we were being pursued, giggling a little bit at our cleverness in eluding Tommy, saying how we hoped he wouldn't be offended.

We made it to my apartment. Leo opened the wine bottle, and we drank together in the candlelight, reclining at opposite sides of the king waterbed. We talked and talked.....rather stupid efforts. Touching, really. It never turned out to be the conversation I had in mind.....and this other conversation hung there, and we were unable to break through and get to it. We said very little that made any sense.

Still, it was very tranquil. I felt as if the late hour might deprive Leo of a place to crash because friends wouldn't be too turned on by an unexpected guest at three in the morning. So I said it was fine if he crashed at my place. The kid wasn't there. With her grandparents..... in the country.

"All right," Leo agreed. He didn't want to hurry away either.

Then he took my hand and I was surprised into loving.

Nobody had ever held my hand as if it was *MY* hand. Leo made a journey of discovery through my hand, searching for clues of me. I lay there feeling it happen, shocked into a new awareness of touch.....it was Eden..... As if no other hand had ever come into his, he felt mine to know what kind of creature I was.....looking for an Alison. And I held my breath as a new lady full of wonderment was shaped under his hands and lips. It was as honest and personal as his singing, his lovemaking.

He touched me as if he had never relied on books or statues or movies or friends' advice when it came to handling a woman. Perhaps he had always been like this, or perhaps something in me set him free.....but he was more than a man.....he was a spirit of *LOVE*. I saw his features in a haze, but there was no identification in this realm of no words. All I saw was living protoplasm identical to my own. Emotion melting the face into ripples of sensation like wind on a field of wheat reflecting emotions I felt within myself. Leo was not a man or a woman or even human. He was the face of the life I felt inside me moving.....and the face of my response.....nothing mirrored there that I did not simultaneously feel.

What kind of creature can we be, that lies like a Siamese twin connected organically with a cord of flesh, breathing in unison, pulses beating so singly as if it has only one heart? The blood in our veins runs parallel courses. The breaths we inhale together, like dancers, share a steady togetherness that makes each second a growing love call. New nerves blossom with every move he makes. From the raw material of my body and my brain, Leo awakens a new woman capable of loving a man.

Never have I been as vulnerable to another human being, and never have I seen a man's face so vulnerable in return.....tangling our spirits in an innocence of brand new meeting, becoming aware of new worlds and space travel, holding each other in another dimension, secure in togetherness.

And there was passion also. All that love stored up and never wanted by another person emerged from each of us freely, stretching its wings for air like a butterfly breaking out of a cocoon. We grasped each other with the hunger of all the unsatisfied love we had ever felt, with the haste to feed of hungry babies, sad for our pasts and happy for our *NOW*. We dizzied each other with outbursts of intoxicated reeling. We'd both cling as our brains spun like tops, and then we'd get back into focus together and make each other smile and moan and call out.....

And as I felt his shuddering approach a climax, I gazed at his face and saw that passion had engorged his mouth so much that it was a blooming red rose in his face, lips swollen a deep crimson. I had never seen such a beautiful sight in all my life. Leo's face reflecting shock, his breath held in his lungs, transfixed, as the blood rose to the surface of his skin, a network of red lace. He was so hot to my touch, it seemed his inner fire would incinerate us both with a physical speech of passionate yearning..... I passed Mercury and headed straight into the sun, all senses shrieking, exploding into the solar system and becoming it, revolving on itself, an expanding and contracting universe. My flesh saw and felt it all.

When I surfaced to consciousness, Leo was the whole world to me at once and necessary to me. His touch was *LIFE*. He was the most beautiful experience I had ever had, and I could not let go.

When I asked had he found pleasure, a dumb question, but suddenly, I was urgent to hear him vouch for it, to make certain this hadn't been a one-sided dream, all Leo could say was, "Do anything you want with me."

I was so very unsure of myself. All I knew rationally was that he hadn't said '*YES*.'

"Everything I have is yours," he told me quietly. But I was still desperate because this one time with Leo, redefining all the man and woman relationships I'd ever had or heard about, was enough to make me helplessly, hopelessly addicted. I grasped him for dear life, tremulous with defenselessness.

It seemed to me suddenly that I'd lost myself and so needed reassurance. I kissed him and then lost his mouth and started to cry, tears streaming down my cheeks. Then emotions flooded the boundaries of my being and I became hysterical, sobbing next to him, truly a messy sight.

Leo, who had never experienced such behavior in a woman, was startled. "Are you all right?" he asked, frightened he had done something to cause pain, stroking and cuddling me.

I breathed in his concern, guiding my shaking as much as I could.....unseen music still reverberating in my body. I had not thought of Leo as a man until he took his clothes off. Had not imagined what he would be like as a lover.....had never imagined the chemistry that he should taste so right or smell so wonderful. Had never expected the first time with any man to reach this effortless soaring climax of the spirit. Nothing about him was alien to me.

And I was afraid to speak the word, *(LOVE)*, and frighten him away.....although from the very first touch of his hand, it could have been nothing less than that.

Coming back to a world filled with the realities of past experiences with men and stories of how men were likely to behave, I became terrified of using the word *'LOVE'*.....of losing Leo by saying too much or perhaps not enough. Because I had to keep him..... He was now necessary to going on living.

All my independence, of which I had been so proud dissolved along with my self-restraint. I asked the question I religiously never asked of a man.

"What are you thinking?"

"Just lying here, being with you.....not thinking," Leo answered.

* * * * *

I AM BACK AT WORK. I come to the office early, and I'm the first one here. This is the first time since the two weeks I have been on vacation I can meditate on what has happened. I will be asked.

I have a new lover, and I don't want to speak his name. It is a secret so fleeting and tenuous, sometimes even breathing spoils it. I breathe air as thin and rarified as the air in the highest mountain peaks covered with snow, suspended in that ethereal atmosphere.

I am fucked up beyond recognition, raw, but relaxed and very mellow, vowing to improve every one of my bad habits and be the ideal lover-woman.

Mirages float across the office wall, projection of Leo's waistline, as lean and slinky as a greyhound..... We have been living, more or less, on my waterbed for the last three days. Oh, it is so good just thinking about it, it hurts.

I write religious thank-you notes to God for existing and sending me Leo as proof and making sure I didn't die before having him happen. I define religion in little notes to myself as having faith and explain to myself why, if I continue to purify myself and behave well, Leo will stay with me.

I look at my past for claims on deserving him so I can be sure he won't be taken away. Also, I explain to myself how, no matter what happens, the experience will never be lost and it means everything I think it does.

The non-committed barrenness of the person I was is tragedy, I remind myself. Even the pain of not knowing how long it will go on is worth the caring. I write myself a long ecclesiastical monologue:

In order to feel alive, it is necessary to have been dead.

In order for happiness to be, grief was necessary.

In order to be alive, one must not fear change.

In order to completely respond, it was necessary to have been frigid.

In order to be good, one must be as good as one's ideal best friend.

Good. Now the ground rules are clear. I thank the fates that I have the understanding and the luck to know how to deal with the situation. All I have to do is *BE GOOD*.....and that's as close as I can come with a guarantee to myself that I will be allowed to keep Leo.

Jack looks at me and says, "You *PROMISED* me in our last discussion of the subject, (last month), that you'd wait at least two years before 'falling in love'!"

"What a cold-hearted little bitch I must have been then," I laugh at him. He shakes his head, the grouch. Who would want to postpone love?

I am sweating away while Jack fills me in on the dramas which have happened in my brief absence. One of our authors, a little lady friend of Jack's, has committed suicide by leaping from her terrace. He has been trying to explain why to himself ever since.

"She was a millionairess," he says incredulously. "Her rich and

220

ailing husband, of whom she was fond but not, (let's face it), madly in love with, was about to kick off with sickness."

I recall the petite brunette, always sharply dressed and nervously aware of her status. A rich man's wife? Paid for with interest apparently.

Jack is remembering her as a former friend, a former fuck. "Her life was full of riches ready for her to just reach out and pick. So why? Why?"

"Are you certain it was suicide and not an accident?" I ask him.

"Everybody is saying it was. She was too smart for an accident. She was a good kid."

I have a happy thought. When Babette is away this weekend, I will take Leo and write on his body in washable crayon: 'I love you. I love you. I love you.' I have visions of the color running into patterns and marbleized designs with our sweat.....being madly, gaily happy.

"Why did she do it?" said Jack. "She didn't even call me."

* * * * *

Leo hasn't called me since the weekend. But why should I want to be happy at the expense of somebody else's freedom? Let him call when it is appropriate for him.

I want a man with a bouquet of flowers in his hand, with his head circled by a rainbow or a halo, to make dreams with me and speak poetic words. Instead, *he* is the one who is *PARANOID* about being owned and going through all these freedom speeches I have been jamming these past few months.....whether seeing me means more than he wants it to mean. What an irony. I want to go out and blast off.

After the first day's work and no call from Leo, I tuck myself into bed, coasting down the slope of exhaustion, drained of all energy. My mind shuts its commentaries off, agreeing to a cease fire. No more explanations tonight. No more smart answers arguing their correctness to unspecified questions. Retirement is the only possible resort.

I turn the television on and all the lights off and watch Humphrey Bogart rescue Lauren Bacall. But she doesn't make it easy for him.

I love the morning and each second of life. I love the book I am writing, not knowing what it is. I love my lover. I love the Jefferson Airplane on Channel 13. I love my dentist. I love my scale. I love my cup of coffee.

The phone rings, and who do you think it is? *YOU GUESSED IT.* Old Tommy himself. At once, we are mad at each other. Where does he get his nerve, his unreality? He makes all kinds of impossible demands on me, crying and saying he will give up music forever, cut his hair, and die. That seven-foot *IDIOT!* I hate the thing in me that cares when he goes to these absurd lengths. He's using me.

On my lunch hour, I meet one over-friendly elevator man, a Latin Lothario, who offered to teach me how to ride a bicycle, a hot-dog man who pestered me until I moved, a man with two Bouvier des Flandres, and a girl who wanted her bag watched while she ran around Washington Square Park. Also, I met a Hungarian dressmaker, three young student types from a local school, and a caucus of gossiping old ladies. What does it all mean?

I had a strange dream about group therapy. I've never been to group therapy, but it sounds a little bit like a class in creative improvisation in a theater department. The room in the dream resembled the Alcoholics Anonymous meeting Elaine dragged me to when I said I wanted to find out what she did. There is a large placard of *DO*s and *DON'T*s in front of the room. Around the third from the top of the list was <u>*LOVE SEX*</u>. I really think about this, and it occurs to me that in my father's mind, all the screwing around I've been doing, (such as he knows or imagines), is bad. There has been a recording in my head that has been repeating: Sex is *BAD*. Sex is *BAD*.....all the while, and I never knew where that came from. (My father doesn't think *SEX* is bad. Only <u>me</u> doing it is somehow bad.) I've seldom allowed the voice to make up my mind for me, but this dream brings it to my attention, and I turn it off forever.

* * * * *

Oh Leo, I am getting stage fright. I am afraid you will not like me as much as you did before. I'm getting as fussy as an old woman of fifty with a blind date. I try to lose weight and wash my face repeatedly .....

* * * * *

POSTCARD FROM PETRA AND RUTHY (from their vacation in Maine):

> *HOW YA DOIN', TOOTS? This place is gorgeous.*
> *Will show pix.*
> *We're planning to do in enough lobsters and clams*
> *to kill a whale tonight.*
>
> *YAY!*
>
> *P & R*

Wait until they hear my latest news.

Chapter 17

I spent the Memorial Day weekend with Leo, my lover. Three days and three nights. And today I walked downstairs with him, used up and still wanting him. That's how crazy I was. We kissed each other with brief parting kisses, carefully not to start something again that would leave us feeling unfinished.

I am totally a wreck. Did he know it, this morning, as he arose from the bed and headed for the shower? My cunt is so raw from marathon sex, I can barely lubricate anymore and even noticed flecks of blood.

I think I could kill myself with unlimited lovemaking. Even after last night, my head dizzy, my stomach upset, and a slight fever from last week's virus, feeling as though a touch to my crotch would be like a sword thrust, and all my energy calling for a break, I still want him. Why am I so insatiable?

Leo has taken me over. "Take me..... Please take me."

"I am. I will....." he says very reasonably.

I laugh at myself shakily as I slide back into wordless orgasms. How much more is there of Leo that I haven't seen? My bed rocks me to sleep. I burrow into it happily.

* * * * *

Jack looks at me, the walking zombie. I am debilitated, and show it. I hear him muttering to himself under his breath: "They don't screw right!" Deadpan, I volunteer no information. Inside, I am filled with mirth.

"I'm going to lunch," says Jack as he goes out the door with Dale.

"Do come back sometime," I tease him.

Off he goes. I am very fond of Jack, but for the first time, he doesn't faze me. My desires no longer come from anything he has taught me: the vocabulary of positions, that talent show attitude..... that is all mechanics.

On my lunch hour, I run to the bank and the stationary store and then to Gristede's where I bought lots and lots of lettuce and tomatoes and a book full of <u>Playboy</u> jokes to make me laugh and restore a little perspective to my over-serious, gushy passions.

Friday night, I got home, having spent most of the afternoon drinking with Jack. I felt like cheering myself up, and I was scared in case Leo didn't show up. In which case, I wanted at least one enjoyable thing to happen in a day. I knew I'd be waiting in my house for Leo.....and if he didn't come.....

By the time I got home, I was tipsy. I washed and dried my hair and was organizing some papers when the doorbell rang. It was still pretty early. I was pleased.....and it was *HIM*.

He was grinning at me in a reserved fashion and holding out a bottle of wine. What a doll. Probably had to sing for an hour on the streets to get it.

I let loose on him, poor unfortunate fellow. I drenched him with words describing the whole week. I bounced around the house. I was a pain in the ass to myself and apologized for talking so much. Leo just sat with a patient and slightly bewildered smile and said, "It's all right."

He didn't kiss me. I wanted to kiss him. Just kiss him so I knew how matters stood between us, not immediately rape him or go into a clinch. Just kiss him "Hello." I was frustrated, wondering if he had stopped desiring me.

"Want to smoke some grass?"

"Sure," I said. So we smoked.

I started telling jokes. A rap ran out of my mouth at an unbelievable speed. I was super witty, unable to stop. I fluffed up entire airy constructions of works and deflated them. The grass didn't slow me down.

"Do you mind if I trip here?"

"You don't have to ask."

So he dropped his pill and sat cross -legged on the braided rug. It is mostly gray now; the colors are very faint, but old and pleasant.

Leo takes out his guitar and sings. I feel a faint strain in the way his throat works. Why? Is he worried about what I will think of him now that we have become lovers? Does he have to be perfect all the time for me? Why should he be tightening up on himself? Is he tired? The beauty of his voice is clouded by tension. I become self-conscious too. ('I love you, I love you.' Idiot. Delay. Delay. Keep those words down..... It isn't the time. But find some words, quick.)

I curl up, head in hand, near Leo's knee; his thigh sleek under his blue jeans.

"I have a question for you. Why didn't you kiss me? When you walked in the door, I mean."

Leo thinks for a while about all the implications behind the question. "Wouldn't that have meant making certain assumptions?"

"But you know I want you to make them. I don't mean we should have grabbed each other and headed straight for the bed. Though I want you. But why didn't you give me a kiss when you walked in the doo..... just a *HELLO* kiss?"

Leo gets lost from his nervousness trying to think of an answer. He isn't angry at me for asking this. It was the right question. It will help things out and make us all right with each other.

* * * * *

I am lying face to the ceiling, replaying my weekend, trying to make word poems of it all. Leo has a pliant strength. Was able to collect his emotional gear and just walk out of the house when *Sesame Street* was over. He kissed me goodbye, but lightly, putting on his other life a few seconds before leaving. I am still a little in his body, and feel his stride as he goes down the hall. Suddenly, I am tired.

Leo scrambles time for me. That is one symptom of his having visited. I live with memory for a week. It's not such bad company. The memories don't come in order but in layers, like a Napoleon pastry. I get a bit off the whole weekend, a layer of crust and a layer of cream, a layer of crust, and a layer of cream.

I fall asleep in front of the TV. I placidly accepted the fact I was dopey. Every quarter of an hour or so, I'd crack open the corner of an eyelid, give the tube a mindless stare, and say to myself, "Oh. I am asleep." I get sick and hate my own unhealthiness. Unhealthiness is definitely *NOT* sexy.

The phone rings. Somehow I already know who it is. Another case of Leo doing something just as I am thinking of him.

"Hello."

"Hello. This is *YOU*, isn't it?" His voice, a supple tenor, so comforting. Make him talk some more. Just soak in the sound of his voice.

"Have you been good to yourself this week? Where are you?"

"At a friend's house. I had nothing to do and figured I'd call."

I imagine Leo reclining near a telephone, legs encased in faded blue-gray denims, his hard thighs.....

"Can you come over? When? Tonight?"

"I guess so."

Everything is so tentative. I want to scream and shatter the delicacy of all this: "I have been loving you in my sick thoughts all week and worrying about being contagious. I have been worried, don't you understand? If I can get sick, how do I know you aren't lying somewhere in a feverish coma, unable to reach me?" (I suppress this litany.)

"I have some grass," Leo offers.

"Should I get us a bottle of wine?" Silence and deliberation at the other end of the phone.

"Well.....if you feel like it. It doesn't sound like such a bad idea."

(Wait till I get my hands on you!)

I buy the wine at the liquor store around the corner, choosing a bottle of Liebfraumilch. I race back to the apartment. Tonight I will open my door, and Leo will be here at seven. When Babette goes to sleep, I will kiss his mouth.

In the back office, the corner office, I watch the rain and hear rain music. I think of *LEO*. Half the time, I still don't call him by name, even to myself. I think *HIM*. Him, lovely waving hair, snaring my fingers. Him, Japanese eyebrows and twinkling amber eyes. Him, thighs under blue jeans. Sometimes I feel he is unpossessable. Half my acquaintances would sneer if I claimed to be in love. But this time it's different.

It is raining. How is Leo going to make his money? God, why

don't you shut the rain off? Who will listen to Leo sing on the streets? It's raining enough to fill his guitar up in minutes.

"Every time it rains, it rains pennies from heaven....." Oh, Billie Holiday, Billie Holiday...... I have a man......

* * * * *

After work, I have a drink with Jack. Leaning on the bar, Jack says, "OK, Alison. Tell me what it is you love."

"There isn't much I want to tell."

"I don't want to know what you do in bed." (As if I would tell him now.)

"Can I be really nasty?" I question.

"Go ahead." Jack shrugs. "We wouldn't be friends if you couldn't." And this third person, this man around the corner of the bar, is smiling at all of this and has somehow gotten into our conversation.

"Well.....one thing I love about *HIM* is that he listens to every word I want to tell him, without interrupting, until I'm finished." This is really devastating as Jack never lets you get even a sentence properly done. "It isn't just me. He listens to everybody that way....." A partial explanation to gently show Jack why I'm now out of circulation.

Phone rings. Old lover of mine whose wife and child are on vacation. New job, salary doubled, and wanting to celebrate. I tell him too that I'm out of circulation.

"What do you mean?"

"I'm only screwing one man now."

"Good God. Why?"

"I'm in love." Dear old buddy, you have enough heart to be happy for me, I hope. "It's like this....." I sing, "I'm in love. That's all there is to say." I'm beginning to sound dumb to myself. "You'd like him. He's great."

Before I parted from Jack, we stood outside the bar; Jack beamingly drunk, looking like a Blake-ian hero about to blossom prophesies right and left. He is the Rain King. The sky lets loose at his command. He props himself against a metal canopy brace and lets the rain water trickle onto his hand. Pulls me by the shoulder.

"Listen. Did you ever make love on a beach during a hurricane? Do you think you would like that?" His image sounds like a scene from a World War II movie. I picture a wild unruly sky.....but damn, I like comfort.

"Actually, I prefer the beach on a calm night in the Mediterranean, when you can see all the stars."

"You've been to the Mediterranean? Where?"

"Israel, Greece, Italy, France....." I start telling the countries.

"Don't mention Israel to me." Hastily, I think of something else to say and get him off politics. He is too happy now, and I can relax. He is tipsy as all hell, and I am wondering how to perambulate him to his subway station and whether it is my responsibility.

"You know, you're nutty, Jack."

"I like to make love on the beach in hurricanesh. It's magnifishent. The rain and the wind and the shky..... everything all going *BANG, BANG, BANG*, right along with you." I go into gales of laughter. Is there anyone else who would be standing in the rain conducting an aesthetic discourse on why hurricane weather is good for fucking out of doors? I think it unlikely.

I kissed Jack good night on his cheeks, on his nose. He wanted me to kiss him on the mouth. That I couldn't do. Oh, Leo, don't grudge Jack a few kisses of compassion. Someday you may be an aging man, feeling your health eroding beneath you, drunk and delicately balanced, and needing a sweet young thing to give you a goodnight kiss.....and tell you you're still a man.....still in the game...

Jack doesn't let himself dream dreams of love like ours. And he's lonely despite all his fun.....has to get drunk before he can go home...... Somewhere in this city Leo is coming to me through this rain. We'll stay indoors, listening to the rain fall.

* * * * *

In the morning, I brashly jump on the scale. It is full of rusty water. I drain it and wipe it off. Will it tell me the truth? I can't believe my eyes. That damn gadget is telling me I am *FAT*. But that fat? 135? How can it be? I am enraged with myself and start cursing. Fat Bitch!!! Ten pounds of sheer torpidity.....useless fat. How can you be fat and dare to be in love? Get that fat off, woman! How can you love me, Leo, with this extra ten pounds? *CRASH DIET* again. This calls for drastic action.

Last night at the bar, Jack says to me, "You won't get mad if I tell you something?" I already know what it is. That man is nothing if not candid.

"Go ahead. Say anything you want."

"You've gained weight!" *(This is news?)*

"I know."

"When I first hired you, I mean, it was a treat to see your ass go tripping down a flight of stairs, but now...."

"I know, I know...... Instead of a little trippy-ass secretary, you've got a big, draggy-ass secretary."

He tries to make gallant amends. "It's just a visual thing, understand? I'm not saying a big ass might not feel good, all things

231

depending." He is trying to make me feel better, exploring this possibility. "It might feel pretty good. But just somehow, it doesn't look....."

Man, don't you tell me about my ass. The big legs and ass man of the office, Danny, has already run it down for me. ("I *LIKE* zaftig women.")

Visions of an infinitely expanding ass, rotundity. Ugh! Fat..... white layers of fat.....such as pork lard on sale in the grocery, heavy dead.....that is what is lining my hips under the skin, soft, gushy, oily, fishy.....

Leo, my bed is empty without you there. I want to love you. How will I keep your love if I get into a state where I can't even love *myself*?

* * * * *

WHAT IS LOVE?

(I look it up in *Websters*.)

love (luv), n. (*M.E.* love, love; *AD* fufu; akin to *OHG.* luba & more remotely *G.* live; *IE*, base 'leubh'—-to be fond of; of. *LIBIDO, LIBIDINOUS, LIEF, LUST*) *(Good grief.)*

1. strong affection for or attachment or devotion to a person or persons. *(Right.)*

2. a strong liking for or interest in something. *(What have I been telling you?)*

3. a strong, usually passionate, affection for a person of the opposite sex. *(Leo, I have a strong but not unusual passionate affection.)*

4. the person who is the object of such an affection; sweetheart, lover. *(Far out!)*

5. sexual passion or its gratification. *(Aha. Fucking!)*

6. *(L)* a) Cupid, or Eros, as the God of Love. - b) *(Rare)* Venus

7. par. <u>play for love</u> i.e., play for nothing, in tennis, a score of zero. *(Like tonight, but what the hell.....)*

8. in theology a) God's benevolent concern for mankind. *(I hope he'll show some.)* b) man's devout attachment to God. *(Where is it?)* c) the feeling of benevolence and brotherhood that people should have for each other. *(should, could..... I wish they did.)*

v.f. *(LOVED* (luvd) *LOVING)* 1. to feel love for. *(Leo)* 2. to show love for by embracing, fondling, kissing, etc. *(Leo)*—*(note Webster's delicacy: <u>etc.</u>)* 3. to take delight in, take pleasure in, *(as Leo takes pleasure in me),* as she <u>loves</u> good music. *(I do.)*

v.i. to feel the emotion of love; be in love, *(Good advice!),* fall in love, to begin to love; feel a strong, usually passionate affection,. *(It's driving me crazy!)* For love, as a favor, or for pleasure, without payment for the love of, *(Free love, YAY.),* for the sake of; with loving regard for, in love, feeling love, enamored, *(Whew.........Whoooo),* make love, to woo, embrace, kiss, etc., *(('<u>etc.</u>!!!'!!'),* as lovers do. *(I wish it was Friday!)* no love lost between, no liking or affection existing between. *(I should have thought it was going to advise not to waste any.....)*

I should use the dictionary more often. It's hotter than *Playboy. Webster's* makes it all seem so easy, so simple to define. Anyway, according to the authorities on the English language, love is supposed to mean all those things.

Leo, will I really see you on Friday? I need a hand to hold between now and Friday across the two day span. I've cheated myself, not asking you enough questions to feel I know who you are. How can I have permitted you to leave out so many important details? You've retreated to a life I can only guess at. Why am I not clairvoyant?

Why are you different from other men? Why do I want you to stay when we have finished making love? Why do I like to see you sleep? Generally, I detest men who sleep. They should do it elsewhere, not in my house. Your sleep is not an interference. But why? You sleep! Other people sleep. Why do I like to watch you eat? It makes me want to laugh.....and when I do, you look at me as if to say: "Ohhhhh.....*UNFAIR!*" But I'm not laughing at you.

Jack is now taking me to Chinese restaurants and ordering me vegetables.....low calorie food. We didn't drink. Jack is trying to be 'on the wagon.' He said he thought the key to my behavior was that I enjoy the falling in love but not the loving. Where does he get his ideas? He couldn't be more wrong.

Leo has stayed away all week. Probably right. I should know how to handle it and work also. Worrying about this could kill me with fatigue. I am blue, frantic blue, but slow melancholy blue, full of unanswered questions.

Petra calls to say, "I'm home and teaching part of a German course." Her natural competence is making itself felt very rapidly.

I explain how depressed I am.....the not knowing what is going to happen. She said she understood, and what I described reminded her of the intense affair she had with Steve.

"You are vulnerable. That's what it is. But that's not bad. You wouldn't have gotten so vulnerable if you weren't sure he wouldn't hurt you. It is when you are vulnerable that you are open...... Learn and grow."

Friday afternoon. What's the matter? I feel as if I've taken a million pills of speed. Nothing has happened, except I've been to the dentist. He has cleaned my teeth and they are gleaming like a shark. *(GNASH!)* My mouth is better than a commercial for the right toothpaste, (the Kiss- and-Tell kind).

It's Friday. I am berserk with joy. I can take on tigers and revolutions, parades and intellectual chitchat, hikes through NY streets; rain, thunder, and hurricanes won't phase me. I could somersault myself to Heaven. I want everything. I want Leo.

My cunt is a radioactive field, a sonar device..... I feel time with Leo getting closer and closer. My heart is a light bulb, and the switch has turned on, and Leo is coming.....with his prick like a diamond.... and I'll drink the light from him like a camel, taking off for a long caravan, to live on for the rest of my life.

I'm waiting for five o'clock so I can leave the office and prepare. The rest of the staff is waiting also, trading quips, feeling themselves to be enormously witty.....

"Why don't we have the nerve to just leave?"

I'm the world's deepest well. I'm the Grand Canyon of Colorado. I'm the burning bush on the Sacred Mountain. I'm a lake full of blue lotuses. I'm the lost continent of Atlantis, rising again.

"I'm healthy." I smile gleefully at Leo when he appears as I'm drying my hair. I was so glad to be clean when he arrived. This time he kissed me at the door, which helped a lot. But it still seemed to take time before we reached the point where we left off last time.

We're off to the movies and home, by-passing the supermarket to equip ourselves with Mexican TV dinners and wine. Leo, on the street, promising me to sing ten songs in place of the one I asked for. Knowing when I need an arm around my shoulders.

Leo, with a blissful expression, splayed across the waterbed like a tripped-out antelope, all graceful loose limbs. I stroke his legs. From the hip down he is very furry, blondish hairs that let the light shine through them I would know these legs anywhere. Do his legs feel how much I enjoy them? He lies there willing to be handled, eyeing me from behind his glasses.

And between his thighs, his prick is a growing thing, stiffening with pleasure. I take him in my mouth trying to make more pleasure, filling my throat..... Until I need him in my body, and he enters. We are both 'oh-ing' and he says he wants to stay in me forever, and I love him. We come and start laughing at ourselves for no reason and lie there, drunk with coming.

Saturday morning, I inform Leo that the next time he trips, I want to trip with him. He is hesitant, knowing my history of low physical tolerance of acid.....but understanding why I want this. He also knew where to get pure *LSD*, which, in our calculations, minimized the risk considerably as it wouldn't contain either speed or strychnine.

I call Petra on the phone. I wanted to check it out with her, my medical adviser. She was sleeping but when she understood what I was asking, said, "I think, in view of the way you take acid, it's a *VERY* bad idea." I promised to take a low dose. "Aren't you the lady who said she was never going to touch the stuff again?"

"True," I responded, "but aren't you the lady who said she was staying away from that stuff and then took a trip in the country? So it seems that under certain circumstances, it is all right to trip."

"Well," she contemplated, "I guess you *can* handle it now, having gotten yourself so much more together. So if you're going to do it, do it. Call me if you need help or rescue."

"I don't know why I should," I said. I can't reject the trip as a means of getting closer to Leo, even if it means risking my life. I trust his love will somehow pull me out of whatever the trip may bring.

Leo and I walk hand in hand over to Cruisan's. Cruisan's house is dark, and we nearly stumble over Tommy who is asleep in the hall on a couch that takes up most of the passageway. But then we get into the tiny red room with the table and the stereo, and there is Cruisan, bearded, *(sparsely),* and long haired, *(thin stringy long hair),* and a happy smile on his face, having just played and won a game of chess with Sidney.

"How are you doing, Cruisan?"

"I get high, and then I get strung out, and then I get higher and more stoned and then more strung out, and then I get even higher, and this goes on for days.....and finally, I fade away, and I sleep for a few days......"

Leo asks, "Do you know of, or have, any acid on hand that you're willing to part with?"

Cruisan goes into a rap about the virtues of chemically pure 'Clear Light.' It is expensive. $5.00 a hit. But worth it not to mess around with bad stuff, so we made a deal.

On the way home, we sat for a while on a bench in Washington Square Park, taking in the trees, the fountain, the people, and the *'Fuzz.'* The Jesus-Freaks set up to the right of the arch with a truck complete with bank and speaker system. They started to play "Jesus, Son of God, can set you free—eee--eee." Then all the musicians testified over the mike about how Jesus really loves you and you should find God in your hearts.

"Look at this world without Him. It's a mess. He didn't make it this way. People have made it this way." They were all extremely exalted, having found God and having been saved from themselves, and..... very sectarian. No other way to God, except through his son, and never in the history of the world has there been a man who was so *PERFECT*, and everything he said was TRUE, and everything he said was *PERFECT*.

"He claimed to be God, so either he was or he was a liar. Give it a chance. Look in your hearts and see if you can't find him..... *Hallelujah*. John come up here and praise the Lord for the people.....,"

Slowly down the avenue, in a walking hug, we discuss it all.

"It's all true," Leo starts recounting how a Jesus-Freak interrupts a Yoga disciple who has just invited him to hear a Guru speak on meditation. "Those people can't help you find it. Only Jesus." We both grumble words about how exclusivity is shitty.

"Still," insists Leo, "it's all true."

"What am I going to do with you? Grrrrr....... You're so open to *EVERYTHING*....." Leo laughs. He knows perfectly well what I shall do with him. I shall love him.

I make us grilled cheese sandwiches for snack and started Leo reading my beginnings of a book, which he got interested in. I nervously went off and puttered in the kitchen and finally fled to my typewriter so I wouldn't have to watch Leo read. I wanted the words to stand or fall without me.

When he had read all he could, he came and put his arms around me. "You have been through a lot of interesting experiences."

"Do you still love me?" and he said he did, and I hid my face in his shoulder.

"Do you want to go on that trip now?" We hunted for the acid and couldn't find it. I knew we couldn't have lost it, so we combed the house and discovered it in with my diet pills, (smart lady), and Leo sliced the pill with a razor-blade and took half. I took a sixth.

We went into the other room and lit candles. Leo got his guitar, and I got my notebook. Wrote down:

Item #1: Permitting one's self to take acid is as important as taking it. (Allowing myself to plumb my feelings as they would be without the censorship of my conscious mind is a risk. And I'm glad I am daring to do it.) Then I looked at Leo and had another thought, so I wrote it down.

Item #2: What do I see? Only the man I love playing his guitar. Is that all there is? That is all there is.

With those words, I felt the acid coming on, and thought: 'Uh-oh, it's *SPIRITUAL* acid.' I heard Leo playing his guitar, playing his music with an uninhibited passion and also a control I had never heard from him before. The acid was giving him a preview of the singer he was to become, and if he could do this with acid, someday he would get there without it.....and the music reached out for me like a soul..... and the notes stirred in all my nerves.

I got myself a blanket and a pillow for my head, and lay down near Leo, shaking and hoping I wouldn't have convulsions. There were Indian designs all over the frets of the guitar and Leo's face, and I mention this to him. "Perhaps it's the reflection of my guitar strap," he said. Green and blue lights were flashing all over Leo, and I came just from looking at him, sensing the high speed of his energy, and the wax in my ears.....melted.....

* * * * *

IN THE HEART OF THE GREAT SPHINX

Leo and I are buried alive, dying of unanswered riddles. Twenty-two needles, a chaplet of wires, have pinned my brain in place, and the scientists tap my head for neon words. Electricity rains on those convoluted gray furrows. Another miracle of modern technology: synapse by automation, the computed harvesting of human ideas. I have been electrified.

The moon takes its last curtain call in a sky of royal purple. It hangs over me like a lamp over an operating table, the night-eye of the sky cyclops. My blood is sweet nectar. I am stung many times. The parasites that feed on me grimace. I contribute my red heart into the collection plate. My blue eyes yield their colors to a cloudless sky. Soon I will be only a mound of sand. Children will make me into pies and build castles out of me.

The Angel of Death whistles at me as I cross the river of concrete. I am drowning in the relentless street. The people look at me through glass eyes. Polluted with helplessness and the defeat of possibility, we lie between the pages of books on *UTOPIA* like flowers pressed and dried, preserved in a family Bible. Dead flowers merged with the name of our ancestors, with our membership cards and our birth certificates, withered, faded, crumbled roses......

Atlantis, a hungry city, waits for its population. Its towers are scythes. Its streets are graves. Its coliseums are omnivorous, saluting the list of names who have perished for the sport of soundless spectators lusting for violence. The Con Edison men drill endless holes in the metropolis for imitation lights that will make money. Light must be paid for.....imitation lights. The garbage trucks digest the filth of the city, grinding away. The Grand Coulee Dam is a mammoth freezer of TV dinners. The farms of America are fields of tin cans with brand names on their labels. The clouds shower us with radioactive rain. The Rush Hour subway shrieks under the ground, stuffed with human beings, docile willing cattle. There are no jobs left anymore for our*SELVES*. We are bodies with unnecessary minds, hauled to and fro.

This toy factory produces dolls, one after another. All alike. They come with strollers, tea sets, appliances, doll houses, and call to their mothers in identical metallic voices: *"Mommy! I want a bottle. Change my diaper! I love you."*

Fresh dreams of children modeled into factory plastic simulated stereotyped cardboard surrogates for love. Even monkeys could detect a conspiracy of malnutrition.

It is the Age of Aquarius, we are told. Aquaman leads the human school of fish to the sterile alcohol of the Mermaid Cafe. The laurel wreaths for our champions have turned into greenbacks paid to cabbage heads. Canned laughter and tears are channeled into our mini-minded brains. And America's ears listen only to the machine hearted magnified voices of the owners of the microphones and the electricity. It is election time, and they turn up the volume, telling us we are represented, should pay our taxes, and this is *JUSTICE*. We live in triplicate. Who represents us? Liars, blackmailers, cheats, thieves, false-faith-healers, phony witch doctors, slave traders, quislings, mercenaries, scientific brains milked like herds of contented cows while their milk will raise a generation of nuclear babies. They are branded U.S. and so is the moon, and as we look up, there is our fate waiting.....more of the same.

America, land of the free, are you conscious of necessity? America, land of the flag of my childhood, you're going backward. This is not *Renaissance*. It is *Denaissance*.....and you give us no alternatives. We must drop out. From high school and college, from your armies, from your sweepstakes, from your competitions, from your country clubs.....from your political parties, from your fraternities and sororities, from all your games, from your factories. We are *BURNING*: Not only draft cards but credit cards and membership cards in your clubs......not just flags. We burn our identification, and some of us have even burned our bodies to dissociate..... We need *Strawberry Fields.....Wild Strawberries.....*

I don't want to take a test to have our relationship approved, Leo. I don't think a stranger with a badge reciting words over us can help us. I don't want to be told by the law how I must *BE* to you, only by my heart. God invented hearts, and Man invented *CONTRACTS*.

Swear me to tell the truth. I am Earthborn of the family *Homo Sapiens*, and I know nothing. My ancestors were salamanders and dinosaurs, and their ancestors were amoebas.....dividing perpetually.....and it is still happening all around us. Down with the cost of living. We don't need a Space Program. We need an Earth Program to make this world a home for mankind instead of a Welfare's Island. Across the billboards and the office buildings, and the subway cars, I see graffiti, the people's epic novel of our time: John was here and Mary was here and Suzy was here and Rex was here.....scrawled messages.....by the people, for the people, of the people, a chronicle of lives expelling souls in spray paint protesting the walls......

I pour the primal screams of my unborn children into alabaster vases, into the craters of the moon; a treasure of might-have-beens, gambled away by strangers in games of chance. I want to be a citizen of a land with no name, with no nationalities, where only 'people' live, without labels, without partitions, without senseless brutalities.

My Orpheus, Leo, sing me to life. A song has no body. A song is only a soul.....stop the twilight with your voice. Sing a siren song to the mercenaries and to the generals. Let's make a world for children instead of out of them..... The brain-readers stop the current. I volunteer for relocation to a better world. The EEG reads normal..... *OH.*

* * * * *

My head is a furnace, and I am a glowing charcoal, but I am coming back to a clear picture of Leo, and I think I have been saying something because he looks worried. He puts his guitar down and says, "Shall we talk now?" and I say, "Yes. But I have to stay lying down."

I keep getting lost in his nearness and trying to hang on to the sight of him to keep from drifting away. His hands shield me lovingly as if I were a child. I know that if he made love to me, I would die of it. Yet I cannot say 'No' to him.

He seems to sense that too. His heart racing with acid and strained, he held me to his chest. "Let's just be still for a while," and then, "I'm not sure what happened."

I think I said "I love you," many times, in case I did not survive. I wanted Leo to keep that.

"You're getting very far away from me." I saw his face from five hundred miles away. "The rushes are so heavy."

"Contain yourself, Alison....." Leo whispers gently, cradling me at the brink of his own trip. "You'll be all right."

"If you tell me I will, then I will. But I'm close to dying."

"But you *won't* die."

We decide the trip was a test and that if we could make it through the trip then we would make it. So we rose and walked about in the room as if it were a street, letting our brains settle. Leo left me to go to the bathroom and I found myself dancing alone.

"See," I told myself, "when you thought all you could do was lie on the floor and fight for survival, that was all you could do. And now you think you can dance, and you *CAN* dance."

Leo came back.

"Look, Leo. I'm dancing." And then I stopped, feeling silly, and asked him to play music again because I thought I could listen better.

Leo sat in one of the green chairs, soft dull green corduroy armchair, still with an aura of flashing aqua lights, and his hair streamed like rain onto his shoulders, waving softly at the ends, and his chest was naked, and he started to play. And I take my notebook and write:

"Premise #1: When you lose your mind, you lose your senses as well."

And I glance up at Leo and see he is playing for himself now, searching the guitar for logic, exploring the interconnection of chords and melodies, trying to master the logic of music, not playing any song. And I listen to him growing himself, his intuitive choice-making as he picks out chords. The way he is using acid as a fuel for creativity is more beautiful to me with each new note.

By this time, we were both on top of our trips and so were able to embrace each other, and my unspoken insecurities were gone, and we blended into each other on the bed. I was a deep lake and Leo a blue lotus floating on the surface with a long trailing stem sinking deep into me, and then we were as one person answering each other's desire. I listened to his pleasure.

"I love the way you receive me," he told my ear, and I nipped him on his ear lobe and his neck and his shoulders and slid my hands over his back painting pleasure with my fingertips into his skin. He held me tightly, and we came in a dawn sunburst.

Later I went into the kitchen for juice and found myself naked, bare feet feeling the floor turn to sand. And I was as happy as when I had been a small child naked on the beach and stood there innocent and released, looking at Leo sitting up in the middle of the bed, smoking a cigarette. And I brought him juice and sat next to him wrapped in a blanket, telling him all memories of happy times and finally fading out to him making more music.

I found myself half awake, drowsy, and apologizing for not being able to stay conscious, and Leo kissed me goodnight many times, holding a cigarette to my lips because I had no strength to do it myself. So I curled up next to him and drifted off into a tunnel, speeding like a car into an evening sky filled with wild hawks flying circles. I woke up to find Leo exhausted and ready to go to sleep. I kissed him and held him and let him sleep and woke up again.....at noon.

Finding Leo sleeping peacefully and soundlessly, I tiptoed into the shower and then went to my typewriter and stayed there until I heard a cough that told me Leo was awake. I ran to him, shedding my dress and diving into the bed.

"How long have you been awake? -- Good morning."

"Five minutes. -- Good morning."

"Why didn't you call me?"

"I heard you in there typing and didn't want to stop your thoughts."

We made love again, and talked and made love, and soon it was five-thirty, and Babette was dropped off by Dave, and all our time alone was gone. Leo made eggs, and I made the bed, and we ate and parted. I read Babette a story and put her to bed, and then went to bed myself trying not to miss Leo, and when I woke up, it was Monday and time for work.

* * * * *

The scale says 129? I haven't been starving. From where this extreme loss of weight? I remember asking Leo why he hadn't done any exercises in the morning. "I don't need to," he laughed at me. "I've done enough exercises as it is." Oh *LOVE*. It is so *GOOD* for the health.

I remember telling Leo I want to be his woman, and he looked at me sadly. "How easy it is to lose yourself."

"I don't know who the people are who made you so afraid of losing yourself, but I'm not like them."

He examines my face. I am self-conscious but leave my face to be looked at, hoping he will see something that will give him confidence in me.

"No.....you are not like them."

I search for words to tell him what it is I want of us, knowing I will be exposing myself while I am doing all this, and Leo says with a defenseless look that tears my heart to pieces, "I am very vulnerable now."

"I am very vulnerable too. Haven't you seen this?" I beg him to share his doubts, to trust me enough to do that before he flees, to explain to me how he thinks because I don't always know.

"Always tell me what you're thinking," Leo said..... You are opening for me like a flower in slow motion. Your nostrils contract while you breathe in, and your eyes dilate very widely, and I see red sparks on your eyelashes and your mustache and the deep gold of your eyes..... How will I ever get my work done?

Chapter 18

All my friends are coming back from California, hitch-hiking: Pierre and Maryann, Howie and John..... Jack is making me do a drawing for a book cover to save Academia Books money.....and I work it and rework it.....and there is filing and telephones, typing business letters..... and at home, there is cleaning and laundry and all the ordinary chores. I am worried that Leo, jealous of his freedom, will run away.....not seeing that I don't want to chain him and I have to work.....

* * * * *

Dear Alison,

I am writing this letter saying goodbye to our past relationship, except for memories of an experience I'll never forget. And saying hello to new experiences with you.

I have seen many of your faces, and I think I have seen the face of love and revelation within you.

I really have no fear of the future and no reason to worry about what will become of us. We will grow together, and when I go down, I'll always come back up.

I think my feeling of fear comes from thinking that I will have to leave you some time and will never see you again. And I don't want to let you go.

Maybe I torture myself with an illusion of my inability to love so I can love. There is always a question of love. I don't doubt that you love me, but I doubt the love within myself because that has become a way of life.

I am fascinated by the way you are growing. I think you are extraordinary. I need you to help me be a whole being. I don't have many true friends and have never had a relationship with as much emotion and movement as I have with you. We should try to do everything we can for each other. I don't want you to deny yourself to please me.

Love can only be triumphant when we are equal and in unity. I don't want to love you by glorifying your being to dullness because then you would be something you are not really.....I'll never hurt you.....

LEO

***

Dear Leo,

I begin by saying I love you. Your troubled look frightens me, because we can't bear to hurt each other, and so we leave questions unspoken and unanswered. I am outside your gates, begging to be let in.

I cannot wish to trim your wings. I want you to fly. It seems a part of my nature to love you. You are God to me, not a frozen idol or a fixed image in time. You are the unfolding of my life, part of my chase for perfection. You are my home and my mirror and my wishes..... I want to live as intensely as I can, as long as I can feel. I want the best.....and you are that for me. I want permission to love you as much as I can without your being afraid of it.....wanting you to love me as much as you can.....

ALISON

I love / you love.

Meet me in the middle of your dream, sometime during the week. Love yourself till then.

LEO GLASS

I love you. Eat breakfast. Have a good day. See me when you want to see me.

More love.

A. G.

* * * * *

I call up Petra, and she tells me that Ruthy doesn't even want to see me anymore, and she will tell me about this when she comes to visit me. I feel death inside me, closed doors. Ruthy hasn't even bothered to discuss it with me, whatever it is I've done this time. Is it Leo? Leo won't even talk to Ruthy or Petra and doesn't explain why.

They came in one night, and all he did was sit wordlessly on the floor, stubbornly silent, not even returning their hellos. He idly picked isolated chords on his guitar, not even playing, limping music filling the space for himself as if to obliterate my visiting friends from his awareness.

Ruthy and Petra have passed judgement.....I can see it. They don't quite understand what I can see in someone who hasn't been to college. They ignore Leo's presence after a half-hearted attempt at cordiality. Oh, why can't my friends all get along and love each other? Now Ruthy has dropped me..... again.

* * * * *

Alison,

I don't know if I will see you tonight. I want to get in touch with

248

someone who owes me money.....will call and let you know what's what.

Always, L. G.

"Leo, I need you. Please come over....."

I lie in candlelight and Leo walks in in a neat yellow shirt with a letter he wrote for me, and I feel him to make sure he is not just a memory, and he wants to know, "Is there such a thing as love?"

"I'll show you." Oh, how can I get that idea across the confusion.

"I love you, Leo. I love you."

"Oh. I thought maybe you just had a stupid crush on me or something....."

"Of course not. I mean, well.....yes, a very heavy crush....." We laugh, cutting through some of the fears. "I'm paranoid about your loving me," I disclose. "It isn't *you.* I've been conditioned not to expect men to really love me. So when you notice yourself loving me, please tell me.....if you see me looking confused."

Spaced out. "*OK.* I love you. Now."

"But I don't look confused now, do I?"

* * * * *

Babette marches in on us, pale in the darkness of the candlelit room, finding Leo and myself tangled up naked. Myself saying, "Hello, darling. I think you should go back to bed." She did quite happily. And it seemed to me that there was nothing in our loving that could disturb even a child. No violence. No frustrated vibrations. No atmosphere of hostility. Even a child seeing us would have to conclude we were hugging or dancing, not fighting.....no sign that we are experiencing anything else than pleasure.....

Freudian theory posits that the sight of parents in coitus is a primal trauma for children. The sinful connotations even the psychologist dumps on sex, how it is really bad for children and humans..... I know that if I had chased Babette out screaming and punished her, then it would be a trauma, and she would feel excluded, and *THAT* would be a crime against her development.....

I see a brand new Leo with a sinless face, guiltless as a saint after a visitation, stretching and purring, smoothing his mustache and humming.....

I am afraid. What is this world going to do to us? How are we going to be able to keep what we have? I have awful premonitions.

Dave takes Babette away for the weekend. Leo and I lie on the bed wondering what to do with all the time. We decide on taking diet pills and going out to the Village. Leo sings in the street, on the front steps of the Hotel Earl. People throw money at him. One dude gives us a five dollar bill and some I Ching coins, "to throw the I Ching" should there ever be the need. I finger the old Chinese coins, looking at the inscriptions. Leo gives them to me as a gift to remember the evening.

It is too early to go to Gurdy's Folk City, so we head for Cruisan's house, stopping in front of a bakery.....and there we find a birthday cake. We decide that Cruisan should have a birthday and buy him the cake and walk in singing..... "Happy Birthday, dear Cruisan....." Who should be there but Tommy, plugged into Donnie's Gibson guitar, making amplified traffic noises.

Cruisan, excited about his cake, slices it and gobbles it up. Then he bustles around with wires and pickups so a jam session can happen. Tommy has a tantrum. He wants Donnie to leave with him. He's become so unreasonable. Donnie is speeding and so are we. Leo jams with him until midnight because we have decided Gurdy's is too expensive.

We take the red bus for Chinatown, and Leo tries out chopsticks.

We order Hon Shu Chicken and Shrimps in Black Bean Sauce. Leo tells me over the food how it was in the army, how his roommate went crazy in Germany and how he was put in the stockade. Leo tries to explain about Germany and hash-hells and prostitutes and driving an ambulance, about getting drunk and smashing chairs, about telling the army he wants out.

There is a fog in the streets so dense it is like walking in a private cloud. We kiss under the trees of Washington Square.....looking at the arch looming out of the mist, watching the frisbee players who are up late, listening to some smashed musicians bawling the blues to bongo drums and guitars not exactly in tune. Screams of "Help! Help!" cut through the fog. No one can see anything. And I am bleeding and need a shower.

We walk home. I shower, and Leo reads poetry. I have bummers, wondering if I am having a spontaneous miscarriage or a hemorrhage or what is with me, because the bleeding won't shut off.....and I don't want not to feel well. Here is Leo next to me, and he looks fine. I decide to just lie down, and my eyes begin leaking silent tears, and I am low and lost and far away. Leo kisses me and brings me chocolate ice cream to eat in bed, saying, "I love you."

* * * * *

8:30 a.m Sunday morning. The doorbell rings. Leo is sighing gently in his sleep. It is Tommy.

"We're still asleep." I hear retreating footsteps down the hall. No words from him.

10:00 a.m. The phone rings, and I have been trying to get back to sleep. It is Tommy.

"But we are still sleeping!" He sounds mad.

"Still?"

"Yes. And I'd really like to get back to sleep."

251

"Catch you." And he hangs up.

I go back to bed crying, "Oh, Leo. I want to be asleep, and I can't." Leo arranges the blanket around me and draws me close and I soak up his sleepiness.

When I wake, he has been watching me and tells me he is going to get a job as a cab driver because he needs a new guitar and also so that we can live together soon. I ask if he is sure?

"I don't want you to be pressured because of me..... I don't want to hang you up." Leo says I will never hang him up because if I do, he will tell me, and I will stop.

"What did you think of me, that first night, when I invited you over to my place?" I tell him now how hard it had been to get the words out.

Leo says that because he was tripping, I was completely transparent. He thought it was a really groovy thing because he would never have been able to come over on his own. He tells me that he always thought I was beautiful and had a beautiful head. That he had been dreaming about me for several weeks before, wondering would we ever? I love his eyes.

* * * * *

Monday morning Babette comes over to the bed to stare at a sleeping Leo curled up in a heap of blankets.

"It's Leo. Why is he here?"

"Because Mommy wants him here."

"I wish he would stay here always, Mommy."

I whisk her off to the day care center. Walk into the house during the lunch hour with two shopping bags full of groceries to find Leo gone. The bed made neatly. The kitchen counter and sink clear of dishes. Blankets folded professionally on a chair. There is something to be said for boot camp. Did he leave a note? I scan the house. Found it!

Thanks for letting me sleep..... Later, L.

I am so tired I am collapsing like a telescope, like a tripod with adjustable legs.

Leo picks me up at the job to go to a concert. Benny, who I guess got a glimpse of Leo, comes to my desk the next day and advises me earnestly and sincerely that this is *THE* ugliest young man he has ever laid eyes on in his life, and certainly at least five years my junior. I am shocked. I had to bend my mind out of its usual patterns to try and figure out what Benny was saying. Why the hell does he think it is his business to let me in on this observation of his? I don't tell him what his wife looks like.

I always see Leo as devastatingly beautiful and fantasize women chasing him on the street, and Benny says he is ugly. The ugliest. *'Loathsome!'* How can this be?

I try to look at my image of Leo with Benny's eyes to see what he finds 'repulsive.' Thick glasses? Nasty complexion? Doesn't like long hair? Maybe he thinks Leo should wear a suit?

All I feel is the first touch of Leo's hand, not taking me for granted, not treating me as if I were a doll, trying to find *me.*

* * * * *

My head is blasted into incapacity by pain. These past few weeks it has been growing..... and the bleeding hasn't stopped, and so when Leo hasn't been around, I have been lying in bed with attacks of pain, wondering if I have to see a doctor or what? Tonight, leveled by excruciating cramps and twists and shortness of breath, there is no position in which I can be comfortable. Ruthy calls to make up and hears something is wrong in my voice.

"Wait there. I'll be right over," she tells me. Runs all over the Bronx, rounding up some Darvon to kill the pain. And just when I feel ready to faint, there are Ruthy and Petra with Darvon, which I immediately swallowed. "Oh, Ruthy, you're here....." and I passed out. I wake to Leo, reading a note from R & P saying they had gone home having done all they could. They have set up a doctor's appointment for me on the morrow. I should not be a fool and go.

Leo is miserable, not knowing how to take care of me and feeling helpless and unable..... no job and no money.

* * * * *

After a brief internal exam, the doctor decides it is either gastroenteritis or a spastic colon and gives me a prescription for pills. As soon as I take them, I start hemorrhaging very heavily with severe cramps, expelling large clumps of bloody jelly the size of half fists.....and becoming very pale from loss of blood.

"Oh God. Alison, what am I going to do if you get really sick?" cries Leo. "Oh, please don't have cancer..... Please don't die and leave me." We cry together like frightened children..... feeling unprotected from fate.....waiting for the doctor to return our calls and tell us what to do.

When we locate the doctor, he says his diagnosis is obviously wrong and I should stop taking the pills, all pills, including birth control pills.....and I want Leo more than I ever have, in spite of the bleeding and the pain, because I may die and I want to die in his arms..... What are we to do?

And so Leo moves in to care for me. As I convalesce slowly, he starts hunting for a real job. We provide ourselves with prophylactics against the irrationality of desire.....and my heart is telling me this is the last love my life will have, the last man.....no more changes.

* * * * *

Either my alarm clock is unreliable or I turned it off in my sleep, because when I wake up, I had only a half hour to get to work. I had to start the day in a hurry, clenching my teeth; rushing Babette through her breakfast; berating her, the clock and myself, apologizing for my loss of temper; and getting mad all over again, mostly at myself.

I look into the future and groan because there just isn't enough money....and how are we going to afford our lives? Leo gets more drained than I do from lovemaking these days. I have to restrain myself from making demands or feeling insecure. I know Leo goes out of his way to do things just for me. He's job-hunting really hard and coming home angry and tired. First, he thinks he has found a job, maybe.....and then they don't call him back. He's been so gloomy, he doesn't have the energy to play or sing. And he is catching a cold. Most of our spare time is spent recuperating, lying in bed, dozing, and reading.

I am methodically reading all of Hermann Hesse.....and Leo is reading Krishnamurti and copying into a notebook, (with a dictionary by his side) all the words that puzzle him. He is determined to educate himself, college or no college.

Winter is coming. And prices are rising. I feel our life is as fragile as glass, ready to be shattered by one harsh note. We pare down all our expenses.

When we talk, Leo allows me to get sucked into long monologues, and he doesn't say anything. I wish he would talk to me and not be so distant. I'm certain something is bothering him, so I ask, "Why do you let me ramble on and on?"

"Why not? I have nothing to say, really."

I insist he does have things to say but is keeping them to himself, which is hurting me. It means a lack of confidence that I will love him through a disagreement, or a wrong thought or problem. Then it begins to come out.....

"I've been thinking of the difference in our ages, and what it means....."

"Does it really matter, Leo?" I cry. "Do you think you can't love me because of it?" And he says he has thought that he loved me. The use of the past tense really scares me. I ask, "And now?"

How contagious fear is. I try to smile and be less afraid.....and Leo says he does love me, but because of the age factor I have moved with people on a different intellectual level.....

"Not so," I protest.

"Alison, face it. It's true. I haven't been to college and I haven't lived that long....." and his lack of experience is bothering him and all the books he hasn't read and his not having the vocabulary and feeling unequal.....

"But you have a very fine intellect," I reassure him, hating to hear him put himself down, and I list all the things I have learned from him. He starts to feel a little better and some of the remoteness goes away, and comfort comes in its place. I tell him how many of the words which have been coming out of my mouth, startling us both, are brand new to me and were made possible because of his love.

Leo falters, saying he wants to give me something to make me happy. I am not sure what he is talking about. He says he is trying to love me the best he can, doing the best he can.....and he looks so helpless.....and it is terrible what is happening to us, probably only for lack of money.....and I put my arms around him, swearing that nobody but him has ever.....and that even his needing me is doing me good.

* * * * *

Leo gets hired at minimum wage at a cheese factory, operating a machine, grating cheese for Parmesan shakers. He comes home every night, dusty with cheese crumbs, hating Italian food now, and his poor hands are cut and blistered. I wonder again what our love is doing.....yet we need the money. My salary isn't enough to cover bills. No more little checks in envelopes from my father who completely disapproves of Leo and tells me I should feel guilty for getting the poor boy into trouble. He zooms in on me with the admonishment that such a relationship will never, *NEVER*, work..... Don't I see the big cultural gap between Leo and myself? Don't I see he is nine years younger? Don't I see that the pressures of a relationship with a woman who has a young child are unfair to the young man? What is the matter with me?

"Dad, you don't understand how I feel," I stumble incoherently, trying to defend something that cannot be explained.

"Alison, sometimes you make me ashamed to be your father. You are thirty, almost, and you still want candy like a baby. What you have with this young man, it is like wanting candy. Isn't it time you grew up and were sensible about your life ? And what about Babette? You lack all the biological instincts of motherhood..... You ought to be protecting her, not thinking of yourself....."

Leo comes home and finds me on the telephone trying to ventilate my pent-up anxieties and fears to Petra. I get off the phone, pinhole poor Leo who is slightly stoned having passed by Cruisan's house. We can't have secrets. I proceed to recount the entire conversation with my father, and I see Leo's face contort with rage and feelings of inadequacy.

At least I'm not letting all this fester in myself. We fret, mentally counting our pennies, in the midst of our financial crisis, panicked. I imagine myself stranded and forced to go crawling on my knees back to Daddy's feet, acknowledging "You were right. You were right. I'll never do it again," in total humiliation.

"But I won't leave you, Alison," swears Leo.

"I wouldn't go back unless Babette was starving....." Leo looks at me with expectancy; my knowledge should exceed his perhaps.

I've been to college. He waits for me to compose his discords, and all I can play is a game of love and speculation.

We sit across an ashtray filled with nervous cigarette butts, looking at our room, our oasis in the middle of a jungle of a city. I spend my hours working, supporting this dream.

"We can move and get a cheaper apartment," I suggest. We start planning all over again.

* * * * *

After several hours of doubting, we resolve not to let the world split us up and make love, and it is fantastic. Then we sit in bed looking at pictures in art books and reading poetry together and staying very close. It is cold outside.

Naturally, the next day when I was in the office, all the bummers came back in magnified form. Money problems fill me with dread. I am chained to New York City since Babette must be able to see Dave and chained to the day care center area and so if we move, it must be within a radius close to it. How long Leo can endure this job of his? I really do not know. He comes home from his job numb.

I have to hold him for several minutes before the tension drains out of him. He showers. He reeks of Italian grated cheese. He has no appetite at all.

Leo is hardly interested in jamming. He says the guitar fails to inspire him and his hands are all tight and bruised from work. "They don't feel like a guitar player's hands at all anymore," he confesses, holding them up so I can see.

What is happening to Leo's beautiful hands, the elegant square tipped fingers, supple and sensitive? There are open cuts and scabs all over them.....and I feel that I have done this to him, that I am no good for him. And still, I worry about money.....because they are not paying him enough..... It hurts to see how work wipes away his usual verve. He just gets quieter and quieter. His identity is up in the air for him. He used to believe he was a musician, but now.......

* * * * *

I was coming down the hall on my way back from getting cigarettes, and some of the neighbors invited me in for a few minutes. I threw my coat in the apartment, told Leo I would be back in ten minutes, (he having previously said he wanted to be alone.) When I got back, he was shaving and shaking like a leaf in a heavy wind and looking extremely upset.

"Darling? What's the matter?"

Leo blurted out that perhaps he was getting on my nerves or maybe I was getting bored with him. "Why did you go down the hall without me?"

I explained that I had thought Babette should have someone in the apartment. It hadn't meant to be for longer than a few minutes and that if anyone had turned out to be a musician, I would have come home and let him go instead. Still, this shook me, that Leo had been so easily rattled. I think he is growing insecure about me. And I love him so.

Ever since my father mentioned the age difference it has come to the forefront of my awareness that when I am forty, Leo will be thirty and wanting children of his own. How can I have a baby at the age of forty? Leo resents Dave and cannot feel toward Babette as if he is her father. But he has an affectionate temperament and is trying to be her friend.

"Leo, when are you going home to your house?" Babette asks him one day.

"This is my home."

"This can't be your home?" I see he's hurt.

"Why not, Babette?" I intervene.

"Because you're not Leo's mommy..... She's my mommy, so she can't be your mommy, Leo. Mommy, are you going to be Leo's mommy?"

"No, Darling. I'm Leo's friend. I'm your mommy. Leo doesn't want to have me be his mommy, do you, Leo?"

"Don't be ridiculous." He frowns at me.

"You can be Leo's friend too, Babette. I don't have to be his mommy for him to live here with us."

"But," she still needs to know, "will he be Barbara-Debbie-Ann's friend?" Barbara-Debbie-Ann, *(the 'real baby'),* is Babette's favorite doll, who has a lot to say about what should go on in the house.

"Barbara-Debbie-Ann, will you be Leo's friend?"

"I think she says 'Yes' Mommy."

* * * * *

"You have a healthy sex life, Baby." Leo laughs at me standing in the kitchen, naked, holding a frying pan. "Stop being so conceited, Leo." I snap a towel at his ass. "You know very well, *YOU'RE* my sex life." Leo reminds me of an Egyptian sculpture with a frying pan..... absurd.....his shoulders emerge very square and broad from underneath his shoulder-length hair.

We make love, and it is still wonderful, although we are tired, ailing from the winter's cold.....depressed because of poverty.

IT HAS BEEN A ROUGH WEEK. Leo has been flipping out; being hostile; throwing his glasses on the floor, and curling up in a tight unmoving ball. Being angry and then turning his anger against himself, saying he doesn't want to live in this world anymore.

He took some Mescaline this weekend. I think it wrecked his brain. Monday and Tuesday, he stayed home from work with Babette who was home from the day care center, recuperating from a cold and he says she was really mean to him.

"She doesn't like me. I know she doesn't. She only likes me when you're around.....to please you."

"Perhaps it's natural you argued, being stuck together in a house for two days, both sick."

The subject of the discussion waltzes in. I send her to her room, out of harm's way, to bed. Surely Leo shouldn't be jealous of a small child? I hope it's not that.

"Just don't talk to me. I don't want to be picked on or picked at," he says. "I just want to be alone."

"But, Darling, what could she have said that hurt you so much?"

"She said she doesn't like me and doesn't want me to live here. And all this right after I'd been reading stories to her. I felt like punching her in the mouth.....but she's only a little kid, so I chased her away....." I could tell he was thinking about quitting me. He's so insecure with me, with reality, with the job, which really does stink. "She's not even my own child," he croaks. "How can I ever feel the same about her?"

I know Babette can be irritating. Who would know better? But she's only a child..... and I see Leo is little more than a child too right now because he's hurt and bewildered and the world isn't treating him very well.....and I'm little more than a child, thinking I can have Leo *AND* Babette, and somehow, if I keep a pure heart, everything will work out.

"Alison, I'm losing my mind. I'm not in touch with myself anymore. I have no values anymore and no morality. I don't even know what things feel like anymore..... Oh, Alison....."

I feel the rejection of the child, and rejection because maybe I am not worth it to Leo to keep himself together for us.....but his pain is larger than mine, and I cannot bear for him to feel so alone.

We hold each other, silent in the darkness, wondering how long we can last.....how long?

Oh, Leo, I am the source of all your unhappiness. I am no longer good for you. *You* have been good for *me*. In the five months we've been together, we've made love more than Dave and I did in that seven year marriage. And it has always meant something. I'll have it to keep, no matter what happens.

I feel that a day will come and you will not be there because it has been too much for you.....because if you weren't living with me, you wouldn't have such a lousy job, and you'd have energy to make music again. Maybe dreams aren't really real. Maybe even the best things do end. If only I could get rid of the bad thoughts that keep repeating in my head, that you don't love me, that I am not really lovable, that I have no reason to go on.....

You say you love me, you love me still. You will go on loving me, you will always love me. I don't know. I don't know. I don't know how you can under the circumstances.

Would it be better for you if we broke up? Would you just be wandering around from place to place with no home and no one to love you, upset and lost inside, not knowing what to do? Or would you find happiness in wandering, free from cares, responsibilities, except to yourself, singing for your supper, taking your chances with the world?

I don't want to turn you into a retired suburbanite with a house outside of New York City, commuting every day to a job you hate..... with a wife and children, safe, and laying your musical dreams aside. I'd rather have you chasing phantoms, looking for your self-fulfillment at the cost of everything rather than cripple you, making you just like all the others.

It is open school day at the day care center. I know that Babette will be very disappointed if I don't go. I walk through the projects with their lawns of tended green grass, across streets littered with crumpled bits of paper, broken glass, cigarette butts, and dog shit. It is a gray sky, and I'm depressed. I pass people on their way home; people trying not to look at me and I'm trying not to look at them. The trees that are covered with pink blossoms in the spring and summer are bare now and look half dead.

I walk into the day care center building and Babette's classroom. The kids are messing up with various materials: glitter, feathers, construction papers, and glue. Parents are also invited to dabble if they want to. I don't.

I exchange words with Babette's teacher. Babette has adjustment problems, but they see a marked improvement in her speech. She occasionally lapses into deep thought. In general, she eats well and does not attack other children. She is a bit of a problem at nap time.

I gather Babette's coat under my arm and try to extract her from her constructions. She starts demanding ice cream. She will misbehave if I don't give it to her. "Not today," I tell her in a voice of finality.

They say children's IQs are definitely improved by parents speaking to them. But I have nothing I can say with patience at the moment. I don't feel gay. All that comes out of my mouth seems to be reproaches. I shut up.

I make Babette's dinner, meatball stew from a can, and give her juice to wash it down and Fig Newtons for dessert. Then I chase her to her room to play. I *NEED* quiet.

Babette makes the usual grotesque mess of her room and balks at cleaning it. I am uptight because she is not even trying to be helpful. I cannot be so strong that I never break down.

Leo is in a jealous fit because the other day, as he came

by to collect me from work, he saw Steven, one of the editors, propositioning me while I was at my desk.

What happened was that Steve, when he got back from his vacation, decided he wasn't meant to be monogamous because his relationship with his girlfriend wasn't going well. And so he decided to make heavy passes at the first available-looking female, me. I told him *SORRY*, but I was now a reformed character, being faithful and monogamous and all settled down. He said, "Too bad."

In the middle of all this, Leo came around the corner, convinced that I was enjoying it all and I wasn't.

"Why should I be the target of your wandering urges, Steven? What the hell are you trying to do?" I asked.

"Dunno," he said. "But I thought of you because I've been dreaming about you lately." Oh. Not again.

I told Steven I wasn't on the lookout for any affairs and that he wouldn't like it if I looked at him as a 'challenge,' which he nodded to and trouped off. Today was really an exception. Normally, Steve treats me as an older brother would treat a small and insignificant sister. That's because he's an editor, and I'm only a secretary, even though I have a BA.

I had to hurry and catch up with Leo who was striding at a fast pace, in a fury, refusing to even talk.

"Why are you mad at me, Leo?"

"Who says I am?" Then he said he didn't care anymore.

* * * * *

I HAVE LUNCH WITH DAVE. I waited for him on 14th Street for about ten minutes, feeling alienated from the people passing by staring at me, trying to figure out what I was doing standing still in the street like that. Everyone else was moving.

Finally, I see Dave's head a block away, and he is running easily down the street. I had been curious as to whether I would still recognize him from far away because when we used to live together, I always would. As it turned out, I did recognize him. He came to a halt in front of me wearing a middle class business coat, a flashy tie, and a printed shirt. He never would have worn anything like it in the days when we were married. Lately, he has begun to look dapper, 'but in good masculine taste,' of course.

He'd recently had a haircut, I noticed, and was cleanly shaven. The skin around his chin looked slightly smoother than a plucked chicken's. His throat is shaped a little like a bird's too. His neck plugs into his head, and the muscles between his ears and his collarbone are pronounced cords.....but he manages to look fresh and clean and full of vigor and strength.

His hair is receding, as we all knew it would. (His father is bald.) But this makes Dave look dignified, a strange contradiction with the muscularity of the rest of him. His deep set eyes are still bright and friendly and, as usual, do not see the person in front of him, *(me)*......

We took our seats inside the luncheonette, at a booth for two persons, already prepared with silverware and placid yellow cups. I start to sit facing the door, when Dave orders summarily, "No! You sit there!" and points to the other seat.

I was amused and moved to sit with my back to the door. Dave always did have a fetish about sitting facing the door, though why he should expect to find an assailant in back of him is beyond me. Dave's repertoire of foibles is very diverting, now that I don't have to live with them.

"Still sitting facing the door, always?"

"Well, I'm still alive," says he. "Therefore, I'm going on the supposition that my theory works." To Dave, everything appears in the light of this or that theory.

We settle into our seats and look at each other. We just look. There is a certain blankness I feel, so I examine this man to whom I was married for so long. It still feels familiar to sit across a counter from him, yet we are now strangers. We still assume we know the other person. What fools we are. And though he is looking at me directly, I still feel I am being overlooked and his mind is not really taking stock of who I am.

We have very little to talk about, except Babette's progress at school and little stories about things she has said and done. And it's all a grim preview of how people who were close can lose each other.

* * * * *

Leo is suffering. He is working 8 to 5 with a half-hour off for lunch. His hands hurt and they don't feel like part of himself. He gets paid a flat $100 a week, less taxes. and barely has money to spend on himself after he gives me his share of our expenses. We have our first real arguments. He starts talking about leaving and going after himself. I feel it may be the right thing for him to do, and feel humiliated. My love hasn't been good for him at all.

I don't exactly know how to face Leo. Each time I look at him, I start cracking up and crying, feeling ashamed like an unwanted person. He can't bear to see me cry and stomps out of the house, saying he has to make arrangements with himself. I lie by myself waiting to hear him unlock the door and come to bed.....wondering..... "How long?"

* * * * *

Oh, Lady Arcana, won't you please help me? I've never needed your help so much before in my life. I've been trying to be as good as I can be, love Leo and love Babette, and I've been writing some and painting, even though I'm not good at it yet.....

Oh, Lady Arcana, I think I'm going mad. Leo's unhappiness is too much for me. You've got to do something to help us, or we won't be able to make it. I've been trying as hard as I know how by myself. But it isn't enough.

Oh, Lady Arcana, can't there be a miracle? Don't let life take Leo away from me. I don't want to live without him. And I can't live with him, seeing his hands get chopped up and his throat hoarse from all the cheese dust, coughing all the time. I know that it's my fault he's come to this. And it wouldn't have to be this way if only we had some money, just a little more money.

Lady Arcana, how can it be like this in the world, where money can spoil love by not being there..... Where Leo can only get a lousy job because he got kicked out of the army and hasn't got any skills except playing music? I work like everyone else, and just because I'm a woman, I'm a secretary and don't make enough money to take care of my child, my lover, and me.

Lady Arcana, I know you're there. I believe it. Please explain why all this is happening? It must mean something.

I've finally found love, real love, and it's dying.....because of the world being the way it is. I only need time..... Leo needs time..... If we can only have some time without all these pressures, I know we can do something.....

Oh, help me, please help me.....help me..... I need help.

Chapter 19

I'm sorry, Alison.

I don't think I could say I'm sorry enough for the way I acted last night. Although I didn't know what I was doing. I wish there was some way to forgive myself. I wish I had another chance.

I'm sorry, Alison. Beneath the rage of psychic storm, somehow I love you. I don't know how you would want to speak with me again or even consider me any kind of friend. I never cheated on you or lied to you, and knowing I hit you puts pain in my heart. I realize how badly I've treated you almost every day because everything is so confused and forced from me now. I wish I could change what happened last night.

I will never drink again. I wish there was some way I could make up or apologize for what I did.

I wish to God there was some way, Alison. I could kill myself for what I've done to you. I'm sorry. I'm sorry. I'm sorry. I'm sorry.

LEO

* * * * *

I'm so sorry, Alison. I guess it would be best to leave you even though I don't really want to. It's a terrible tragedy, what happened last night. I wish I even had some recollection of what I did. I've been in states like that before when I drank too much and forgot what I did for some amount of time.

I wish there was some way I could talk to you. I wish I wasn't a man. I wish I wasn't a brute. I'm sorry!

I'm going to miss you. If you're ever in trouble or need anything, I'd run to help you. I don't know why our relationship began to get sour. I wish I could've kept us together but it seems like nothing goes right for me. I don't know why I begin destroying myself and my world so often. I'm just a greedy pig and I hate myself.

Our relationship began as a marvelous loving experience about six months ago. After having spent a weekend with you, I left and existed wrapped in an invisible blanket of aromatic sweetness. You were a different person then in the way you treated me, and I was different in the way I treated you.

What happened? Why did I begin to feel so much hate and anger that I never felt before? Once I had hardly anything but a guitar and I felt like a flower. Why did I turn into such a monster?

Once I was never jealous and could be very generous. Now I have a place to live that is very comfortable and plenty of food to eat, and I'm greedy, jealous, envious, obnoxious. I can't quite make any sense out of these feelings which I don't even want to consider my own. I stomp all over the floor and scream out my bad feelings, my frustration, of having doubts about what maybe I consider reality's superficialities, and my mistrust of monogamy; while you lie in bed crying, afraid of me, because you think I might go to bed with someone else.

I become exhausted from manufacturing sympathy until I lose my mind. I never made any dates with other women and I never screwed anybody's wife, and really, I don't intend to.

I'm sorry I became violent. Knowing I hit you tears me apart inside and frightens me.

Once, when I was in the army, I went into a state of unconsciousness while drinking. I wrapped a long thick cord around my neck and began strangling myself. If it hadn't been for some friends, I would've killed myself and probably never even have known it.

I'll never drink a single drop of wine or liquor again. I guess the last thoughts or feelings I remember of last night were of feeling worthless. I began to get uptight because I thought that you thought because I was a drunk, I was worthless, not worth talking to.

LEO

* * * * *

I guess you can't really accept my apologies. I can't either. I want to tell you goodbye, and I'm sorry I messed us up. I realize how stupid and immature I am. I will try to learn from this experience. I am too violent.

You are a very fine person. You never really hurt me or meant to intentionally screw me up. I want to call you in maybe a month after you restructure yourself. I do really care about you. I have no hopes of ever being your lover again, but to know that we could still be friends would make me feel better. It will take some time to be able to find myself and earn any kind of respect from you. It means so much to me.

I try to face the truth about myself. There is so much bad truth and good truth. I try to suppress the bad truth so things don't feel bad, but suppressing it only makes things worse and makes me feel guilty about myself.

I want to get married someday and have a family. I wish I could have married you, but now I've destroyed all hopes of even having your love. I hate myself for it. I swear to God I do.

I'll be okay and will make music and write songs and change myself to be more patient and stronger. I hope many good things come to you. I hope someday you will be happily married because I feel it means so much to you. I wish it wasn't so painful to love.

Alison, I feel as if I've lost the most beautiful friendship I've ever had. I lost so much in you.

LEO

* * * * *

The more I write letters to you, the more stupid I appear to myself. Everything I had was here. I don't want to go back on the street, with no money and no place to stay. I'm very hurt and I don't want to see anyone. I can't stop breaking up all over the place every five or ten minutes. I feel worse today than I did yesterday.

I still find it impossible to leave this place because it has become a home to me. I can't say I'm sorry enough for what I've done to you. Alison, it's so hard to go outside because I am liable to start crying. I can't stop putting myself down for being such a fool. I don't want to leave you, and I don't know if that's a very irrational feeling to have.

I'm missing you, hating myself for feeling I haven't been right. I don't think I would leave you if you hit me because I'm not afraid of you hurting me.....but I'm afraid of myself hurting you.

It's getting more painful not seeing you than it would be to see you. I don't want to love anybody but you because then I would lose you altogether. If I can't love you, then I can't love anyone.

If I knew we would still be friends, I'd be able to leave easier. I still don't remember what happened. I just woke up feeling tragic and thought I had a bad dream about you leaving me. And when I called you at work and you told me what I did, I just started crying.

Please don't believe that what I did was all of me. If I said anything bad, that's not the way I really feel about you, only my own hate for myself. I couldn't hate you.

I wish I could find my way back to you. I see all your faces and changes, and I've only known you such a short time. I don't want it to end now.

271

I really have never trusted anyone as I trust you. Somehow I need you. I don't have to need you sexually. I need you in a way that's so important and means so much to me. I need you as I need to live and love and be a good person to myself, and I want to be a good person to you so badly.....

Goodbye, Alison.

LEO

* * * * *

THREE YEARS LATER, I bump into Jack Livingston on Fifth Avenue. I'm now a full-time art student, and they are really teaching me how to paint as I have always wanted to. I'm still writing.....and that's getting better also.

Jack is a little more corroded by alcohol; his hair is almost all gray, but he is still his friendly self.....whisking me into the nearest restaurant for a bit to eat and a drink.

We sit there together over the food as we used to do. I'm glad he still cares about me enough to feed me.

"What's happening, Jack? How is life treating you these days?"

"Pretty much the same. But I'm no longer with Academia. I'm still director of a publishing house, a bigger one. Academia was getting too tight for me." He takes a sip of his martini just as he always used to do. "How about you, Alison? You're in art school? Good. That's where I always thought you should be. And how's your love life? Mine goes on just the same....."

Hesitantly, I wonder how I can tell him I am back with Leo and all that has happened since I left Academia.....as if I have to justify love.....but I start telling him about Leo.

"You see we're in love and always have been.....but always, there are problems:

272

First, Leo had to get a job, so he got one in a cheese factory, and that was because of love, but his hands were cut up by it, so he couldn't play music, and that was love.

Then he hit me because he was drunk and depressed, and that was love. And I threw him out because I was afraid, and that was love.

But he still wanted to be my friend, and that was love.

And as soon as we saw each other again we went straight to bed, and that was love.

Then he lived elsewhere with a friend but was my lover, and that was love.

And then he got a job repairing office machines, and that was love.

Then *he* broke with *me*, and that was love.

But we missed each other so much, we got back together, and that was love.

Then Leo split New York City for Mexico, and that was love.

And I didn't make love the whole time he was gone, and that was love.

Then he wanted me and came back, and that was love.

Then he gave me the clap and lied about where it came from, and that was love.

I believed him for three solid days of confusion, and that was love.

Then I threw him out again, and that was love.

But then we missed each other again and didn't want it to end that way, and that was love.

Now we're living together again, both of us in school..... I'm going to be an artist, and Leo's going to make it in music.....and that's what's been going on in my love life.

NOW....... What do you think?"

Jack Livingston raised his martini as if to toast me and said:
"I think you're crazy."

PSL020USA